Heart of the West

A stunning novel of passion and adventure

He kissed her. Not a tender kiss like those he'd given her in college, but a deep kiss and greedy, the way he might drink a glass of water when thirsty. That quality moved her, a sense of need mixed with passion. His hands gripped both her shoulders. He leaned into her body and pressed her backward . . .

He deepened the kiss. The thrum of her blood drowned out the ocean. Citrus cologne tickled her nose. His fingers plucked her finely spun blouse sleeves, sliding over her skin and tightening . . . He pressed tightly against her, trapping her in a half-sitting position . . .

He bent down and nipped the curve of her neck. A thrill spiraled through her. She'd relived his kisses so many times, but she didn't remember this darkness, this velvety texture and bolt of sheer joy . . .

Jove Titles by Kathleen Sage

MANY FIRES
OUT OF EDEN
HEART OF ALASKA

Heart of Alaska

KATHLEEN SAGE

JOVE BOOKS, NEW YORK

HEART OF ALASKA

A Jove Book / published by arrangement with
the author

PRINTING HISTORY
Jove edition / October 1997

The Putnam Berkley World Wide Web site address is
http://www.berkley.com

ISBN: 0-515-12158-4

A JOVE BOOK®
Jove Books are published by The Berkley Publishing Group,
a member of Penguin Putnam Inc.,
200 Madison Avenue, New York, New York 10016.
JOVE and the "J" design are trademarks
belonging to Jove Publications, Inc.

PRINTED IN THE UNITED STATES OF AMERICA

10 9 8 7 6 5 4 3 2 1

This book is dedicated to the public librarians of California.

When I was a child, there was a poster. It said: "Books are our friends." No one had to tell me that. Books were my best, steadiest, most constant, and often only friends. Not only were books my friends, but they were also a solace, an education, and most of all a conviction that if I could make friends with Shakespeare, if I could love and commune with the finest minds our culture had produced, I could do anything I wanted.

I grew up and did exactly that.

I became a successful attorney, with a seventeen-year marriage and three lovely children, and went on to write popular fiction.

This was not the future anyone predicted for me.

So this book is dedicated to the public librarians of California, for the fine education I received with their help, and accompanied by a plea to all my readers: Support your local libraries. There are still hope-filled urchins haunting those stacks.

Acknowledgments

Special thanks to Karl Gurcke and the staff of Klondike Gold Rush National Park for their patience and courtesy in answering my questions. Have a great Centennial! I'm sorry I didn't get to hike the Chilkoot.

Thanks also to Jane Hollister Wheelwright, author of *The Ranch Papers: A California Memoir*. Her graceful description of her parents and their ranch served as a springboard for this novel.

As always, thanks to my husband, Larry, and my sons Todd, Tim, and Tony, gentlemen all. May my royalties someday buy you Porsches.

And finally, a special thanks to my sister-in-law Kathy, who baby-sat more times than I will ever be able to repay.

Hi, Brian! Hi, Kimby! We miss you.

A twisted limb touches the sky.
The perfect form is always a lie.
Bettina will live within me forever.
Such desolate secrets.
And she never cries.

—Zachary English, American poet
and short-story writer, 1875–1916

One

Christmas 1897
Santa Ynez, California

Dancing couples whirled through soft candlelight—men in black suits trimmed with velvet; women in gowns of bright-colored satin. Jesse Wheeler threaded his way through the swirl of bodies, attracting attention as always. Though few of the dancers looked directly at Jesse, their gazes strayed toward his dark figure. A glance here and there. A whispered remark. A slight sway of attraction. There was something so exotic about him—the untameable mane of curly black hair; the copper skin that glinted like a new penny; the extravagant grace of his slim-hipped body—that even the most jaded noticed.

"You want to dance with him, don't you?" Don Daniel Wheeler took Bet Goldman's elbow. He steered her to the edge of the waxed parquet dance floor.

"No." Bet pressed one hand to the small of her back, doing her best to straighten her spine. She'd never make true ramrod posture, but she made a serious try at looking normal. From the waist up, she succeeded, but her lower back curved at an odd angle. "Not really."

Out on the floor, Jesse Wheeler bowed to a lanky blonde in a gray satin ballgown. The violins welled with the movement, as if the musicians had picked up the grand gesture. The lithe woman stepped into his arms. They made a fine couple. Jesse—black-haired, six feet tall, and strong-featured with the graceful carriage of his Spanish forebears. His companion matched him in all but his coloring, a slender aristocrat, a gold complement to his darkness.

Pain flared in Bet's spine. She leaned lightly forward. She'd wanted to dance with Jesse all her life, but she'd go to her grave before she'd admit it. "I don't like dancing really." She accepted Don Wheeler's arm, feeling the fine wool sleeve beneath her silk one. She flushed, correcting her previous thought. She'd known Jesse since she was eleven. It only felt as if life had begun when she met him. "I like riding better."

The older man smiled, chucking her chin. "That's our Bet. Always the liar."

"Who is she?" Bet asked, turning away from the don's piercing blue eyes. She did not recognize the tall, graceful woman, but thought her a local ranchowner's daughter, judging from her confident posture and the tasteful tailoring of her low-cut gown. Her matchless perfection worried Bet just a little.

In the nineteen years since she'd known Jesse Wheeler, many women had thrown themselves at him. He'd never returned the affection of any. He claimed he'd never found the right partner, but Bet knew better than that. That commanding man—heir to this ranch and self-assured dancer—had grown up in vast baronial splendor with mostly horses for friends. His controlled exterior hid a lifelong shyness; he was as wary of strangers as an untamed mustang. Bet put her worries out of her mind. It seemed too unlikely and too depressing that Jesse would finally form a serious attachment just when she needed his help. Still, it did not hurt to ask. "Does Jesse like her?"

"You'll find out soon enough." The silver-haired don tugged at her sleeve, pulling Bet toward the outdoor veranda. Candlelight glinted off his old-fashioned conchas, accenting the matching curls on his head. He tried to guide her by the waist, but Bet shied away lightly and lingered by the sideboard. The cool night breeze leaked through the French doors, mixing with the warmth from the bodies and the dry heat from the fireplace. The scent of cut pine drenched the air. She adjusted the drape of her paisley shawl and paused as if she wanted a drink.

Gallant as always, Don Wheeler stopped. A certain sadness haunted his eyes, but Bet didn't question its presence. She'd known Jesse's father for many years. Though a fortunate man in many ways, he often seemed slightly dejected. With a slight bow toward Bet, he lifted the ladle and dipped it into the claret-colored liquid.

Bet accepted the drink and turned toward Jesse. She searched his face for some hint of expression, but he'd always been opaque in that aspect. His bold features gave lie to the boast of his mother that no Indian blood sullied her lineage. No verbal description could capture his beauty and probably no photograph either. He had a long face, smooth-skinned and high-cheekboned, whose allure lay in its pride and aloofness. He might have been made of obsidian really, at least until he kissed a woman. Bet knew something about that velvet experience. She smiled, sipping the punch. "Do you really think me a fearful liar?"

"Certainly, darlin'. Look at these ladies." The aging former sea captain nodded his head toward the room's center. "Everyone wants to dance with my Jesse."

"True." Bet laughed through the tension in her corded muscles. She wanted to knuckle the ache in her back, but did nothing more than lean into her corset, letting the special stays take the weight. "I don't know why I should be different."

"You are special, though. And don't you forget it."
Don Wheeler pulled a flask out of his vest and spiked
his punch with some of the liquid. "Why don't you ask
him? You know he'd teach you."

"And let everyone laugh at the cripple?"

"No one would laugh. And what does it matter? You
didn't let that stop you from riding."

"That's not the same."

"Why?"

Bet swallowed the cool, sweet-flavored liquid. "It just
isn't, Don Wheeler."

He leaned over and whispered a whiskey-scented suggestion. "Then ask him when you two are alone."

The night air played with Bet's neck, lifting the fine
spray of hair at the nape. She'd known the ranchero for
almost twenty years. He'd never tried to play the match-
maker. "Who's the woman, Don Wheeler?"

But her old *compadre* just smiled sadly.

Jesse tightened his grip on Christine and scowled. He
could feel the tension in her stiff posture. A frown
tugged at her pretty pout. He couldn't read her expression exactly, but her gaze slid toward Bet, then skittered
away.

"Is that Bet Goldman?" she asked.

Jesse nodded.

"I thought we agreed—"

"Mother agreed, but evidently not Father."

The musicians segued into a contra dance, a pretty
song, a little bit faster than the waltz they had been playing. Christine's dress rustled stiffly as Jesse twirled her
toward one side of the ballroom. She followed, sure-
footed and graceful in spite of her height. "Is your father
in charge of our engagement party?"

"No, but he's in charge of this rancho. This is the
annual Christmas party—"

"Does Miss Goldman celebrate Christmas?"

Jesse was about to explain Bet's father was Jewish,

which made Bet a Gentile in Jewish tradition, when he realized the whole conversation was pointless. He shouldn't have to defend his friendship with Bet. His father, however, was another matter. Though they often disagreed on small matters—and Jesse would like to strangle the old man at this moment—he protected him against all outsiders. And he included Christine in that number. "She's spent Christmas here for many years. I suppose he didn't want to be rude."

Christine looked doubtful. Without any prompting, she whirled into Jesse's embrace. He stepped politely away and glanced at Bet. She stood by his father next to the sideboard, huddled with him in deep conversation. Jesse tried to read her expression, but she turned away just as he did. Fawn-colored tendrils trailed down her neck, accented by a curled scarlet ribbon. The old longing rose up in Jesse. He squelched it. That way lay madness. He already knew it, though he'd go to his grave without understanding how a woman could delight him so much on some levels and hurt him so badly on others.

He tightened his grip on Christine and drove her in the other direction. She must have been watching Bet Goldman as well. She tilted her head toward the retreating figure. "She's prettier than you described."

Jesse scowled, dipped, then tucked Christine under his elbow, facing her forward, promenade style. "If you like the Gypsy type, I suppose."

"She still doesn't walk perfectly well."

"No. But she does damn well for a woman who spent her first twelve years as an invalid."

Christine didn't like riding cow ponies, but she had a fine education in English riding and could jump with the best in a valley filled with fine jumpers. Some of that training showed now. She kept her voice level, her face composed. "I suppose you're proud of having helped her."

Jesse shrugged. "It was just a little boyhood adventure."

"Have you heard the scandal about her and the poet?"

"Yes."

"It's quite romantic. Though I can't quite see why he's so devoted. They say he's half her age really."

Jesse's neck muscles tightened. He hated this subject. He especially hated that Christine knew about it, though why this should be so he couldn't imagine. All literate California knew about the wild young poet Zachary English, and his mad affair with Bettina Goldman. "She's barely thirty."

"He's just over twenty."

He glared, probably harder than he intended. Christine missed a beat in their dancing and stumbled. Jesse paused and waited for her to recover. While she took a minute to regain her composure, he silently counted to four. She picked up his rhythm, his unspoken cadence. Bettina disappeared out the door. Christine lifted a bare and elegant shoulder. "Of course, arithmetic was never my strong suit."

Bet waited in the room known as the study, though the spaces in these old adobes had too many uses to be narrowly labeled. A pool table dominated the center of this one. Books lined the walls and glass bookcases. Blunt beams defined the home's former limits. Over time, however, the house had sprawled outward, becoming a lovely and capacious mansion, the heart of it still this thick-walled adobe, a cool retreat from those more modern places where sunlight poured through mullioned windows and reflected off shimmering white walls.

Bet had sent word to Jesse through one of the servants. She wanted to see him in their old play space, not in the garden where they'd gamboled as children, but here in the study where they'd spent time as students trying to ignore their growing awareness that each had become a man and woman.

Bet smiled, taking one of the books off the shelf. She

wished life could be so simple once more. It had been the sunniest time in her life, those teenage years when Jesse had adored her and she'd returned his favor. She opened the book. Robert Stevenson's *An Inland Voyage.* She didn't have this volume in her Oakland collection and wondered if Don Wheeler could be asked to make a donation. She caught herself on that thought. No one would ever make another donation to a library she headed if she didn't find that scoundrel Zack English and get back the money he'd taken.

"You look lovely, as always."

She turned and faced Jesse, her heart constricting a little. "You also."

His expression evoked a day clouding over, but she'd grown used to that over the years. She advanced from the side of the room and ran her hand over the black velvet collar of the finely cut suit he was wearing. "I see you've found a new tailor."

"I have, though he's not as good as your father."

Bet winced. "He loved this study, you know."

Jesse pulled away. He ran his fingers over the dark green felt of the pool table, then lifted a cue from the rack on the wall. "It's a good thing he did. It wasn't much use to the Wheelers."

"I didn't mean to imply—"

"I know you didn't." He picked up a small piece of chalk and dusted the tip of the polished wood stick. "You can't help it if your whole family's brilliant."

A song floated in from the party, a passionate Spanish cantata complete with guitars and a warbling male singer. Bet could not follow the words, but the song made her lonely. Heartbreak in music did not need translation. "I still miss him, even after ten years."

Jesse lifted the triangle enclosing the balls. "I suppose it's worse now that your mother's gone."

"It is, but I do all right."

Jesse paused. His fingers tapped lightly over the cue stick, as if he, not the singer, held the guitar. He remained that way for half a stanza, then scowled as he peered over the table. "I'm sorry I couldn't come to the funeral."

"You couldn't have made it in time."

"Still, it must have been bad."

"Zach was a help."

Jesse scowled hugely. That didn't surprise Bet. They'd never discussed Zachary English, but she knew perfectly well Jesse would be jealous.

"How is that going?" he asked.

"Not so well really."

"Oh?"

Now came the hard part. How do you ask your best friend to help you look for your lover? "He's gone to the Yukon."

Jesse bent down over the table. Bet wished desperately she could read his features, but he'd perfected the trick of hiding his feelings, and she knew she'd get nothing from observation. He squinted, taking aim down the line of the cue stick. "That doesn't mean he doesn't love you. Half the youngsters in California have trekked off to the Klondike goldfields. If it weren't for the ranch, I'd be there myself."

"Really?"

"Why not?" Jesse broke the neat cluster of balls, scattering them with a solid *thwack*. They rolled toward the walls, two of them dropping into side pockets. "A chance like that comes once in a lifetime."

"I haven't heard from him since he left."

Jesse circled the table. He cut an elegant figure in his black jacket, gold-embroidered vest, and white linen shirt with a softly rolled collar. For all his reserve, he had flamboyant tastes, a legacy no doubt of his mother. "I doubt letters get through very often."

"Maybe."

"Maybe he does not like to write."

"He's a poet, Jesse."

He bent down, sighted again, and sent a red ball into a pocket. "Letters are different."

Bet sank into a brown leather chair, her fingers curled tightly over Stevenson's volume. She didn't know how to approach this subject but seldom wasted time on self-pity.

"Don't look so glum." Jesse abandoned the table, tossing the cue stick on its surface. He lifted her chin and perused her face. His gaze was dark as the tar that sometimes washed up on the beaches. "If he makes you unhappy, I'll have to thrash him."

Bet smiled, doing her best to look worthy and valiant, but her insides were melting. They always melted in Jesse's presence. That would be the hardest part of this plan. Maintaining the slender thread of their friendship, while the two of them looked for the wayward poet everyone believed was her lover. "I'm worried, Jesse. What if he's hurt?"

"From what I've heard of young English, he's just as wild as those gold fields."

"He's scrappy. It's true. But that reckless streak will get him in trouble."

"So?" This he said with a lift of one eyebrow.

"He's very young, Jesse."

He let go, returned to the table, and picked up the cue stick. "Old enough to take you as a lover and shock all California with poems so erotic they had to be censored."

She laughed, lifting the book as if to toss it. "Don't be so provincial, you silly. In the circles I run in, it's considered quite chic to outrage the censor."

"Do the girls who read your horse stories love it?"

Bet grew suddenly serious. She'd considered this subject quite closely. "It adds to my luster. My fans think it's romantic to sneak-read the poems he wrote me."

"And you approve?"

"Yes. At least I think so." She flipped through the

pages, trying her best to look casual. "It's a good way to prepare them for marriage."

He tapped the stick on his thigh. "Since when are you such a great fan of marriage?"

She snapped the book shut, jumped to her feet, marched to the shelf where she'd found the volume, and slipped it onto the shelf. "He's a real artist, Jesse. Something I'm not."

"I disagree with that assessment."

What could she say? Young women loved the stories she wrote, but she had no illusions about their artistic merits. Her horse stories would never outlive her. Zack's poetry was another matter. "I liked the poems."

"I'm sure you did."

She retrieved her own cue stick from the wall. "Will you play me?" she asked.

Jesse nodded. Bet watched him closely, trying to get a sense of his feelings. He gave away nothing in expression or posture, simply leaned over the table, racking the balls with a fluid motion.

"You're jealous, aren't you?" she asked.

"Don't start with that, Bet."

She dropped her shawl to her waist and knotted it tightly, then leaned over and broke up the cluster. Two balls dropped into the pockets, one striped and one solid. She assessed their positions, then called out "Solid" and sank three balls in a row. She missed the fourth ball on purpose. With a bright smile at Jesse, she stood back and waited. "Don't ever be jealous. No one can take your place in my heart."

He picked up the small piece of chalk and dusted the cue stick. "That's a pretty lie, but I don't believe it. Especially not after these poems."

"You taught me to walk."

"Another falsehood. I taught you to ride. You learned to walk by yourself." Slowly he circled the table. They were good at this game. They'd played it often, for ten years at Christmas and before as children, though they

hadn't been so skilled at it then. He made a run of four
balls, then missed in a way that blocked her best shot.

Bet grinned. It was an unspoken rule from their childhood. Neither truly outdid the other. His little trick lifted
her spirits. They'd been friends forever. Surely he'd
help. He'd have to leave his beloved rancho, but she'd
already talked to Don Wheeler. He didn't mind if Jesse
went to the Yukon. "I need to ask you a favor."

"Shoot."

"If I don't hear from him by spring, I'm going to go
to the to the goldfields this summer. I'd like you to come
with me."

"You must be joking." He threw back his head with
a flare of his nostrils. A queer light shone in his eyes.
The music had stopped in the other room. She waited
out his pause to the babble of voices and the smell of
pine boughs. He tapped his fingers against the felt, then
slotted the cue stick into the rack on the wall. He retrieved the balls from the table's far corners and arranged them neatly inside the triangle. Bet waited
through his actions with patience. Evidently their pool
game was over, though she didn't know what that fact
signified. As a polka started up in the next room, she
mustered her courage.

"Well?" she asked.

He jiggled the chalk in his hand. "To find this poet
of yours?"

Bet nodded.

"Why lower yourself?" he asked in a husky voice.

Bet reslotted her cue stick in silence. She trusted Jesse
with her life, but not with the truth about Zack's indis-
cretions. Jesse didn't have a temper exactly, but he
wasn't above violent reprisal when it came to protecting
those who were weaker. The wayward young poet had
stolen some money. Not only her money, either, but also
funds she'd raised for a library she'd started. She felt
pretty certain he had good intentions. He'd left a note

saying he'd repay with interest, as soon as he returned from the goldfields.

She hadn't heard from him since. Worried and frightened, she wanted to find him. She knew what a foolish gamble he'd taken, thinking he could increase their money by panning for gold in the Yukon. Not the least of those risks was Jesse's reaction if he ever found out Zack had robbed her.

She straightened her shawl, considering excuses, reasons to give for chasing down Zack. Discarding them all as too far-fetched, she decided finally on dignified silence. Fluffing her curls over her shoulder, she winced as Jesse tossed the chalk on the table. It bounced off the sidewall with a rattle.

"You've got a lot of guts, Bet."

Two

Jesse strode to the ballroom, his heart pounding and his jaw muscles tight. "Guts" wasn't really the word he wanted. The dancers swirled in the gold candlelight. He ignored them. He paced toward the front of the long room. Bet's nerve knew no limit. He wanted to seek out his father and tell him that he could take the Flying W rancho and rot in hell for the dirty trick he'd played by inviting Bet Goldman this evening.

He didn't. Soon enough he'd have his revenge. Bet drifted into the room, pretty as always, but chewing her lip and for a moment he almost regretted he hadn't told her in private; but damn it, he couldn't, not after she'd hurt him like that.

She wanted him to look for her lover. He could have wrung her slender neck. Only one thought appeased him. He could announce his engagement and see her expression. It was too much to hope he would hurt her, but at least she'd know it had finally happened. She'd been replaced by another.

He circled the edge of the room. Christine was talking to a chubby old woman with pom-pom-shaped buttons marching up toward her bosom. Jess took his fiancée's arm and tugged her toward the bandstand. She balked, looked in his face, then toward Bet. Her expression sobered, and she followed quickly. Gray satin rustled as she hurried beside him.

Jesse silenced the musicians with a wave of his hand. Immediately couples stopped dancing. The conversation took longer to silence, but Jesse stood on the bandstand and glowered. He hated speaking in public, but for once he had anger to suppress his discomfort. Anger and the thought of his vengeance.

He looked directly at Bet. She stood next to his father. The old don had taken her arm and held her so tightly you would have thought he still saw her as the little cripple who'd come to the rancho so long ago and captured the hearts of so many people.

Well, she didn't have *his* heart, damn it. He grabbed a guitar and strummed out a flourish, using the noise to silence the last of the talkers. The crowd moved in, both men and women. Jesse could not see his mother. He thought about waiting, but rejected the notion. Mother approved of this marriage. It was his father, the schemer, who'd pined and pined for a grandson, then thrown Jesse completely off balance by disapproving of every woman he courted.

"I have an announcement." Jesse took Christine's hand. She stepped slightly inward and lifted her chin. To the left, the pom-pom lady tittered. Jesse took a deep breath and continued. "Most of you know Christine Deutch. She's almost a neighbor." Several of the younger girls blushed. Jesse wondered who already knew, and it hit him. He was about to make a public commitment to a woman he admired but didn't love. He fixed his gaze on Bettina's green eyes. He pulled the emerald ring out of his pocket, but even its deep green fire and sparkle couldn't make him take his gaze from the pale face he'd known since childhood. "As of June, she'll be more than a neighbor." Bet's eyes widened slightly. The old don gripped her waist. Jesse tried to shift his gaze to the left, to take in his fiancée, but green eyes and scarlet ribbons held him. He closed his hand over the ring. "I've proposed, and Christine's consented. We're going to be man and wife."

Polite applause, punctuated by sighs and coos of envy, broke out in the room. None of that mattered to Jesse. Nor did he look at Christine, though he knew he should slip the ring on her finger. He studied Bettina and wondered if she regretted what she was hearing and if she would still run after the poet.

He could not tell what Bet felt, however. She turned slightly pale, but showed no expression except a thin white line at her lips. Jesse scowled. He slipped on the ring and kissed Christine abruptly to a scattered crescendo of clapping and giggles and the ascending flourish of the guitar players.

Bettina ran. Don Wheeler attempted to follow, but she fobbed him off with a smile and excuses, controlling the pace of her exit until he fell behind. Then she broke into an awkward gallop that jarred her back and insulted her body with painful reminders of her physical limits. She felt like a roof had fallen in on her—for the second time in her life. She didn't know why Jesse's announcement should hurt her. He deserved to marry and have someone love him. His timing was lousy, of course. She still needed to get to the Yukon, but she could figure that problem out. So why did she feel like a puppet who'd suddenly lost the strings that moved her? She doubled her pace with an oath to herself.

She reached the familiar red barn. She knew Firestriker was in there. She sensed his presence before she arrived. He must have recognized her odd gait, however. He nickered in greeting as she approached. Bet's heart lifted a bit at the noise. At twenty-five, he was almost ancient. His death would leave her so lonely. She liked to think he might have some years in him. She'd heard of horses that lived to forty, though she also knew they were as rare as men who live to a hundred and twenty.

She opened the side door and slipped in. "Hello, boy." She'd not taken the time to get a lantern, so she felt her way to the tack room, picked out a bridle, and returned to the horse. The well-kept barn had several mounts in it, but she knew Firestriker based on instinct and habit. He knew her, too. She could tell by his nicker. He poked his head out of the stall. She slipped on the bridle and led him out. Murmuring softly, she walked him to the pasture. She had not intended to ride him, but when they reached the grass paddock, he looked so forlorn that she pulled up a stool and leaned her weight on his bare back just a little. He braced himself, seemingly eager. All Bet's problems fell away for a moment, as they often did in the small chestnut's presence.

She'd never forgotten, not in all these years, that wonderful, miraculous summer when she'd ridden and ridden this marvelous creature. At first Jesse had taught her in secret, so convinced was he the adults would be angry when they discovered what he had been doing. And certainly there had been vast consternation when she, Bet, tiny and crippled, had first showed off her newfound skills.

But both her father and Jesse's had defended the children against the hysterical pleas of both their mothers. She'd been allowed to continue riding. By the end of the summer, Bet was glad that she had. That autumn, the miracle happened. She, who'd never walked a day in her life, had begun to be able to move her legs. A surprised doctor explained the mystery much later.

The childhood accident that had left her a cripple had damaged her back and hip bones. If her spine had been severed, she could never have walked, but the problem had not been quite that serious. The injury kept her immobile so long, however, that her leg muscles had withered. No one had thought to try to rebuild them. Although no doctor would have predicted this outcome,

Jesse had found a way around her impairment. If she kept riding, she might learn to walk, though she would never be normal, as her spine had a permanent curve and one leg was a different length than the other.

Bet smiled, stroking Firestriker's coarse mane. When had her life ever been normal? What would she have been had she not been a cripple? The daughter of a world-famous writer? Would that have been normal, that unconventional life? If her father had not been a struggling writer, would the tenement roof have fallen in on her? And if he'd never become an itinerant tailor, how would she ever have encountered Jesse Wheeler?

Firestriker nickered. Laughter drifted out of the ranch house, bringing Bet back to the present. Jesse was engaged to Christine Deutch. He wouldn't go with her to the Yukon. Not that he'd turned her down directly. He hadn't. He'd simply loped out of the room and made this announcement. It hurt. Far more than she expected, though she'd waited many years for this day.

Firestriker's brown ears twitched back, questioning her delay in mounting. Bet's weight did not seem to hurt the small mustang, and she let herself exert more pressure. She could feel the warmth of his old body, the patience bred of so many years, but she also felt that thin thread of his tension. He remembered the times they'd had in these mountains, when he'd been a wild young mustang and she and Jesse had been wilder still.

Bet frowned and blinked back her tears. By the time she'd reached sixteen, she'd developed a full fantasy life as Mrs. Wheeler. Bet's mother must have suspected as much, though they'd never spoken about what kind of a future a girl with Bet's history would have. Mother took her instead to a doctor.

Bet would remember that day for the rest of her life. He hadn't been old for a physician, a modern man, perhaps a bit blunt. He'd explained her limits in front of her mother, skirting carefully around certain parts, which her mother had filled in a bit later. Bet could never have children. Or carnal knowledge. A true cripple could have had children, as her damage would have been higher. Bet's injury had taken her womanhood only, all of the injury involving her pelvis. She'd beat all the odds in learning to walk. She should never test her limits so far as to attempt sexual function or childbirth.

Riding home, Bet hadn't cried. She never cried in front of her mother. For all her childhood affliction had warped her, it had been in some ways harder on her parents. Bet's care had stolen their greatest treasures. Her father's dreams. Her mother's great beauty. Everything, really, except their love, which had grown stronger over the years, a remarkable feat all by itself, considering their differing backgrounds. Bet struggled always to make their life happy, and never more so than on that day when she sat at the side of the carriage, her heart going to her desolate mother.

She threw herself into her father's arms, though, with passionate sobs and silly excuses. She'd never explained her problem to him, too shamed by the doctor's brusque manner and her mother's silence on the ride home. Bet did not follow the medical side, though she had it confirmed by other doctors much later. She did not understand that her back had been damaged, that the doctors believed her hips had been crushed, that lovemaking would likely be painful and she had no proper passage for birthing. She understood only one fact from the visit.

She would have to have an unusual husband.

Three

That husband wouldn't be Jesse. Bet pressed her cheek to the brown mustang's withers. She learned that the first time Jesse kissed her, beneath the gargoyles of the South Hall Berkeley. He wouldn't be the man she would marry. Not that she didn't like the brief contact. She loved it. His kisses went through her like lightning. Which was exactly the problem. She couldn't imagine how she'd resist him. Not to mention the question of childbearing.

Firestriker switched his tail in impatience. The conversation came back with a jolt. At seventeen, she'd put the question to her mother obliquely. "Do you think Jesse will want babies when he gets married?"

"Of course, darling," her mother had answered. "Most men want children, especially Jesse."

"He's kind of a loner."

"Jesse might not want many, but he loves the rancho. It's been in his family for three generations. He'll want to pass it on to his son."

"And if he has a daughter?"

"That might suffice, but I don't think he'd like to be

childless.'' Bet frowned as her mother undid the corset encasing her waist. She helped Bet with the contraption at night, a childhood ritual that left them both fatigued, as she wore an unusually rigid foundation garment to give her a more normal posture.

"Maybe he could adopt one."

"I don't think Doña Wheeler would like that." Mother unrolled the steel and cloth casing, freeing Bet's waist and small bosom. "Her bloodlines go back to an admiral who served under Columbus." She smoothed cream on the welts in Bet's back caused by the torturous bite of the stays. "She only had the one child herself. I strongly suspect she thought childbirth a duty. But she'd expect no less from a daughter-in-law." She lowered a soft lawn nightgown over Bet's head. "Why do you ask?"

"No reason," Bet lied, smiling at the sensation of freedom, the smooth touch of the cloth on her unconstrained body. "He seems so lonely. I worry sometimes about his future."

"He'll be all right." Mother pulled out the first of the haircombs. "That's why the don sent him to Berkeley. For both a wife and a fine education."

But Jesse had not found a wife. Bet straightened her spine to ease her aching back. She could only guess why, for many women had been quite attracted, but Jesse remained shy and wary of strangers, especially when those strangers were women.

"You can ride him, you know." Jesse's low voice slipped out of the darkness.

She turned toward the husky sound. "I don't want to tire him."

"Don't worry." He moved through the night. He'd flipped the black jacket over one shoulder. His white shirtsleeves glowed in the moonlight. "He still loves to be ridden. The children ride him. You're scarcely bigger."

She leaned on Firestriker's back. The white-faced

mustang tensed, his ears flicking rearward. Jesse tossed the jacket over the fence and placed his hands around her waist. Bet's heart constricted. She knew that firm grip so well. Those long, blunt-tipped fingers nearly encircled her waist. He eased her onto the gelding's brown back. Firestriker relaxed and moved slightly forward. Bet urged the horse toward the edge of the paddock. Jesse fell in beside them, not talking at all.

Bet attended to the animal for a moment, but his old bones seemed to hold her quite well. His spirit seemed easy as he stopped at the gate. Jesse held it open. She looked anxiously back toward the ranch house, its windows ablaze with light from the party. "Won't your guests miss you?"

Jesse smiled. "Christine's showing all the ladies the ring. It'll be a while before I'm needed."

He led her out of the paddock and down toward the stream. Pepper trees shaded this spot in the summer, their feathery leaves wispy and fragrant, but in the winter their fine branches rustled and made the refuge a little bit spooky. Bet could hear the rush of the water, an airy, whispering counterpoint to the laughter and music of the Christmas party. She and Jesse rode here often as children, and a sense of peace returned to her. "Congratulations on your engagement."

"Thank you."

Perched on the horse, she couldn't see his reaction. She knew he'd be tense. It had been a sore spot forever between them, the time she'd turned down his proposal of marriage. "You deserve every happiness, Jesse."

"And thank you again."

She wanted to shout that she meant her good wishes, but she stifled her protests. From the time she knew they couldn't be married, she'd tried her best to make Jesse Wheeler hate her, but in some perversion of human nature, she'd only succeeded in making him love her. He'd asked her to marry him the year she finished high school, the year after he finished college.

She smiled, glad he couldn't see her. All her life, she'd cherished that marriage proposal, even though she hadn't accepted. Of course, life might have been simpler if she'd been more truthful in explaining her rejection to Jesse. But she found those intimate details too painful, so she'd pleaded the rancho instead. Its isolation. Her own ambition. The fact that she'd been accepted to Berkeley. It had taken him seven years to forgive her, but when they'd caught another unbroken mustang, the don invited her to spend Christmas at the rancho. And she and Jesse had gone back to their friendship—silly, amiable, easy, and lovely—as if those long years had never happened.

"Will you still go to the Yukon?" he asked.

"I think so."

He stepped forward a little and took Firestriker's head by the bit. "Bet, don't be stupid. If the man doesn't want you—"

"I just have to, Jesse."

"It's no place for a lady."

She waited for him to go further. He didn't. He never referred to her as a cripple, never cited her limp or small stature as reasons she couldn't accomplish some goal. She sometimes imagined he didn't see her defects—her crooked back, her awkward gait. Perhaps he thought her legs looked normal. She never mentioned the ache in her back. Some part of her hoped she had fooled him, that he'd been so impressed by her learning to walk, he didn't see these residual problems that marked her so strongly with everyone else.

One thing was certain: His had been her only marriage proposal, at least until she'd met Zack English.

"What's he like?" Jesse's low voice broke into her thoughts.

"Zack?"

"Yes."

"He's young. Wild. Full of himself."

"Is he handsome?"

"After a fashion." She let Jesse lead Firestriker through the darkness. She knew the way perfectly well, but this seemed so much like the old times, Jesse guiding the horse while she rode, that she didn't dare pull back on the reins and break the spell.

"Do you love him?" he asked quietly.

"Also after a fashion. Certainly I love his writing."

"Does he love yours?"

"No." She thought she ought to get down. This seemed too sad, riding the horse who'd been her salvation, telling the man she loved like a brother how she felt about the unruly poet who'd stolen her money, and whose verses had made her famous in a way she'd never expected. "He thinks my writing's too sentimental." Bet waited, but Jesse said nothing. They'd come quite a distance from the ranch house, and the Christmas music had faded away. "He's probably right."

She pulled on the reins, tapped Jesse on the shoulder, and motioned for him to help her down. He complied, his hands lingering briefly on her tightly cinched waist. She took Firestriker's reins and hooked her elbow in Jesse's. "I've known Zack since he was twelve. He was just a street urchin really, devouring every book I could lend him. He did not even know I was a writer until around two years ago." By the stream the air was perceptibly cooler, and a light breezed played in Bet's tendrils. Jesse adjusted her shawl over her shoulder, though he didn't put on his own wool jacket. Bet enjoyed his touch, the warmth of his presence, but ignored her reaction and went on talking. "By sixteen, he'd started writing. Stories. Poems. Everything really. When he found out I was a writer, he asked me to critique them and—"

"I know. I read the poems."

"My heart went out to him, Jesse. He's terribly foolish, but it took so much courage to rise so far above that background."

He stopped, turned her toward him, and lifted her

chin. Her heartbeat sped up, as it always did in his presence. For the briefest of moments she thought he would kiss her. "Was that what you wanted? Someone to mother?"

"I'm not in love with Zack English, Jesse."

"Then why are you chasing him to the Klondike?"

"It's not what you think." She tried to pull back, but he kept a firm grip on her chin. His hold made her nervous. For years their attraction had stayed perfectly balanced, held in check by his shyness, their friendship, and her own air of Gypsy independence. She would have to abandon some of that pose if she kept to her plan to chase down Zack English. "We have projects in common. He's my protégé, Jesse."

"Some protégé."

She tapped his wrist lightly, slipped out of his grasp, and ducked under Firestiker's neck. Jesse tried to follow, but Firestriker moved forward. For a moment, Jesse seemed startled and angry. Keeping the horse between them, she started walking again. Jesse followed, his fine boots and light step making no sound in the grass. They walked side by side in this way until the ranch house faded into the background, the cool night air caressed their warm cheeks, and the lightly salted air tickled their noses. "Don't believe every word of the poems."

"He's not your lover?"

"I didn't say that." Bet didn't quite know what to tell him. She didn't like seeing him jealous, but her love life was none of his business. "I'm just pointing out the poems are fiction, not an objective reporting of facts."

Jesse pushed himself under Firestriker's neck. "He's not the stud described in those verses?"

"Jesse!" She shied toward the stream and slipped. He steadied her with a hand to the back. She stiffened. She knew he could feel the steel of her stays. She wished he could touch a waist strong and supple, but she could not overcome that particular shortcoming and made up her mind not to regret it. "You shouldn't ask me questions like that."

"I don't see why not."

"For one thing, you're going to be married."

He tucked his arm under her elbow and led her away from the gurgling water. "In the library, you told me you'd love me forever."

"I'll always love you, but it's more of a friendship."

"Don't friends have the right to ask questions?"

"Not anymore." Now she felt threatened. They'd come so far from the house. Not that she thought Jesse would hurt her. He'd always been a gentleman really, but his touch made her flustered. His touch and the darkness. For reasons she couldn't explain, those elements made lying harder. She felt like the girl, frightened and crippled, who'd learned to ride Firestriker so long ago. "We can't be friends once you are married."

He pressed a swift kiss to her forehead. "I don't see why not."

"Because . . ." She stopped. Firestriker nickered. She reached forward and touched him, throwing her arms around his neck and resting her cheek against his warm skin. "Because . . ." She bit back her impulse to weep, to reach out and hug Jesse Wheeler instead. "Because . . . I saw the look Christine gave me."

He touched one of her tendrils, a tiny ringlet lying down on her neck. "It was just a small misunderstanding. She'll be all right once I put her right."

"Don't be a fool." Bet smiled and touched Jesse's finely worked sleeve. "You can't put a friend ahead of your wife."

He leaned close. For a moment she thought he would kiss her, but he whispered near her earlobe instead. "Now who's being provincial?"

"Surely not me." And she laughed. For the briefest of moments, she savored the warmth, the pool of heat in her stomach, the aftereffects of Jesse's close whisper. She would miss his friendship, the sense of excitement, even the light scent of citrus he wore. She drew in her breath. "But I would ask one favor."

"What?

She buried her face in Firestriker's warm neck. "You'll look after him while I'm in the Yukon?"

"What a silly request. He's always well cared for." He pressed in behind her, one hand rubbing the mustang's forehead. His warmth and scent mingled with that of the horse.

"You won't put him down? No matter what happens? I'll be back by the end of the summer and then I'll be able to care for him always." He turned her toward him. His gaze searched her face. She tried to read those dark eyes, but she'd never had any luck reading his expression. It had gone through her mind that her beloved horse might be in danger if Christine turned out to be jealous or spiteful. "Jesse?" She touched his black velvet jacket, still slung over his shoulder.

He leaned so close she thought she could feel him, though he didn't quite seem to touch her. "Give him up, Bet. He doesn't deserve you."

"Do you find Christine Deutch worthy?"

He scowled.

"Well, then." She leaned her cheek against the velvety muzzle. "Promise you'll take care of Firestriker for me. I'll be back for him by the end of the summer."

Jesse returned Bet to the ranch house. He noticed Christine under the banyan, a pale, silent figure staring pointedly at the small woman whose hand Jesse kept snugged in his elbow. Ignoring his fiancée's glare, he led Bet up to the porch, planted a brief kiss on her forehead, and smiled at a gathered group of young ladies. They tittered, then drifted back into the ballroom, assessing Bet with sly glances. She lifted her chin, waved gaily at Jesse, then disappeared into the soft light and music. Jesse turned and strode to the shimmering figure shadowed by the heavy tree branches.

As he approached, Christine bolted. She headed down toward the garden, a champagne glass dangling from her languid fingers. He followed, annoyed. Her measured retreat conveyed her disapproval more clearly than than any amount of explicit displeaure. When she reached the grape arbor, she paused. He joined her, his jacket still slung over his shoulder.

She took a swift sip of her drink. "You're testing my patience."

"It's not what you think."

She touched her neck lightly, a nervous caress. "Really, Jesse. I know she's a cripple, and I shouldn't be jealous, but everyone knows you chased her for years."

Jesse felt a twitch in his jaw muscles. He liked Christine Deutch and admired her riding, her fine social graces, and her cool beauty. He did not like her possessive nature, but he knew no wife would be perfect and made up his mind not to regret it. He held his anger in check. Bet had been right in one observation. He did not want to choose between these two women. He might be upset with Bet's request, but he didn't want to lose her friendship forever. "Are you jealous?"

"No. But I do have my pride. You put all my friends in a tither."

"She's thinks she's losing the poet."

Christine paled. Even in the shade of the arbor, he could see her creamy complexion go chalky. She turned and fled, her full satin rustling along the brickwork. Jesse hurried after her, his heart pumping strongly, trying hard not to be angry. She slowed when she reached the great circular well, the heart of a vast and exotic garden collected from all the places his father had traveled before he settled down on the rancho. Sitting down on a small wooden bench, Christine lifted a silver bell and rang it.

The dark water swirled. A dozen gold shapes drifted up from the bottom, lit by the glow of a Japanese lantern. She tossed in a leaf, watching intently as the black waters parted and the exotic koi imported by his father nosed the twig, testing for food.

"What a pity," she said. "They're so trained to the sound, they don't even know the leaves aren't for eating."

Jesse put down his jacket and rolled up his shirtsleeve. "Sure they do. They just have to taste them." He dipped his hand in the water, stroking the belly of one of the largest, a multicolored beauty, gorgeous as a pinto. "They're surprisingly intelligent creatures."

She took a delicate sip of her drink, leaned back on the wall, and gazed at the garden. Though the ranch house was modest compared to his income, the don had spared no expense on the surrounding grounds. Botanical wonders were pampered like children, the one passion all three Wheelers shared.

"It's funny," Christine said. "She suits you so poorly."

More koi bumped Jesse gently, looking for food. "I haven't broken off my engagement to you."

"But you would in a moment if you thought she would have you."

"I suppose you think me exceedingly foolish."

She took another sip of her wine. "No more foolish than I, pining for someone who doesn't want me."

"*Touché.*" He picked up a few small pellets of fish food from a bowl kept by the well. He tossed a few into the water. The surface roiled with confusion as the pellets drifted downward and the competing koi ate them. "You can keep the ring no matter what happens. We'll talk again, when I get back—"

The clink of glass hit the brickwork. The fish disappeared with a flourish. "Where are you going?"

"The Yukon."

She touched her neck lightly. "With her?"

"She's chasing the poet."

She drained the whole glass, then touched Jesse's shirtsleeve. "And you're chasing her."

He flinched. "That's one way to put it."

"What if I'm not waiting when you return?"

"That's a chance I'll be taking."

"You know I've had suitors."

"Of course." He lied just a bit in this assessment. Christine had beaus, but she'd schemed for years after Jesse's proposal, though not for the most flattering of reasons. The daughter of a neighboring rancher, she loved nothing so much as this idyllic valley with its close-knit group of horse-mad romantics whose way of life had been fading for years. The Wheelers had money. The Deutches didn't. For Christine to hang onto her rancho, she'd have to find a wealthy husband. "But you'd give a great deal to spend your life on this rancho."

"My point exactly." She rang the bell and tossed another twig in the water. "That's what makes our marriage so perfect. We're bred to this life, you and I."

"Maybe."

"So you'll gamble our marriage for a half-Jewish cripple, just because she turned you down in college?"

"Yes."

"Why? Our ranch is not doing so badly. With a little infusion of cash—"

"It's not the money."

She touched the pearl button of his white linen shirt. "Is she really so much the temptress? I've read the poems—"

Jesse stilled her hand. "That's none of your business."

"I think it is. It's Christmas Eve. You've announced our engagement. Ten minutes later I find myself rejected because a little tease—"

He squeezed her wrist tightly. "I've not withdrawn my proposal. This is just a request that you wait a little bit longer."

"Give me one reason why I should do that."

He stared pointedly at the horizon, the vast tract of land that belonged to his parents.

She slipped out of his grasp, rubbing her wrist just a little. "I don't understand the attraction. That woman's a Gypsy, if not by blood, then by inclination. Have you read the poems? Why would you want a woman so wanton?"

Jesse smiled to himself. The koi were cruising under the surface, waiting patiently for a genuine feeding. "I'm not sure I do. But I have to be honest. If she can't find the poet—or he rejects her—I might try again with my proposal of marriage."

"And if she accepts?"

"Then you keep the ring for your troubles."

She pulled the ring off her finger and held it over the dark well water. "The emerald means nothing. I could use it for fish food."

"I'm sorry if I've hurt your pride." He watched the koi briefly. They rose to the surface, attracted by the light and movement. "I know it was cruel to announce our engagment, but we'd already planned it. I lost my head when she came and asked me to help her hare off to the Yukon. Now the whole idea is making me crazy because if she's stooped to chasing this poet, it might mean she's ready to marry, and if he doesn't want to accept her—"

"I could sue you for breach of promise."

"You're fooling yourself if you think you can thwart me. It's the land you want, not so much what comes with it. And you might very well have it, if you can be patient. But I'm going to try one more time for Bet Goldman."

Her blue eyes narrowed, stormy beneath the delicate light of the Japanese lantern. "But no little emerald is going to repay me for what I lose if you call off this marriage."

"Of course." He picked up a food pellet and tossed it into the water. "Perhaps it would help if I found an infusion of cash for your rancho."

Four

July 1898
Oakland, California

Bet grasped the handrail as the two-masted steamship chugged out of the harbor. The black-coated figure couldn't be Jesse, though she couldn't imagine mistaking him. Tall and reserved, with an elegant bearing, he always stood out in a crowd. This was especially so in San Francisco, where the proud heritage of the aristocratic Californios had long since been supplanted by more recent immigrants. Such men crowded this steamer—small-statured men mostly, with varied complexions, the diverse flotsam of a great port city, with nothing in common except their pretensions and dreams that exceeded their home culture's limit. Still, Bet thought she must be mistaken, for why Jesse would be here she couldn't imagine. He'd turned her down firmly that day at the rancho, and she'd never made a second request.

One hand on the rail, Bet inched her way down the wooden deck. The elegant stranger had planted himself on the prow, feet braced like a sailor, hands clasped behind him, clutching a slim leather-bound volume. Bet's breath caught in her bosom. She recognized the little book by its covering.

"Jesse." She stopped, jostled by the press of the crowd.

He turned, tucked the poems into the breast pocket of his chinchilla greatcoat, picked up her bag, and snagged her elbow. "Good morning. May I escort you down to your stateroom?"

"Where are we going?"

"I told you. Down to your stateroom."

"Why?"

"I'm accompanying you to the Klondike."

She twisted away, perusing the crowd for feminine figures, though she'd been the only woman she'd noticed amid the restless crowd of hard, hopeful faces. "Christine?"

"Gave me permission."

He was lying. Bet knew it. She'd made inquiries about Christine Deutch in the last few days she'd spent on the rancho. Jesse had betrothed himself to a type like his mother, self-assured and commanding, strong-willed and possessive. A woman like that did not give permission for her fiancé to stray to the Klondike, especially with a potential rival. "I didn't mean to imply—"

"Forget it. It's done." He jerked his chin toward the receding shoreline. "The next stop's Vancouver and beyond that Alaska. We'll be back by next Christmas in time for my wedding."

As he hustled her down the narrow staircase, Bet worked over the problem of what she'd do now. The whole situation had become unnerving. When she'd asked Jesse for help she'd been frightened and worried. She hadn't known about his engagement and hadn't intended to interfere. His current expression, dark and determined, the pressure of his hand on her back—and the

volume of poems he'd tucked in his pocket—told her
what a mistake it had been.

He confirmed her impression the minute he guided her
into the stateroom. As he planted her in the room's center, his arm brushed the side of her bosom. The movement might have seemed accidental, except Bet knew
Jesse much too well. He might be shy, but he'd never
been graceless. He tossed her bag into the corner, pulled
out the thin volume of poems Zack had written, and
opened the book to the flyleaf.

"Now, Jesse." She edged toward the door.

" 'To Venus,' " he read from the ornate inscription,
" 'and the muse erotic.' "

"Stop"—she placed a hand on his sleeve—"at the
cost of our friendship."

To her relief and surprise, he halted. The look in his
eyes hadn't changed, however. She backed away quickly
and pulled off her gloves, her mind churning over what
to do next.

"Jesse." She moved around the small stateroom, exploring its corners. It was the best stateroom on board
and had its own water closet, but she still didn't have
much room to maneuver. The walls seemed thick, the
ship's labors noisy, which didn't leave much hope for
screaming. "We have to talk."

He stripped off his coat and draped it over a chair in
the corner. "We're long past talking, Bettina Goldman."

She stepped back farther, nearly tripping over her bag.
"It's not what you think between me and Zack English."

He lifted one eyebrow. "Then he's quite a convincing
liar."

"Well, of course." She stepped back one more time
and met the wall behind her, which made logical thought
come rather more slowly. "All writers are excellent liars."

He moved and caged her. "Then why should I believe
you, my dear little author of children's horse stories?

Are storytellers more truthful than poets?''

''That's not what I meant.'' She had no idea what she should do now, and the thought flashed though her mind that she should confess the whole sham, but that would be such a betrayal, not just of herself but of Zack English as well. ''Look. I fudged a little that day at the rancho. Zack does think we're going to be married.'' She lied easily in moments of panic.

He lifted her chin. His eyes were dark and hungry, angry and possessive. ''Do you think that matters to me?''

''If Zack doesn't matter, then think of Christine.''

''She doesn't matter much either.''

Bet doubted this statement. She strongly suspected she'd destroyed his engagement. The idea made her sick to her stomach, but she needed to keep up the fiction that he had reasons not to seduce her. ''You're not being fair, Jesse.''

''Look who's talking.'' He moved his lips over her earlobe, but he didn't kiss her, not really. A light brush of velvety texture, then he dropped his hand and regarded her coolly. ''You're frightened, aren't you?''

''No.'' Now she lied truly.

''Too bad.'' He pushed off the wall. ''Because you frightened me, and I'd like to get even. I've made inquiries into the trip to the goldfields. Do you have any idea what you're getting into?''

''I'll be all right.''

''There's a killer pass.''

''They're building a railroad.''

''You have to carry a ton of supplies.''

''I'm sure there are porters.''

He pulled out the poems again and held the thin volume under her nose. ''I want to make sure you're back for the wedding. I think it will be the only suitable vengeance, to have you watch me stand at the altar.''

She tossed her paisley scarf over her shoulder. ''You're jealous.''

"No. Not a bit." He snapped the book back into his pocket. "A trip to the Klondike fits my plans nicely. A man ought to have at least one great adventure before he settles into his marriage."

Jesse cursed Christine as he hustled down the narrow hallway. He didn't regret his broken engagement, but he'd be damned if he'd give Bettina Goldman the perverse satisfaction of knowing she'd ruined his life. Not when she might be in love with Zack English. Jesse wasn't jealous. Bet had been wrong on that score. Oh, he'd gotten a little upset when she'd first asked him to go to the Klondike. The gall of her had annoyed him the most, the arrogant confidence in their friendship that made her believe she wouldn't hurt him with a request so oblivious to his former feelings. Once he'd gotten over his burst of anger, however, he realized he had been incredibly lucky.

With a silent chuckle, he took the stairs to the deck two at a time. Bet Goldman, free spirit, freethinker, and just lately notorious wanton, had stooped to chasing after a lover. A lover, what's more, who did not seem to love her. Jesse had read Zack's poems quite carefully. He'd never been much for fiction reading, excepting, of course, Bettina's horse stories. But he'd learned a great deal from those. Bet thought herself disguised by her fiction, but she stripped herself bare on those pages.

Reaching the deck, Jesse pushed his way through the dark-suited miners, city boys mostly, dressed in their finest, broadcloth and wool already rumpling. Jesse wound his way toward the mountains of baggage, searching for the stack that contained his belongings. He had studied the poems quite carefully. If Zack were half as honest an artist as Bet was, he wasn't in love with his Gypsy-like mentor. The poems had a coldness, a distance and fury, that completely belied their apparent content. Technically brilliant and beautifully written but clearly written to shock the reader, these were the poems

of a man driven by artistic ambition, in love with his
goals, not with the woman who was said to inspire them.

Jesse's jaw twitched as he reached the largest mountain of bags. He practically threw himself on the rubble,
a great stack of jumbled luggage. Around him, dozens
of men picked through the arrangement, but Jesse ignored them as he tossed the baggage from one spot to
another. Of course there were risks involved in this
chase to the Yukon. Bet might be engaged to Zack English, though Jesse doubted the truth of her statement.
She wasn't a liar exactly, but she wasn't above twisting
the truth, especially if it suited a higher purpose. She
had strong feelings about this young poet, and Jesse believed she was trying to protect him. Why this should
be so, he couldn't be certain, but perhaps the beautiful
poems explained it.

For as long as he'd known Bettina Goldman, she'd
been obsessed with becoming a writer. Though her horse
stories were quite popular really, she believed them to
be silly and female. She was always fretting about how
to improve them and never happy with how they came
out.

He paused, stretched his muscles, took a deep whiff
of salt air, and blinked the fog off his eyelashes. He
thought himself six kinds of fool and probably something more stupid than that. He'd loved Bet Goldman
all of his life, or at least since the first summer he'd met
her. Some part of his heart had clung to the hope that
she'd finally accept his marriage proposal. Why this
should be so, he was not certain either, for they made
the world's most unlikely lovers, worse even than his
mother and father. She, the worldly, cosmopolitan
writer; he the inarticulate recluse, who could have spent
the rest of his life on the rancho without ever once leaving the valley his family had settled so long ago.

Still, for as long as he'd known her, he'd admired
Bet's courage, her grace and beauty and her sense of
humor. For just as long, he'd treasured their friendship,

which is why he'd believed her excuses. She was probably right about her and Zack English. Another writer would most likely suit her. And why should Jesse care if the scoundrel didn't love her? After all, it was none of his business. Except it was.

Because—he pulled out his leather cabinet bag—the poems had ignited an emotion in him, a soul-deep fury and not very pretty, but natural enough and hard to ignore. A hunger. An anger. A possessive nature. Jesse might be shy. He might be reclusive, but he was a man like any other. He'd have gambled the ranch and a thousand engagements for one of the nights described in those verses.

"What have we got here? A dandy?"

Jesse ignored the speaker, one of three slickly dressed men with matching straw hats, brocade vests of scarlet and purple, and identical black-and-white houndstooth-checked trousers. He sighed to himself, silently cursing the stampede to the Klondike and every hopeful, naive young fellow who lusted to make his life's fortune in a quick trip to the goldfields. By the time Jesse had found which boat Bet had taken, he had been unable to book a private cabin. Or even a cabin at all, for that matter. He'd paid six times regular passage to be guaranteed a space in a horse stall. He expected some privacy for his money. Evidently that had been an illusion. Three gaily dressed men lounged on the hay bales Jesse had thought reserved for himself.

"Good morning." Jesse eased through the door of the stall. He deduced his bunkmates to be professional gamblers, as much by the paleness of their long, slender fingers as by the flashiness of their clothes. Jesse wasn't much for that class of people. Not that he held gaming immoral. He never judged another man's vices. But ranching was already a gamble. Jesse seldom wasted his luck or his money on any less serious high-stakes diversion than the gut-wrenching business of holding together a heritage that time had passed by. Suppressing a groan, he dropped his steel-framed leather bag on the one hay bale lacking a bedroll. "I hope I'm not intruding."

"No. Not at all." One of the gamblers pulled out a cigar and lit it. Jesse thought this a risk all by itself, considering the hay and the hold's closeness, but he kept his thoughts to himself.

"We're always happy to have company." One of the gamblers tipped his flat-brimmed hat.

The third, almost a duplicate of the first one, except for a pale handlebar mustache, stepped forward and held out his hand. "We're the McReedy brothers. Hank, Hal, and Handsome. I'm Handsome." The gold mustache quirked into a smile.

Jesse had to laugh. The brothers made a kind of human rainbow, ranging in age from oldest to youngest, in shade from darkest to lightest, and in height from tallest to shortest. And the youngest was Handsome, though palest and shortest, and probably not such a bad man. But Jesse still didn't like sharing his quarters. He clasped the soft hand Handsome offered. "Jesse Wheeler."

"Of the Flying W ranch?"

Jesse nodded. His rancho was well known in California. Not many of the land grants families had kept their holdings intact. The Flying W's links to the past and his father's shrewdness in preserving its profits had made the splendid acreage famous.

"My goodness." Hal, the middle one in every respect, reached into his pockets and pulled out a well-worn deck of cards. "Perhaps this will be a pleasant journey." The rectangular pile whirred through expert fingers. "Would you care to join us in a game of poker?"

"Not really." Jesse shrugged out of his coat and folded it neatly over the hay bale.

Hal seemed unperturbed by Jesse's refusal. He laid the cards down in rows of seven, the beginning of a solitaire hand. His brothers watched with languid interest. Hank, the tallest, darkest, and oldest, puffed slowly on a cigar, which clouded the already much-befouled air. Handsome hefted himself onto a hay bale and pulled out a cheroot to match his brother's. Jesse suppressed the urge to cough. Generally he loved the smell of a stable and didn't too much mind the odor of smoke, but the roll of the ship and the closeness of the hold began to make his stomach queasy. He unbuttoned the top of his cotton shirt but grabbed the coat of black chinchilla. "Gentlemen," he said, nodding to his new bunkmates, "I believe I'll go and get some fresh air."

As Bet made her way down the wooden deck, she noticed Jesse had returned to the prow. Hundreds of men milled about on the small surface, jostling their way to the handrails. Mostly they looked back at the land. Jesse glowered out at the ocean. He ignored the excitement and air of nostalgia, the cold mist that turned the green hillsides emerald, dampened the air with its drizzle, and twisted the clouds into weeping gray tendrils.

Ignoring the pitch and sway of the deck, she worked her way toward Jesse's dark figure. "Are you feeling all right?" she asked when she reached him.

Jesse nodded, but he did not look well. He stood rigidly, hands clasped behind him, glaring out at the vast expanse of slate-colored water.

"Seasick?"

He shook his head.

This she believed. Jesse loved the ocean. He sailed quite a bit in the summer, a passion handed down from his father. Still, he looked distressed in some fashion, his finely shaped mouth thinned into a frown.

"Homesick?"

Jesse scowled. The sea breeze whipped through his black curls, which turned darker and wilder with each passing moment. The deck had become a little less crowded, but hundreds of men still prowled its length.

One of them bumped against Bet as she waited. Jesse scowled even more deeply.

Suddenly Bet understood. "Would you like to come down to my cabin?"

He shifted his weight and gripped his fists tighter.

"I'm the only single woman on board."

He did not comment, but interest flickered behind his thick lashes.

"They didn't give me a roommate."

"Thanks." Jesse flung himself onto Bet's bunk bed and loosened his collar, a kind of high color suffusing his normally bronze-colored complexion. "I wasn't sure I'd make it all the way to Alaska without tossing a few men into the ocean just to get more room for breathing."

Bet laughed. "Really, Jesse, I swear you like horses more than you like people."

"I've never denied it."

"I suppose that's natural, having spent your whole life with cattle and cowboys."

"Not to mention a former sea captain father . . ."

He didn't finish the sentence, but Bet understood the implicit finish. He'd been raised by a former sea captain father and a glorious, frivolous mother whose dreams of escape collapsed when she discovered too late why Don Wheeler loved her. He'd not been awed by her impressive bloodlines, or even her dark and exotic beauty. He'd fallen in love with that old Spanish rancho, that beautiful prison whose vast open spaces had trapped her more tightly than the tiniest jail cell.

Luxury-loving and gregarious by nature, she hated that land and in the end her husband. She'd borne her son out of pure pride and malice, the last of her familial duties, then retreated into reclusive silence, bitter and grieved by the age of thirty. Jesse adored his mother and respected his father, but otherwise had very few friendships. He did not seem to think it a failing.

Bet folded her cape over a chair, opened her bag, and

riffled through it. "Want to play a game of Hearts?"

"No, thanks." Jesse adjusted his sleeves and unbuttoned collar. "I just turned down a better offer."

She flashed him a glance.

He shrugged out of his chinchilla greatcoat. "I'm rooming with three professional gamblers."

"Oh." She checked the derringer stuffed in her bag. "Be careful."

"They're decent enough. But it's going to be a very long journey. I can't say I relish sharing a stall with three total strangers."

"A stall?"

"Last accommodations they had."

"Ah. Jesse."

"Don't look so worried." He sprang from the bed and strode to her side, brushing one of her curls from her forehead. "It's going to be a terrific adventure."

"You can sleep on the floor if you want."

"That's not what I had in mind."

"No. I suppose not. Fan-tan?" She pulled out a small box of dark pebbles.

"You brought them?"

"I brought several games for the voyage." She flashed him her warmest smile, still niggled by his sleeping arrangement, or something else, perhaps his expression, or maybe just his double entendre. Jesse had never been much for fancy wordplay. "And you know perfectly well fan-tan's my favorite."

He smiled back and pulled up a mahogany chair. She placed the round stones out on a small mahogany table, then immediately clapped a small metal bowl over them. She'd learned this from Jesse, who had learned it at Berkeley, gambling in the back rooms of the laundries. On a dare Bet had gone with him once to a genuine opium den that smelled of joss and a sickly sweet substance Jesse had explained was the notorious opiate. Their parents would have been shocked if they'd known—and looking back it had been truly foolish—

but at the time it had seemed harmless, and she'd had no subsequent reason to regret the experience.

"How many?" she asked, pulling her wand out of its bag and holding it over one of the rows.

"Three," he answered without hesitation.

She divided the stones into groups of four, then counted the remaining ones. He drummed his fingers on the small inlaid table, a gesture she knew did not mean impatience so much as a sign of his restless nature. "Three," she said. "You win. You haven't forgotten the skills you developed."

"Some skills never leave you." He was eyeing her sharply, a gaze so incisive it caused her to pause.

"Yes?" she asked softly.

"You haven't told me the stakes."

"Ah." She laid out the fan pattern again. "Nickels?"

"Higher."

"Quarters?"

"Small change."

"Surely not dollars?"

"I was thinking of something a good deal more substantial."

She placed the long, slender rod in her lap. She couldn't gamble for very much money, though she didn't want Jesse to know that about her. He thought her secure in her finances, an illusion she preferred to maintain. "We could gamble for time in the bed," she said.

He arched his dark eyebrows.

She felt her cheeks color. "Not together, of course. But I could spend the night in a deck chair."

"I liked the first idea better."

The hot blush crept upward. She pushed up from the chair, walked to the window, and looked out at the still-foggy ocean. She didn't know what to make of Jesse's comment. In the old days she'd have known how to control him, but she wasn't so sure of him now. She drew in a shaky breath. "Is that an improper suggestion?"

"Maybe." His voice had gone a little bit husky. "At least it should be. I know we don't run in all the same circles, but I might enjoy outraging the censors."

"Don't be foolish, Jesse. I told you before, Zack is taking artistic license."

"That doesn't offend you?"

"Of course not." She returned to the table, ignoring the light that had come into his eyes. She'd have to be careful. She didn't believe Jesse's denials that Zack's poetry had not made him jealous. He still had the small volume tucked in his breast pocket, and she suspected Zack's tome had outraged more than the censor. Pain flared in Bet's spine, and she leaned lightly forward. She'd have been gambling her life, though Jesse didn't know it, if she'd done the things described in the poems. Slowly she sat back down in the chair. "We'll play for the pillow. Unless you have one down in that horse stall."

"No."

"Good. Then perhaps the voyage can be made more comfy."

He smiled slowly and watched the rod closely. She drew out the small stones again. They'd played this for hours during the past few summers, nearly always breaking exactly even, as fan-tan wasn't just a game of chance, but depended on the skill of the players.

"Two . . ."

She swept the stones into small groupings, then counted out the remainder. "You win," she said softly, then flashed him a glance. She'd planned on cheating so he'd get the pillow, but he'd won on his own, a surprising result, as he seldom won two in a row.

He reached behind her, grabbed the feather pillow, and set it on the floor behind them. "I've given up a great deal to help you."

"I'd rather guessed that." She clicked the round

stones though her fingers. "Has Christine broken off your engagement?"

"Of course not. I told you."

"Then I don't take your meaning." She lay the stones down on a pattern. "More?"

He stood up abruptly and moved to her trunk. "Did you bring anything to make music?"

"Two harmonicas and one tambourine."

He lifted an eyebrow.

She shrugged and poured the rest of the little round pebbles onto the table. "It seemed like a good idea."

"It is."

He clasped his hands behind his back, turned toward the square window, and stared out at the ocean. This, she knew from long experience, meant she had something he wanted.

"Would you like to play something?"

He nodded briefly.

She knelt down and unhinged the trunk's buckles, wondering again about his engagement. Maybe Christine had let him come without protest. That seemed unlikely, but some people surprised you. As she worked at the clasps, she sensed him behind her, as much from the slight sound of his breathing as from the citrus-scented cologne he exuded.

"We have an arrangement, Christine and I."

She leaned back into her corset. "An arrangement?"

"Rather like you and Zack English."

Briefly she pressed on the small of her back, then she lifted the trunk lid and took out the small instrument she'd stored in a cardboard box in a pocket. "I wouldn't call what Zack and I have an arrangement."

"Then what would you call it?"

"He's my . . . fiancé. I told you that also."

"But you haven't waited for marriage."

"No. Not exactly."

He held out his hand for the small mouth organ. "Well, neither have Christine and I."

"I see."

"I don't think you do." He sat down on the bunk, leaned against the bulkhead, kicked off one shoe, crooked up his leg, then started in on a song. She sank into the chair, her back and heart aching, for other than their shared love of horses, this was the side of Jess she loved best. The reclusive rancher had the soul of an artist, and he showed that side in his music. Cradling the cheap toy in his hands, he blew softly into the fragile mouthpiece. Miraculous sounds swept through the cabin, surprisingly rich and full-bodied. She could hardly believe a man could create such music from an inexpensive mail-order mouth organ. Memories came rolling back, of evenings spent at the rancho, summer nights in mountain pastures, winter scenes on the veranda.

She picked up the small tambourine, tapping it gently against her knee. Jesse's eyes softened briefly, then his expression hardened, and the tempo grew stronger. He filled the room with a low, urgent warble, haunting as the cry of a seagull. She stopped the trill of her tambourine and watched his long, brown, blunt-tipped fingers as they held the little child's instrument. The music held her, that and the ocean, whose deep swells had established a cadence. She leaned against the red velvet cushion and let the music carry her off. Some of the fog had burned away, and the midmorning sunlight brightened the cabin, before Jesse gave up his solo performance. Bet had listened the whole time in silence.

He lay the instrument down in his lap and watched her, his chest blowing slightly from the exertion. "It's going to be a very long voyage."

She nodded. "I'm sorry I didn't bring a guitar."

"I brought a Jew's harp." He glanced out the window.

"Oh, Jesse. That will be lovely." She moved to the end of the cot and sat gingerly on the edge of the bunk. "We'll have something to do in the evenings."

He stared at her from beneath lowered lashes, his expression hooded and distant. "Did you really let him touch you that way?"

"Don't start on that, Jesse." For all the intimacy of their friendship, they'd never discussed their romantic affairs. In truth, she doubted Jesse had any great experience with women, handicapped as he was by his shyness, the provincial nature of the local gentry, and an unfortunate combination of parents.

In a fluid movement, he caged her again. "Perhaps we can make a kind of play of them."

"Honestly, Jesse." She didn't struggle against him, thinking any show of fear would be fatal. It had been years since he'd tried to seduce her, but she still remembered the awful power of even his most innocent kisses.

He pulled the small volume out of his breast pocket and flipped to a dog-eared page in the center. " 'The Virgin Queen.' " He tossed the tome on the floor beside them and brushed his lips over her earlobe. "We can't reenact that one, though I must admit I feel rather foolish." He no longer kissed her, but spoke in hot whispers, both his words and their heat exuding passion. "All the years I schemed after that treasure, wondering what price it commanded. I offered the ranch. My name and protection." He laughed, a short, harsh sound, and the heat from his body made his rich lemon scent spicy. His cotton shirt had lost all its coolness. "And all you wanted were verses." He hovered close, though he did not touch her, except where his thick eyelashes brushed against the curve of her neck. "The irony is he not only took you, but also he described the experience in such exquisite detail that I can relive the event as vividly as if I had been there."

"Really, Jesse." She dredged her voice up out of her throat, though she scarcely heard it for all her heart's pounding. "Don't be so small-minded."

He drew back abruptly. "Perhaps I could read it out loud."

She snatched the book off the floor, her hand brushing

his as she did. She beat him to the verses and held the book close to her bosom. "Now you're not only being provincial. You're being barbaric, verging on loutish."

"You think so?"

"I know so."

His eyes pooled to darkness as one long finger traced the gold letters on the leather-bound volume. "I suppose it does bring out the savage."

He kissed her.

Five

He kissed her. Not a tender kiss like those he'd given in college, but a deep kiss and greedy, the way he might drink a glass of water when thirsty. That quality moved her, a sense of need mixed with passion. His hands gripped both her shoulders. He leaned into her body and pressed her backward. Pain flared in her spine, but she ignored it. A tension pooled in the pit of her stomach, and in those lower, forbidden places that no one ever touched or ever discussed, except to make them off-limits. She tried to think of something to say, some effective way to object, but the easy lies had all escaped her, and she could only think of feeble excuses.

"Stop," she breathed quietly. "This isn't proper."

He deepened the kiss. The thrum of her blood drowned out the ocean. Citrus cologne tickled her nose. His fingers plucked her finely spun blouse sleeves, sliding over her skin and tightening over closely worked stitching. He pressed tightly against her, trapping her in a half-sitting position.

A nerve pinched in her back, and she flinched.

He pulled back, his full lips in a frown. "Did I hurt you?"

"No," she lied, her cheeks heating quickly, her mind working over how to dissuade him without revealing too many details. She leaned into her corset and struggled to get control of her breathing. The ache in all those forbidden places seemed so much stronger than this minor discomfort. Still, she ought to tell Jesse how hopeless this was. Only the lowest tease let a man continue without letting him finish. She wanted to weep and curse all those doctors, but she knew that would be futile, and she never engaged in pointless sorrow. She placed her hand on Jesse's chest and imagined those long-ago days of their friendship when they'd ridden the mountains on Firestriker. "Jesse." As always, the thought of the mustang gave comfort. She noticed the pace of Jesse's heartbeat, slower and stronger than that of her own. "We can't go any farther."

"Why not?"

"I don't have to give you a reason."

"You want me. I feel it." She opened her lips, but he moved swiftly, urging her once more with his hard body. "And don't talk to me about Zachary English. Mention his name, and I'll kiss you silly."

She shuddered. He had the power to seduce her. He had the power to force her as far as that went, but it wasn't rape she feared at his hands. He could end her life far more simply, assuming the doctors were right.

She sighed, and he answered, his breath soft against her neck. Goose bumps formed where he touched her, a combination of terror and wanting. Right now, it seemed almost worth the risk to lose herself in this sensual rush. She pushed him once more. "Stop now. And I mean it. I'll scream if you don't."

Rebellion flared in his eyes, but he squelched it. She could see that struggle and his effort to win it. She'd never been one for giddy reaction, but neither had she been one to be bullied. She rose from the bed. "I promised Zack—"

He grabbed her, shoving her against the wall, one

thigh pinioned against hers, his hips insistent. She panicked. She had no power against this. Not the sheer physical force, but the thrill and sense of unbalance, the need and the weakness, the ache transmuted into raw pleasure. She dropped her hands to her side and froze. She didn't dare any other reaction, for his littlest response would have undone her.

He bent down and nipped the curve of her neck. A thrill spiraled through her. She'd relived his kisses so many times, but she didn't remember this darkness, this velvety texture and bolt of sheer joy.

Her fear vanished beneath this deep rush of pleasure. Reaching up, she touched the nape of his neck. He had soft curls there, downy as feathers, a striking contrast to the rest of his hair, which was curly and thick and more coarse.

He groaned. His silver belt buckle pressed into her stomach. She wanted to laugh at the pleasure and beauty. Her breasts felt heavy, her lips full and bruised, and he really was kissing her silly, traveling among lips, neck, and earlobe, rubbing his cheek against hers, his eyelashes tickling her skin, his chest crushing her bosom. There was an aggressiveness in his actions, heat, need, and passion, and no sense of his usual shyness. His fingers were agile and restless, though he didn't seek to unbutton her clothes, but ran his hands over her arms, her back, and her shoulders, as if he wished to memorize the sensation. "Speak to me, Bet. I'm not the poet, but I know I can please you."

Now she really did want to weep, for she'd never made love to Zachary English. Where the poetry came from she didn't know, though she had her suspicions. Their friendship had been strictly platonic, the poems the product of talent and longing, and a complete education in Sappho and Ovid. She smiled through the threatening tears while something in her thought process niggled. "Ah, Jesse."

He pulled back, turning his dark gaze upon her. He

looked like a prince in all three of the dark races that made up his unusual bloodlines. "Why do you refuse me?"

"I can't. . . ." She ought to tell him. He'd always loved her in spite of her defects, but something in her rebelled. With Jesse she always felt normal, a treacherous illusion but one she cherished. She was his creation, perfect in his eyes. Even if it hurt him on certain levels, she couldn't bring herself to disappoint him by confessing to such frustrating limits. "We have an arrangement, Zack English and I."

He pressed his mouth against her earlobe. "Then make the same arrangement with me."

She shivered. "I can't."

His hand rested beneath the curve of her bosom. Zack had described this very gesture and many more she'd never imagined until he'd introduced her to the classical poets, with their delicate sense of the erotic and vivid descriptions of sensual pleasure. She'd pressed her mother sometimes on this subject, but Mother had been pedantic and stuffy and always declined to go into detail on what the doctor's fierce prohibitions had meant. "You should confine yourself to holding hands," she'd told Bet primly. "Anything else would be risky."

Bet had tried to ask the doctor directly, but he was even more closemouthed than her mother. He got a stubborn look on his face and informed her that normal women did not discuss this subject, and she should see it as a hidden blessing that her oddities relieved her of a painful duty.

In this respect Bet must not have been normal, as she liked the feel of Jesse's hand on her breast. "But maybe . . ."

"Yes?"

This was madness to even think about, she knew, but she'd never before tested these limits. She'd never been told what would hurt exactly, or what could be done and what couldn't. Zack's poems had shocked more than the censors, for she'd never read such stuff before, and his vivid description of the virgin's seduction contained graphic details Bet had never imagined, more startling and blunt than sly, witty Ovid; more specific than even passionate Sappho. But all had been profoundly arousing, and, normal or not, Bet had learned to enjoy their sensual pleasures.

She pressed her hand to Jesse's chest, reveling in the feel of his heartbeat, the heat and scent and closeness of him. "Maybe we can make our own arrangement."

Jesse clattered down the metal stairs into the bowels of the laboring steamer. He was gambling, he knew it. He'd decided to leave her, to give her the evening to sort out her thoughts. They'd agreed to meet in her room for dinner and discuss how they'd spend the rest of the voyage. The concession rankled, for she'd seemed on the edge of surrender, but she'd also seemed nervous, in fact more than nervous—she'd seemed almost giddy with terror. He had just enough respect left for their friendship to agree to a one-day extension. Her anxiety puzzled him, though. She wanted him. He was certain of that. And she wasn't the innocent he'd courted in college.

He stormed into the horse stall and threw himself down on the empty hay bale and pulled the slender red volume out of the breast pocket of his chinchilla greatcoat. Hank, Hal, and Handsome glanced up. Jesse scowled, and they went back to their poker, evidently put off by his temper. Jesse shoved the book back into the pocket, his hands trembling in frustration and anger. He briefly considered going above deck, but realized quickly that a narrow deck teeming with miners would be even less private than his niche in the stall. At least he could turn his back on the gamblers.

He did so, stretching out on his side like a boy in a sulk. He stared at the wall for a few seconds, his heart thumping beneath the volume, the ship's engines churning beneath him. He didn't think she loved the poet, or even that they were really engaged. He thought he knew the key to his charms. Bet admired the writing more than the man, having been seduced by his artistic pretensions and her self-doubt about her talents. For as long as he'd known her, Bet had lived through her writing, always trying to make it better, always frustrated by her perceived limitations, always surrounded by posturing mentors, half-convinced by the lie that she as a woman would never achieve artistic greatness.

Jesse readjusted himself on the hay bale, propping himself on his elbow. His fingers crept toward his breast pocket. He hated reading the poems in public, though he often perused them in private. It seemed such an infuriating, intimate pleasure, reading the poet's description of what had gone on between him and Bet Goldman. The thought aroused him, and he squirmed a little, readjusting himself on top of the hay bale. The three gamblers ignored him, evidently convinced by his prior demeanor. He slipped the volume out of his pocket, and he flipped through the pages, startled again by their contents. Words and imagery seared him. He slammed one fist against the wooden wall that separated this stall from the others.

The three gamblers huddled more closely together, their vests of scarlet and purple accenting the subtle gradations in height, age, and coloring in the otherwise almost identical brothers. Barely suppressing a scowl, Jesse turned onto his stomach, adjusting himself on the prickly surface. The smell made him homesick, but he ignored it. He knew exactly how Zack English had fooled her. But he wasn't going to succeed at that trick any longer. Jesse meant to take her back from the scoundrel. He didn't know how to do it exactly, but he intended to be far more assertive. His polite reserve had served him so poorly, as had his respect for their friendship. The poet had won her with his pose as a wild man. If that was what she wanted, so be it.

Jesse laughed to himself and attracted startled stares from the gamblers, but another scowl forced them back

to their poker. Jesse had never believed he could be forward, especially when faced with her clear-browed expression. He'd always delighted in her heart filled with
wonder and waited for her to return the affection. Once,
at Berkeley, he had come to blows with a fellow who'd
made a rude comment about her virtue. He should have
known better. Bet hadn't cared. She relished the notion
of a slight reputation and had laughed at Jesse for his
efforts, though she cared for his knuckles quite tenderly
and thoroughly snubbed the football player he'd fought
with. Later she'd written a stinging essay for the school
paper on boorish males and their unfounded assumptions, making the cool but accurate point that such rudeness often covered frustration. Jesse had never tried to
kiss her again, afraid, like most of the males on campus,
of enduring a barbed and public rejection.

He sat up abruptly, shoving the volume into his coat.
His movement attracted the three brothers' attention
again, and it took a thunderous scowl to defeat them. He
succeeded, however. They hunkered into a circle, ignoring their stallmate. Their white cards flashed in a mechanical rhythm, the progress of their game expressed
in low murmurs and an occasional cry of satisfaction.

Jesse pulled out the volume, staring at its textured red
surface, the scent of the leather tickling his nose. Somehow Zack had gotten past her defenses. Or perhaps there
had been others before him. Although he had described
her deflowering quite clearly, by now Jesse doubted
even that aspect of the story. She'd said the books
weren't literally true. How could he be certain she'd
been a virgin when Zack English took her?

The engine clanged loudly as Jesse riffled once more
through the well-worn pages. No matter the truth, the
past didn't matter. He, Jesse Wheeler, intended to have
her. He wanted the woman portrayed in those poems,
and he was going to have her. He intended to kiss away
all her objections, make her forget the dissolute poet,

beg to be taken back to the rancho and kept there forever, abandon her fictional horse for a real one, and spend the rest of her life making babies.

Why in the world would she be frightened?

She wasn't frightened. Bet tried to convince herself of that proposition as she improvised dinner with food smuggled in from the à la carte diner. Jesse slouched in a bed too short for his height, watching the ocean, indifferent to the eating arrangements or all her efforts to please him. She should have been annoyed by such rudeness, but his presence made a swirl in her stomach, and she forgot the lapse in his manners. She had a plan and she would stick to it. Or would she?

She turned on the lamp, changing the twilight from purple to golden. To this point in their friendship, she'd been in control. Tonight she wasn't so certain. He'd come in the coat he'd worn at Christmas, black velvet with a softly rolled collar, outrageously out of place on this steamer filled with toughs and desperate men, every one of them lusting for gold like a madman and apt to resent this proud Californio who advertised his wealth with his clothing. She suspected the coat had a purpose, however, as she shared his weakness for finely made clothing. The tiny curl of heat in her stomach told her how close he'd come to his object. She shivered. She was taking a terrible risk with this plan. But the idea seduced her. She could be almost normal, if only for the length of this voyage.

Jesse shifted slightly, still watching the ocean. He still carried the poems in his breast pocket, she knew by the lay of the jacket, a deficiency of an inferior tailor, as a coat made by her father would never have shown a visible outline. She lowered her eyes and unwrapped two sandwiches from their brown paper wrappers, plunked a bottle of wine in the ice bucket, folded white linen napkins into rectangles, and set out silver utensils and two wine glasses, her own filled with water.

She surveyed her preparations and the brooding ranchero, then smiled. "Does this remind you of the old days?"

He didn't take his eyes from the ocean. "A little."

"You never told me much about them."

He stared out of the porthole, still jackknifed into the bed, his hands thrust in his pockets. "What's to tell? You've known me since childhood."

The ship churned beneath her. Fortunately she had a strong stomach, and neither the smell of the food nor the pitch of the steamer much affected her appetite. The thought of her plan did, however. "I mean the time you went mining."

He kept his gaze on the vast expanse of gray water. His black curls turned softly against the black velvet collar, a bit of color coordination that further affected her stomach. "You never asked."

"Are you going to eat?"

He pushed out of the bed, pulled out a chair, took her by the elbow, and guided her to the table. Once she was seated, he sat down abruptly, folded a napkin into his lap, uncorked the wine, poured a swallow. With his luxurious clothes and elegant manners, it was hard picturing him as a miner. Evidently he'd liked the experience, however, if she believed his father. She picked up her own sandwich and bit it, but there wasn't much taste in her mouth, and she wondered how long it would be before he brought up the subject of their romantic arrangement.

She put down her sandwich and took a small swig of water, trying to wash down the dry chicken. "You never told me how you earned the money."

"Not much to tell. I made it in mining."

"Gold?"

"Copper." He picked up the cut-crystal goblet and observed it, tilting the glass so the liquid coated its sides. "Why this sudden interest in my finances? You never cared about money before."

She shivered inside her quilted burgundy smoking

jacket. Though the steamer was fairly well heated by boilers, the ocean damp crept in the cabin's corners, and she doubted she'd ever be truly warm on this voyage. "I was curious why you've come to the Klondike. You've scarcely set foot off that rancho since the last time you tried your hand at mining."

He held the Chablis up to the light. Golden spots shimmered on the white linen covering the small mahogany table they sat at. "I am interested in exploring for copper."

She poked at her dainty triangles of bread. "You think you might find some?"

He sniffed the bouquet appreciatively. "I don't mean to go prospecting directly, but I thought I'd ask a few questions."

She chewed briefly while thinking. They'd played together since childhood, but they seldom talked about business matters. And they'd never approached the subject of feelings since she'd turned down his marriage proposal. Sex they'd never discussed, though to be fair to Jesse, she seldom discussed it with her mother either. Nor with her father. Or anyone else, except a few small conversations with doctors. "It seems so prosaic, investing in copper."

"Not really." He took a tentative sip of the wine, rolled it over his tongue, then poured a glassful. "It's far more interesting than gold. Gold is a classic. Every fool knows it has value. Investing in copper takes insight." Glass in hand, he rose from the table. He paced to the porthole and peered out again, as if somehow the view might have changed. The move made her jumpy, for she didn't know if he would approach her, or what she would do if he did. A few hours ago he'd been so excited, and she'd been on the verge of a rash promise, but her whole plan seemed suddenly foolish, and she wondered what had possessed her.

He opened the porthole and let the ocean's mist spray in his face. "For most human history, copper's been next to worthless. But in our lifetime it's increased greatly in value." He nodded. "Come look."

She scraped back from her chair and approached him. He stepped back from the window, though not very far, and rested a hand on the small of her back. She suppressed a shiver, ignored her corset, and concentrated on the view from the porthole. A pair of porpoises gamboled in the waning twilight, gliding effortlessly next to the steamer, their gray bodies sliding in and out of the waves in flashes of dark and sensuous motion. She smiled. "Oh, Jesse, aren't they lovely?"

He moved his hand to her shoulder. She did shiver this time, seduced by his closeness, his citrusy scent, the ship's rolling motion. In all the years of their friendship, she'd never felt such an ache for his touch.

"And do you know why?" he asked.

She looked quizzically at him, unable to follow his question.

"Do you know why copper will increase in value?"

"No." She tried to clear the fog from her head. It was hard to return to a sensible subject with the sea spray salting her mouth and Jesse's hand weighting her shoulder.

He ignored her confusion and took a swig from the goblet. "You can move electricity through it."

"I see." And see she did, though only a little. Electricity was all the new rage, with dozens of supposedly practical uses, from pushing cars up the streets of San Francisco to lighting the homes of the wealthy. There might well be fortunes to be made from mining copper. It occurred to her with some disappointment that Jesse might have pragmatic reasons for his apparently eccentric decision to follow her on this risky journey.

"You think you see, but really you don't." He took her elbow, returned to the table, sat her down next to the table, and pulled up a chair. "Just imagine the uses." He tapped the white cloth impatiently, his nearness to her a distraction. "The power of fifty thousand horses contained in a cable the size of my finger.''

She stared at his hands, brown and familiar. She preferred to return to the dolphins, but he seemed intent on this subject. "Pretty impressive."

He slanted a glance. "You're lying."

"No. No. I'm not." The scent of him reached her, and her stomach clenched. "It's much better than Don Wheeler's salt mine."

Laughing, he sat the goblet down on the table. "So you know my father's secret."

She smiled. "I know all the Wheelers' secrets." Jesse's thigh brushed against hers. He didn't touch her anywhere else, but this intimate gesture made her uneasy. She inched slightly over and took a cooling sip of the water. "He told me about it when I was a girl. The rancho doesn't make money at all. He gets his income from shares in a salt mine."

He placed a hand on the back of her chair. "Used to. The mine played out over the years. Sip?" He lifted the crystal container to her, a gesture of offering.

She shook her head and refused it. "I haven't gotten used to the ship's rolling. My stomach feels fine, but my head feels hazy." She took a slight, shaky breath. "So you went prospecting, invested in copper, and did rather well in it. . . ."

"Something like that." He glanced at her sandwich. "Are you going to eat?" She nodded and picked up her food. He didn't go back to his side of the table, and she wondered if he would try to kiss her. She'd liked talking about his business because it allowed her to avoid the other subject.

He toyed with his glass, one hand still resting behind her, his gaze still intent on the shimmering liquid. "Ranching is a wonderful business, but it's better conducted as a hobby."

She swallowed the chicken, the flesh making almost no taste in her mouth. "So why do you cling to the rancho?"

He touched one of the ringlets drifting over her shoulder. She suppressed a violent shiver and continued to work on the sandwich. He traced the outline of her earlobe. "It suits me."

She put down her food and faced him. "Your mother hates it."

"My mother likes people."

"And what about Christine Deutch?"

He stopped his small exploration and took another sip of his Chablis. "Christine would sell her soul for the rancho."

"She's very pretty."

"She certainly is."

"Do you like her better than me?"

"Sometimes."

"Oh. Jesse." She touched his shoulder lightly. "You've betrayed me." She said this sincerely, though she knew it was foolish. "I thought this engagement was a business arrangement. You know, her ranch and yours."

"I wouldn't quite put it that way."

He smiled. The moment took her breath away. Jesse seldom smiled, but when he did, the effect was breathless. His teeth showed white against his bronze complexion, and his smile lent charm to his usually gloomy expression.

She smiled back in spite of herself. "Then how would you put it? You've taken up English riding?"

"No."

She reached over and took a long draught of his wine. She knew she shouldn't, but she'd lost her courage. She wasn't at all sure why he'd come with her, or if he was lying about his engagement or what he'd given up to come with her. "Besides her looks, what do you like better?"

"I didn't say I liked her looks better."

"Then what?"

"Only one aspect, really."

She wanted to ask. Oh, how she wanted to ask, but she struggled with pride and self-possession. "You don't have to tell me."

"I told you before. We have an arrangement, an amorous one, to make the point more precisely."

"And that's the only thing you like better?"

"It's an important 'only.' Perhaps essential."

"I never took you to think 'it' so essential."

He threw his head back and laughed. "Now you are lying. I like 'it' as well as most men. And I have to believe you know that."

"You were never so—insistent—before."

"I've changed."

She glanced at his breast pocket, the rectangular bulge over his heart. "Or I've changed in your estimation."

"A little."

"You've read the poems. Now you think me wanton."

"I don't make assumptions. I've wanted you always and I intend to have you, if not in marriage, then at least for the length of this voyage."

"And if I deny you?"

"Then you're on your own when you reach the Yukon. Get over that pass any way that you can."

"That's what I intended from the very beginning."

"That's true. But you're taking a gamble, and a pretty spectacular one. You're increasing your chances exponentially if you take along an experienced miner. Maybe you don't care about me, but you must truly care about Zachary English in order to follow him all this way."

She took another slight sip of the wine, noting its texture and smoothness, gauging the way it affected her thinking. It wouldn't do to get too mush-headed. She was taking a gamble. He was right about that, but a far greater one than he expected. "You'd do that? Use my affection for him to gain an advantage?"

"Yes."

He was right in some ways. She had a far better

chance if she had a protector, though it ought to be someone she could depend on. "Then let's make an arrangement for the length of the voyage."

He took back the wine goblet and stretched his long legs before him. "Such as?"

She moved to the bed and sat down on it, arranging her skirts as she did. She could feel the stays of her special corset, but she ignored their pinch and smoothed down the cloth of her smoking jacket, then lifted her chin and faced him. "You may explore my person; embrace me; kiss me; do whatever you like, as long as you don't achieve penetration."

He arched one dark eyebrow. "Not satisfactory at all."

"It could be. If you're not too provincial."

It was his turn to drink, glancing over the rim as he did. The ship creaked around them, and gulls cried in the distance, but Jesse finished the wine in absolute silence. When he finished, he set down the crystal, pulled out the slim volume of poems, and riffled quietly through the pages. "Are you proposing some kind of perversion?"

She toyed with the fringe of her paisley scarf. "I'm proposing we vary from what's strictly normal." She gazed at him frankly. "Are you shocked?"

"A little." He returned the poems to his breast pocket. "Have you become so jaded you've lost your taste for what's normal?"

She laughed. "No, silly. I've not become such a Gypsy as that. I'm pretending a virtue, even if I can't have one. I don't want to lie if I'm questioned by Zack."

He bolted out of the chair and moved toward the cot. "Why bother?" Hands clasped behind him, he stared out of the porthole. "If I understand your poet at all, he'd probably think it a novel experience, passing his lady around like a plum tart."

She jumped up and slapped him. She hadn't intended that reaction, but she didn't like his narrow assumptions.

"You know nothing about Zack English and me. And I don't like it when you presume to judge us."

"Then don't keep throwing him up in my face." He grabbed her shoulders and pulled her toward him. The handprint on his face did not make a dent in his shuttered expression. "At least not if you value our friendship. I want to help you. And I'll consent to your little arrangement. But let me make this clear, my dear little dissembling writer. You may lie to yourself and to your readers. You may even lie to Zackary English. But I've seen through your pretty facade and I'm not going to be put off any longer." He lifted her chin with one finger. "Do you understand that?"

She nodded.

"Good. Now explain the rules once more to me."

She tried to swallow, but found she couldn't. His touch, his scent, all his closeness seemed to have gone straight to her stomach. She calmed herself by remembering the mustang. "You may explore my person, embrace me or kiss me. Do whatever you like, except you're forbidden from penetration. . . ."

He silenced her with a quick kiss, then cupped one hand under her breast. "You like that?"

She nodded.

He pressed his hips closely against her. "And that?"

She nodded again. She'd never felt a man in this place, though she noticed sometimes what Jesse looked like there, and she had some notion from her days on the rancho of the more animal side of procreation. He felt hot, stiff, and impressive, and she felt awkward and shaky. He swept a thumb over her nipple, and she felt him stir in reaction, which caused her to flush and tighten her grip and wonder what kind of bargain she'd made. He pushed her into the small bed and lay her fully clothed in it. Without giving her time to object, he climbed in beside her and pulled her close. He brought his mouth down on hers in a violent kiss and circled his arms around her. She thought briefly of her stiff stays,

but the pain seemed absorbed in the snuggle, and she
hoped he wouldn't notice the corset.

She kissed him. For the first time in all these years,
she simply gave way to the need in her. His lips felt so
soft upon hers, his body so taut and insistent. Her own
body felt as if it were melting, and logical thought
seemed fragile and scattered.

He pushed her back slightly. "I want to see what I'm
touching."

Her heart thumped in her bosom. She had no idea if
she could control him, once they went past her mother's
limits, the ones she'd learned so long ago after that awful
day at the doctor's office. "I mean it, you know. About
my limits."

"I know."

"I'm not joking, Jesse." She pressed her hand on his
chest. She could feel the poems in his breast pocket. "It
means a great deal to me—what I said."

"I understand, Bet. I'll do as you ask."

His voice had gone husky, his pupils pitch dark, and
she wasn't sure why she should trust him, but reminded
herself that they'd been friends forever, that this was the
man who'd taught her to walk, that he'd left Christine
to help her find Zach, and if they returned and there were
a wedding, she'd never again in her life be given the
chance to come this close to true lovemaking.

She nodded. "But I have two more conditions."

He smiled, slightly amused. "I thought the last condition rather a lot."

"These are smaller." She shrugged. He lifted himself
slightly away and watched her with a serious expression.
She unhitched the square of silk from her neck. "Toss
a scarf over the lamp."

He nodded.

"And only look at me from the front."

He gave her one look of swift penetration, then nodded brusquely and undid the knot in her scarf. She sat
still, almost rigid, halfway between pleasure and terror.

In all her life not even her mother had looked at Bet Goldman naked, at least not within memory, though it must have happened when she was a baby.

He tossed the scarf over the lamp, turning the whole cabin rosy. He returned to her and sat down on the bed, where she sat bravely, worried and frightened. She braced herself for his touch. To her surprise, he unpinned her hair, ignoring the buttons of her smoking jacket or any other part of her bosom. She didn't dare ask any questions, as she didn't wish to look forward or nervous, but simply submitted to his ministrations like a frightened pony to its new owner.

Smiling slightly, he fluffed her curls over her shoulders, gently massaging the back of her head. His touch felt lovely, steady, not the least bit threatening, and the ache inside blossomed wider. "That's really nice," she said softly.

He kissed her again, this time more softly, tender kisses like the ones he'd given in college. To her chagrin, even those had grown stronger in terms of the power of her reaction. She felt almost dizzy, and she regretted that she'd never been one to believe in swooning. "You could do that forever," she said instead.

His lips parted slightly, and he unbuttoned the top of her smoking jacket. She braced herself on the back of the wall. When he reached the third button he stopped and opened her collar and planted a hot kiss on her neck. She sighed, deeply moved by the pleasure. She'd completely lost track of the ache in her back, and it took her a moment to remember that it would be she who would have to stop him. She twined her fingers in his, uncertain of a more forward reaction, but he loosened himself from her grasp and swiftly undid the rest of her buttons.

She grabbed his hands quickly and held them. She wore a silk camisole under her jacket, and beneath that her special corset. She held his hands lightly.

"Stop here, please."

He stopped, his chest blowing.

"Let me take the lead," she said. "I want to make sure you observe my limits."

"I still don't see why you would want them."

"It's just a way to be faithful."

"Faithful to whom? A man who's run off to the gold-fields?" He grabbed her hand and turned it over. "You have no ring even."

"But Christine does."

He looked as if he were about to argue, but moved closer and pushed her into the mattress. "You're a witch and a devil. You have no right to torment me like this."

"You're the one who's being so stubborn. Why can't you just leave me alone?"

"Because I want you. I've wanted you ever since college."

"Then respect my request, and let's do this slowly."

He lay down abruptly, his body limp except for one part. "Do what you will, but I warn you. I won't leave this bed frustrated."

Her mouth went dry, and she shut her eyes quickly, seized by conflicting emotions. She wanted to please him. He'd risked a great deal to help her, and she didn't know how she could repay him. She also wanted to make him forget Christine. It surprised her a little to find herself jealous, as she'd never felt that way about him before, but she had to admit that thought possessed her. Most of all, she wanted a taste of what it would be to be normal. This kind of lovemaking wasn't normal, she knew, though she'd never been given a precise description of what was normal between men and women, except men were supposed to be the aggressors, and women should be meekly submissive.

Zack's poetry ridiculed that notion. He had the wonderful boyish idea that women, too, should have lust's fires in them. He'd introduced Bet to the classical poets and greatly admired the poems of Ovid, Thomas Hardy in England, as well as the forbidden translations of Sir Richard Burton. She remembered a description from the

Kama Sutra, but the thought of something so blatant shocked her.

She clenched her fingers together. "Oh, Jesse, I'm scared."

"Why? Do you think I'd hurt you?"

"No. It's not that exactly."

"Didn't you like what you did with Zack English?"

"Shush." She kissed him lightly. "Let's don't talk about him anymore."

Rising, she turned off the lamp. She needed the darkness, so he couldn't see her, either her fear or her corset. "Just lay there," she whispered and undressed quickly, then slotted herself next to him and pulled the sheet over her nakedness. He lay beside her, still fully clothed as she fumbled for his trouser placket. She found him quickly enough, silky and hot, the way she'd expected, and she knew from what Zack English had written exactly what would pleasure him most, but she couldn't bring herself to be so forward, so she closed her fingers around him.

He gasped, and she kissed his lips, pressing more closely, letting go with her fingers and nesting against him. He flipped her gently and rubbed against her, and she found they were both hot, moist, and silky. She sucked in a breath. She hadn't known this would feel so lovely, though the poems had aroused some of these pleasures and given her a slight premonition of how delicious this sensation might be. She kissed him, suddenly happy. Maybe she'd never make babies, or even make love like a normal woman, but she couldn't imagine another man consenting to this peculiar arrangement and she wanted to please him any way that she could.

"Would you like me to kiss it?" she asked. His eyes widened. He nodded.

And she did, exactly the way Zack English described.

Six

She shocked him. Somehow up to this moment he hadn't quite believed the poems had been true, but this little display of erotic talent convinced him. He'd never been treated that way in his life, including in the expensive bordellos found in San Francisco. He sat up beside her, still virtually dressed. She scooted back to the bed, pulling the covers up over her bosom. He grabbed them and pulled her toward him, kissing her nipple.

"What are you doing?" she asked.

He lifted his head just a little. "Returning the favor."

"I didn't . . ." Her voice faded away as he deepened the kiss and touched her lower, his anger fueled by his own satiation. She'd left him more empty than he'd been before, for while her lovemaking had been both sublime and expert, there'd been fear and deception and calculation behind it. And he'd discovered quite quickly this was not what he wanted and determined now to take his revenge.

He parted her thighs. She'd thought perhaps that between her boldness and odd limitations she'd left him helpless, but he had his own imaginative tricks. He used his hands and mouth to give her pleasure, holding her prisoner when she protested, reducing her to sighs and small whimpers and taking the time of a man who'd been sated, until she grabbed his head and drew him to her, her satisfaction coming in palpable spasms.

"Ah, Jesse," she said with a sigh.

For the first time, he was tender. He crawled into the bed, lay down beside her, pulled up the covers, stroked her hair, and deeply regretted that he'd come on this journey. "This was not what I wanted," he said quietly.

She looked up, surprised. "No?" He could have sworn she had tears in her eyes. "I thought it was lovely."

He pulled her forehead in toward his chest. "It was. It's just . . ." How could he express this? "Bet, do you love me?"

"Well, of course, you silly." She laughed. "Why do you think I let you do this?"

"Don't you ever take anything seriously?" He eased himself back into his pants.

"Is this kind of pleasure supposed to be serious?" She giggled. Her head drifted back. "It felt so delicious. I didn't"—she paused, looking at him as if she'd never seen him—"I didn't know lovemaking could feel so scrumptious."

He studied her briefly. "Are you going to write a poem about it?"

"No. I don't think so. That's strictly for Zack. I'd be condemned as a whore if I wrote so directly."

He tucked her head under his shoulder. "That doesn't seem like the Bet Goldman I know. To plead the limits of the female sex. To be the inspiration instead of the artist. To let a man do for you instead of trying."

She looked up and frowned, her fawn-colored curls in wild disarray, her green eyes gone to emerald. "I'm not pleading the limits of my sex. I'm simply not that kind of artist."

"Hogwash. You're frightened."

"You want me to write about it?"

"I didn't say that."

"Then what are you saying?"

He stroked one of her curls, wrapping it loosely around one finger. "It isn't like you to try to live through another. You never lived through a man."

She cuddled up closely and took a deep gulp of air. "That's kind of you, Jesse, but I do know my artistic limits. I'm very proud of my horse stories, but Zack's poems have a boldness to them that will make people read them for hundreds of years, if not thousands. I can't compete with his verbal aggression and I don't think I should try."

"Enough." He put his hand on her lips and wrapped the white cotton sheets and gray wool blankets around her. "I don't want to speak of that damned little scoundrel. Is this going to be our arrangement for the rest of the voyage?"

She nodded. He felt somehow sad. He wanted to speak to her about marriage, about coming to live on the rancho, about someday raising children together, but he held his counsel. He needed to get her back from Zack English, and that meant making her realize that she didn't need the poet's cachet to be a serious artist. "Have you ever thought about writing a novel?"

"Of course."

"Why don't you try it? You might learn something."

"A novel takes time." Languid and drowsy, she stroked his velvet collar. "Between the stories and the libraries—"

"Quit the libraries."

Her hand stilled. "They're steady income."

"You don't make money on the horse stories?"

"Oh, yes." Removing her hand, she snuggled down into the covers. "I make money. But the library income's more steady."

He could feel her breathing, smell the tang of his

sweat, of the seed she'd refused to let into her body. "A husband's income would be even better."

"I prefer the library option."

"Fine, just be stubborn. You've got a six-day sea voyage before you."

"Your point?"

"How many pages do you write a day?"

"Five, maybe. On a good one."

"In six days that should be the first chapter."

Jesse didn't bother Bet much, though they spent the next two days in the cabin. He'd brought books on mining, which absorbed him for hours, and sometimes he played on the Jew's harp he'd brought with him. In the evenings they played fan-tan, and he spent his nights in the horse stall with the three gamblers. And she did write ten pages, which mostly surprised her, for they consisted mainly of a sort of memoir of the time in her life when she'd learned to ride.

Jesse didn't touch her again. That fact bothered Bet quite profoundly. Her desires might not be normal, and probably weren't, but she wanted more caresses, and did not understand why he didn't. The need for him came to her in peculiar moments, flashes of hot, vivid sensation, more than a memory really, a visitation almost, or an inspiration, as if someone had drugged her and stripped her naked and her nerves had come to the surface.

Worse, she missed their old friendship, a fact that surprised her even more. She had an almost lifelong attraction for Jesse, but their peculiar encounter had subtly altered the balance between them. She'd lost some of her Gypsy-like independence. He'd awakened a need she hadn't known existed, which apparently was stronger in her than in him.

She put down her enamel mechanical pencil, the one she used for writing drafts. He lounged in the chaise reading a book about mining.

"Do you think we've got a chance?"

He looked up from the tattered volume. "Of what?"

She nodded at the tome in his hand. "Of finding copper."

He smiled a little. "Better than of finding your poet."

She went back to her scribbling. They'd been together in here all morning, and she'd enjoyed every minute, but she'd developed a cramp in her hand. "Do they often find copper in gold strikes?"

"Sometimes." He put down the book and walked to the porthole, opened it, and peered at the ocean. A gust of salt air flooded the cabin, carrying the cries of seagulls with them. "The porpoises are still following us."

She ambled over, trying to look graceful, slightly hampered by the ship's movement and, as always, her own limitations. The sleeve of her smoking jacket brushed his, and he flinched. She felt an odd surge of delight. Perhaps she did have some power in this situation. "So you didn't like our special arrangement?"

"No."

"You seemed happy enough at the time."

"An illusion. I promise."

Her heart squeezed in her bosom. Maybe she wasn't normal, but she'd enjoyed what had gone on between them. And in any event, even if it wasn't normal, their peculiar arrangement was as close to lovemaking as she would likely get in her lifetime. "What was wrong with what we were doing? You didn't enjoy it?"

"I enjoyed it just fine, but I don't like the finish. That's not the kind of satisfaction I'm after."

"Then what?"

He pushed away, his voice low and husky. "Read the poems. Perhaps you'll remember."

She went back to her papers, profoundly depressed. She wanted to tell him she didn't remember, couldn't remember, would never remember, would never give him what he sought after. She ought to tell him about those limits. She honestly ought to, for she could see what pain he was in, but she didn't think he was being fair really. He had his own arrangement, after all, and she hadn't meant to disturb it. She hadn't asked him to come on this trip once she'd known about his engagement and didn't see why her secret should be penetrated just to assuage his jealous assumptions about what had inspired those poems. And besides, if she told him, she'd lose him forever. He'd never touch her if he knew he might kill her. And she wasn't ready to give up the hope that somehow she might have just a taste of what it would be like to be a normal woman.

She sat down at the mahogany table, picked up the pencil, and toyed with its built-in eraser. "Truth to an artist is different, you know, than what might be assumed by a layman."

"What does that mean exactly?"

"You shouldn't let the poems make you jealous."

"Bullshit."

She tossed down the pencil, ignoring its clatter. "All right. Be jealous. It's practically the twentieth century, Jesse. Why shouldn't a woman have lovers?"

He turned, glaring at her from beneath those eyelashes that slanted downward so severely that no amount of perception could read his expression. "Because you can have so much more."

"I don't want any more."

"Then let me be your lover."

"Never."

"Why?"

She stood, gripping the sides of the table, using the moment to keep herself steady. "Because you're the one who wants more. You've always wanted too much from me. More than I can really give you."

"That's true." He stepped away from the porthole, the light flooding behind him, outlining his darkness, his velvety beauty. "For the first time in our lives we're being perfectly honest. I want you. I've wanted you always. I want you to live on the rancho. I want to wake

up to your smile in the mornings. I want to make love—
not just for the pleasure, but also to take that cinched-
in little waist, to see it swollen and full with my babies,
to watch you raise them and have you teach them, to
hear you read them your little horse stories. Haven't you
ever wanted that, Bet? A real daughter, warm, living,
and breathing, not just the children you create in those
pages?''

A sharp pain flared up her back, the sharpest she'd
ever felt in her life. She gasped and must have turned
white, for he appeared at her side immediately. ''Are
you all right?''

''No. No!'' She wanted to lie, but simply couldn't.
Her body had betrayed her completely, and there was
no way to cover the tension, to suppress the trembling
or perspiration that had misted her face as she went faint
and dizzy. ''Go away, Jesse, just go away.''

''No. I won't leave you like this. Do you want me to
call for the ship's doctor?''

''I doubt there is one, but no, not really.'' She forced
herself to a passable laugh. ''You give me a headache
when you're so serious.''

''Are you all right?'' Jesse asked again several hours
later, as he sat by the bed and watched her.

She nodded. She lay on top of the blankets, her eyes
covered by a hot compress to keep up the fiction that
her head ached. It wasn't, but his speech about marriage
had been so disturbing it had taken Bet a while to calm
down.

''What are you writing?'' He'd moved to the table.
She could hear him rustle through her notebooks and
papers.

''It's nothing, really. Just an idea.''

''May I read it?''

''No.'' The pain in her back had subsided, but her
nerves still felt raw and exposed. ''I don't like people
reading my drafts.''

He said nothing, and his silence brought the noise of the ship to the forefront, the low thrum of the boiler room engines, the spray of the waves as the steamer slipped through them, the omnipresent cry of the seagulls even this far from shore. "Perhaps I could proofread it for errors."

"No." She opened her eyes, peering at him from beneath the compress.

He had the oddest look on his face, not at all his usual distant expression. "Why not?"

"I told you. I don't like people reading my drafts."

He lifted the tablet of paper and read: " 'The chestnut mustang quivered beneath me, a warm, living creature ten times my size and only recently broken.' " One hand behind him, he paced back to her. "I like that."

"It's only a draft."

" 'Jesse gripped my waist and kept on in a circle.' " He read slowly, his voice low and husky. " 'The downward slant of his lashes veiled his expression. Wet tendrils formed on his white cotton collar. His hands grew perceptibly warmer. But the horizon was moving. The gold grass and green oak trees. The corral and the fence posts. I could see the line of the streambed and wished in vain I had not mentioned I'd like to go there, but would have to be carried.

" " "Have you ever ridden before?" he asked, panting softly.' "

Jesse tossed the tablet on the table smiled. "I recognize the occasion."

"Do you like the description?" she asked.

"Yes, very much."

"Do you mind that I used the experience?"

"I've never minded, though I have to admit it will be peculiar to have it written out in a more straightforward fashion."

She sat up, removing the now lukewarm washrag. "I don't take your meaning."

"I'm already the hero of the Firestriker stories."

"Of course not, silly. In the Firestriker stories, the horse is the hero."

"But the horse is a symbol and not of Zack English. You did not even know him when you wrote those."

She laughed. "What an outrageous ego. You think you inspired my stories?"

He leaned on the bedpost, arms crossed over his chest. "Now you're the one who's being silly. I might not be a writer, but I did pay attention to old Dr. Springfield when we studied Virgil." She shot him a glance.

He ignored her, glancing at the bedpost with an amused expression. "In fiction, animals have allegorical meanings. They generally stand for some vice or virtue. Horses stood for power and courage, but also the brute side of human nature. The unicorn guards the virgin. The centaur rapes her."

She picked at the washrag. His observation amazed her, for she'd followed him in a number of classes and knew from her professor's comments that Jesse seldom paid attention in college, except when his classes had practical uses. Jesse had confessed to only three scholarly interests: accurate accounting, a good business letter, and a passable knowledge of mining. "These are just stories for little girls, Jesse."

"With lines like that." He held up the paper and reread the reference, the one about the mustang quivering beneath her. "You must be joking. I understand perfectly well what your horse stories are. Allegorical tales for little virgins."

"Jesse!"

"It's true." He returned to the table, set down the papers, walked back to the bed, and sat down beside her. "You're the one whose stories prepare girls for marriage, not the trash that scoundrel Zack English writes."

"He's a fine writer."

"All right, he is." He took the compress out of her hand, walked to the washbasin, and ran water on the compress. "But so are you, and I want to know why you're so frightened."

"What makes you think I'm frightened?"

"I can feel your fear in your stories. And also the wanting. They go together in equal proportions. But I can not understand what fuels your terror. You're a beautiful woman and a wonderful writer—"

"Stop." She was laughing in spite of herself. "Don't say any more, or I'll never let you read a draft ever."

He returned with the cloth and sat down beside her. "You didn't let me read this one."

"Ah, Jesse." She twined her fingers in his. "I wish life could once again be that simple."

"You liked it then, those days on the rancho?"

"Oh, yes. It was the only time in my life I felt normal."

He eyed her sharply. "When have you ever wanted to be normal?"

"Never." She drew her hand back, caught in her lie, then smiled sweetly, intending to cover herself. "But I liked the illusion. That was the best thing about riding. It didn't matter that I was bedridden. That I couldn't walk the length of a hallway. I loved the speed and the freedom. Wonderful, but also quite frightening, feeling that mustang moving beneath me and later—"

"That was a long time ago, Bet."

She hugged him, a dangerous business, but she couldn't help it. "Ah, Jesse, that's why I love you. We'll always have that summer together. When you were so lonely and I was so frightened."

He didn't respond to her touch, only held her loosely, his arms scarcely touching. "You don't seem to want to be normal, but I do think you want to be perfect."

"Well, I'm hardly that."

"I think you are." He chucked her under the chin. "I'll trounce any man who says otherwise." Then his eyes became gradually serious, and he touched the top of her thick smoking jacket.

"What are you doing?" she asked.

"Thinking."

"A dangerous business."

"For sure."

He undid the top button, one of black onyx.

"And now?" she asked.

He placed both hands on the top of her shoulders. "Asserting my rights to our arrangement."

"I thought you said you didn't like it."

"I don't, but I'm still going to assert the rights you agreed to." He undid the front and pushed the heavy quilt jacket down from her shoulders. She sat still, suppressing her trembling. For all she'd wanted him to repeat this, she found once he did she was frightened. "Turn around," he said.

"Jesse." She wore only her camisole under her jacket, and the silk didn't disguise as much as the padding.

"Turn around. I know you said that's off-limits, but I'm not going to respect that particular boundary."

"Jesse." Now she panicked. She doubted he'd force her, but he could seduce her, and in her case that would be fatal. Worse in some ways than that terror, however, was the thought of what he was asking. "You have no rights whatsoever if you don't respect all my limits. I asked you not to look at my back. I won't give you so much as a kiss if you can't respect all my requests."

"I'll respect all the others, but I won't respect that one. Turn around."

"Jesse."

"Turn around." He tugged off the jacket. "I won't have any secrets between us. You turn around now, or I call off the whole bargain, including helping to find Zack English."

She did as he asked. He unlaced her tight corset. She trembled. She didn't want to, but she couldn't help it. This seemed so much like those days from her childhood, when her mother would unlace those tight stays.

He ran his thumb over the indentations, the red welts made by the stays. She crossed her arms under her bosom, wondering desperately what he was thinking. Was he shocked? Would he reject her when he realized the extent of her defects?

She held her breath, and he paused, his breath coming slowly, then leaned forward and nuzzled her earlobe. She didn't respond, held by her terror, only waited for him to say something. He didn't. Instead he caressed her, running his thumbs over the indentations, his palms over the curve of her spine. She waited, too stunned by the contact to even respond, waiting for him to remark that she was clearly not normal, but he said nothing, only kept up the slow massage of her back. She shivered. "What are you doing?"

"Admiring your back." He kissed the base of her spinal column. "Is this why you were frightened? You didn't want me to see it was crooked?"

"Maybe. A little."

He lay his cheek against hers, circling his arms under her bosom, pulling her tight to his chest. She relaxed a little. From this angle, she might feel almost normal, once the angry red markings subsided. "You should have more faith in me, Bet."

"I do. It's just—"

"Lie down."

"Jesse!" She tried to force a plea into her voice.

"Lie down on your stomach."

She did as he asked, for the tone of his order commanded obedience, though she was stunned and frightened by his persistence.

He ran his hand down her spine and the curve of her buttocks. "I like this little curve in your back. It's kind of exotic." A small sob escaped her, but he did not seem to notice. He simply kept stroking her bottom. "It reminds me that I taught you to ride."

She ached now, not in her back but in her feminine apex and her buttocks muscles. It felt as if a fist had formed in her bosom. Beneath the lump in her throat tears had gathered.

He circled his hands around her waist. "So tiny, so lovely, if just slightly crooked. I look at this waist and I want to fill it. I don't have to be a poet to say that."

He pushed her pantalets down slightly and kissed the dimple on each side of her bottom. "Such sweet little dimples." He rolled her over and kissed her, then stopped. "Would you like to look at me naked?"

She nodded, aching now in more places than she knew could respond to seduction, her thighs and her buttocks, her stomach muscles.

He unbuttoned his shirt, revealing the smooth bronze plane of his chest. "I don't want to take you this way." He spoke very softly. "And I don't know why you insist on these limits." He shucked his shirt onto the floor. "But I'll observe the others as long as you want to. I have only one request of my own."

"Which is?"

"That you write me a poem about our lovemaking."

Seven

She did not write a poem, but she did continue with the novel. She wrote for two days without stopping, huddled with Jesse in the cabin, ignoring the beauty of mountain and glacier as the steamer slipped through the Inside Passage, to write a long evocation of those days of her childhood, when Jesse had taught her to ride. She found it a moving, unnerving experience, different from writing her stories. In this memoir she was more naked, more revealed to the reader and to herself. The scenes came more easily, but their coloring and emotions didn't. She was describing an event that had happened, after all, but events and their meanings were quite different matters. More even than in her short stories, she had to inch down nerve, bone, and sinew to find exactly the words she was after.

Jesse didn't help her. He left her alone, remaining absorbed in his own studies, but his presence affected her so intensely she could not find the details, the scattered bits of observation that gave the writing emotional meaning.

She set her pencil down and rubbed her back muscles.

She had to relax, she simply knew it, and let her mind form its own purpose. "Do you remember it, Jesse, how you taught me?"

"Of course."

"What were you thinking?"

"You were so pretty."

She laughed. "Don't be silly."

"I'm not."

She toyed with her pencil, then wrote out a sentence, not paying much attention to detail, just taking down the conversation. "What did I look like?"

"You had pretty slippers, bright red with ribbons and tiny feet peeking out from white eyelet ruffles."

She blushed, eyes on the paper, surprised and flattered at how well he remembered. "Mother made me such beautiful clothes."

"Oh. You were gorgeous. Such a perfect Gypsy, with buttons and bows and embroidered patches. Flowers and stars, rainbows and roses. I'd never seen the like in my life."

"Poverty made the patches necessary, you know. Mother simply made them a virtue."

"I know."

She wrote for a while in silence, recording his speech, and made a few drawings of the kinds of figures her mother had sewn on the dresses she'd made up from remnants and patched together. "Weren't you frightened the riding might hurt me?"

"Not really. I had youthful courage and real inspiration in the way you handled your ailment."

"I didn't do anything really . . ."

"Like hell . . ."

She drew a few more of the figures. It all came back in a rush. Firestriker beneath her. The scent of his flesh. The feel of Jesse's hands on her waist. The fear. The elation. The sense of pure terror. The deep ache in her back and buttocks, the powerful urge to clench her leg muscles. She remembered the little girl she had been, filled with longing for movement and freedom, never guessing the rides on the mustang would push her past the doctor's predictions and give her a life that would be almost normal. "I didn't think I was so very brave."

"You were always laughing."

"That didn't take courage."

"Then what would you call it?"

"It was just my nature, you silly. I don't think I'm brave, but I'm pretty resourceful. When you're stuck in a bed, tears are too boring. You have to find ways to make life amusing."

"Not everyone looks at the world that way." He abandoned the chaise and his book on mining, walked to the table, and sat down beside her. "My mother was merely trapped on the rancho, thousands of acres, her own kingdom really. That world should have made anyone happy, but she wanted to travel, to laugh and have parties. She spent the rest of her life brooding about her lost chances."

Bet shrugged, ignoring his nearness, the press of his thigh against hers. "With all due respect, your mother was foolish. It was one of my goals—to never be tiresome. And I have to say, I think I succeeded."

"That I'd agree with."

She wrote down his whole description, then tried to keep writing, but his observations intrigued her. She remembered those afternoons well, as those had been some of her life's golden moments, but it truly surprised her how well he remembered. She hadn't supposed they'd had so much meaning to a young ranchero absorbed in his horses. "What kind of trees was I riding under?" she asked.

"Pepper trees, down by the stream."

"Do you remember the weather that summer?"

"Hot and dusty."

"And how did you hold me?"

"I ran beside you, holding your waist."

"Yes," she said as she continued writing, "and you

had sweat on your forehead by the time we finished."

"I had sweat on more than my forehead."

"True." Her pencil flowed freely, the black letters scrawling across the pages, almost as if there were no connection between her hand and their conversation. "It dripped into your eyes and made your hair curly. I still remember the heat, you and Firestriker running your hearts out, while I simply held on in terror."

"I'm sure your heart got a workout."

"True. True. But not like you and the mustang."

He stretched his legs before him, crossed his booted ankles, and stared at her from beneath a fan of black lashes. "Too true."

Her heart got another workout, for the memories stirred her along with his presence, and she realized how much she really did love him. Not just their friendship, but also this awareness, this palpable tension. "We've done a lot together."

"That's true also."

"You're waiting, aren't you, to see if I go back to Zach English?"

"I told you before. Christine and I have an arrangement."

"You're lying. And I don't believe for a moment you're looking for copper."

"It's a good investment."

"Yes. I remember. Investing in copper takes insight."

He uncrossed his ankles, glanced at her papers, strode back to the chaise, slouched into its depths, and hid his expression behind the book on mining. "Precisely."

By the fourth day of the voyage, Jesse had gown rather fond of Hank, Hal, and Handsome. That fact surprised him, because he didn't like strangers, but the gamblers ignored him, and he found that endearing, so he started a conversation that evening.

"Are you going to the Yukon?" Jesse asked as he turned back his bed on the hay bale.

Hank, the tallest, darkest, and oldest of the three, answered. "We thought we'd seek our fortunes there."

Jesse sat down on his improvised bed, his hand straying to his breast pocket. This was the trouble with polite conversation. He always thought it seemed pointless once you got past the obvious facts, and what was the point of asking the obvious? So what was the point of talking at all?

"Game?" Handsome, the young one with the golden mustache, held out a deck.

Jesse hesitated. He didn't like gambling for money, but he was trying to establish a bit of a friendship. "I play only for pennies."

The flashy young gambler grinned. "An intelligent man, much as I suspected. There are reasons your family's held on to that rancho."

Jesse moved to one end of the hay bale.

"Twenty-one?" Handsome glanced at him as his brothers gathered around the impromptu table they'd set up in the stall. Jesse nodded. The young man dealt out five cards to each player. Briefly Jesse inspected the deck. The cards did not seem to be marked, though he knew from previous experience professional gamblers could be clever in their many methods of cheating. He discarded two cards and waited.

"Are you going to the goldfields?" he asked.

"Only to Skagway," Hal answered. Jesse said nothing, but the quiet man continued in an affable manner. "We're not much for physical labor. We prefer getting our gold the hard way."

Jesse laughed. He looked at his cards and tossed down two pennies. Hank matched his ante and upped it. The betting continued three times around the hay bales until the pot reached twenty-five pennies. Jesse called his bet and lay down a hand showing twenty.

"Twenty-one." Hank put down two queens and an ace. He grinned as he scooped up the money. "I'll own half California at this rate."

Jesse scowled, though not really deeply. "There's plenty of gold for types like you there."

"You judge us harsh, do you, rancher?"

"No," Jesse lied. He did in some ways judge gamblers harshly, though not more harshly than he judged most people. He wasn't a snob, but he did have high standards. It took a shrewd man to make a profit at ranching, and lifelong schooling at the knee of his father had taught him to look closely at those who might cheat him.

Hank dealt out the next hand. "I noticed you reading."

Jesse scowled and stood up, stifling the impulse to cover the pocket where the slim volume rested.

"No offense meant." Hank raised his hand in a plaintive gesture. "I figured you might be a thinker, not just some nabob with his nose in the air."

Jesse hesitated, then sat back down on the hay bale. "No offense taken. I'm a working rancher, neither nabob nor deep thinker. A vaquero at heart, but the scale is grander."

"The point I'm making is this . . ." Hank looked at his hand, then handed back two cards. "My brother's a pretty bad lunger. There's plenty of jobs in the West, but mostly for those with strong bodies. We had to find a way to support him."

"Do you think the cold will be hard on his lungs?" Jesse asked.

"Not during the summer. We thought we'd spend a few weeks gambling, then get out before the winter gets rough."

Jesse inspected his cards as well as the gamblers. In spite of his first lucky hand, Hank and his brothers seemed to be honest. In fact, the first hand had sealed Jesse's opinion that these three were honest. Professional gamblers usually started out losing in order to sucker a mark in. Hank and his brothers had not pulled that trick. Jesse trembled for their fate in the goldfields. He knew also, and from harsh experience, that mining-camp life could be hard on a gambler, honest or not.

"Have you done this long?" He discarded four cards, thinking to test them.

"A couple of years." Hank handed Jesse the replacements. "We've been working most in Nevada."

"I have one suggestion." Jesse looked at a hand that contained nothing but face cards.

"Yeah?" Hank cocked an eyebrow.

"Make sure and leave before the place kills you." Jesse matched his expression. "And don't gamble away your return passage."

Eight

The doctors had been wrong about walking. Bet thought about their error as she started the second chapter of the novel she was writing. She'd considered that fact occasionally, but always dismissed its implications—that if the learned physicians had been wrong about walking, they might have been wrong in their other predictions.

She considered that possibility now as she listened to Jesse play a mouth organ. He sat on the bed, one foot propped up, playing mournfully on the small instrument. She perched in a chair by the mahogany table, struggling to ignore the tug of his presence.

She'd been writing all morning, working to finish the first thirty pages, as they'd be steaming into Skagway tomorrow. She and Jesse had been cooped up in this cabin. The strain had begun to tell on her nerves. He hadn't brought up their peculiar arrangement since the time he'd turned her over so calmly and spent so much time massaging her back—though he sometimes mentioned the poem he'd asked for. Instead, he'd kept up a campaign of seduction, touching her with maddening precision, his lips to her earlobe, his hand on her back, his thigh brushing close when she stood near him.

She knew what he wanted. He wanted more of her. All of her. To make her his wife. He wanted risks and commitment and, in the long run, babies. And she'd always believed all that would kill her.

But the doctors had been wrong about walking.

She put down her enamel mechanical pencil and turned to a blank page in her tablet. "What if we find him?"

He paused in his playing. "Zack?"

She nodded.

"I don't know." He swung into a sitting position, boots on the floor, harmonica dangling between his fingers. "Do you want me to trounce him?"

"No, don't be silly."

"Too bad." He pulled a fine linen kerchief out of his pocket and started to shine the mouth organ's surface. "Have it your way. I'll leave you two lovebirds together, sail down the Yukon, and go looking for copper."

She stood up from the table and walked to the porthole, pretending to peer out. She'd gotten her sea legs and had no trouble standing. The strain on her back, combined with the ship's movement, made her feel a little bit dizzy, especially when she stood so close to Jesse. "And what if Zack doesn't want me?"

"Then you'll have come a long way for nothing."

"Would you leave Christine if I asked you to do that?"

His citrus scent mingled with that of the ocean. Beneath his open shirt collar, she could see the veins in his neck. The damp air had tousled his hair, reducing its curls to dark corkscrews. With his gold complexion and exotic features, he looked far more poetic than Zack, whose street urchin childhood still showed on his face, which was rugged, outdoorsy, and boyish.

Jesse blew a few low notes, then paused. "I haven't decided."

"She'd be a better wife in many ways."

"Oh, I agree."

Bet returned to the small writing table, wishing she hadn't made her observation. She didn't generally think of herself as jealous, but she was beginning to realize she could be, at least under the right circumstances. She had ached for Jesse since she'd known him, but now the ache was more carnal and also more urgent. She enjoyed so much having him touch her and didn't know why he objected to their peculiar arrangement. Except that it wasn't normal. A more normal arrangement was probably better, at least from the male point of view.

She sat down, picked up her pencil, and twisted it so that more lead showed. She *was* jealous. That reaction signaled a change in their friendship. She'd never been insecure about Jesse before. Then again, she'd never felt threatened. He'd always been there—a brooding presence and unfulfilled promise—and she realized, with a deep sense of unease, that she didn't want that promise to end. She pressed the point against the cream-colored paper, watching idly as a small dot appeared on the paper. "If I agreed to your last proposal, I'd submit to your lovemaking without any returning promise of marriage."

"Yes."

"Does that seem fair?"

"You're the one who said you wanted a lover."

She pressed the pencil on the paper, testing the strength of its tip. She wanted a lover. That much was true. And the doctors had been wrong about walking. But she'd already told too many lies. Even if she were willing to test their predictions, what would Jesse do when he discovered she was a virgin? "And what if I conceived a baby?"

"What kind of promise did you extract from Zack English?"

She had no understanding with Zack, but that was a part she couldn't tell Jesse. Nor, though she knew there were methods, did she know how to prevent conception, except hold to her proposed limits, which was part of why she had proposed them. "Zack took precautions."

"And if I produce a precaution, are you saying you'd change our arrangement?"

"No." An outrageous lie at this point. She didn't know what she'd do if he produced a precaution. She'd never wanted him more in her life, not even in the days of her childhood when life had been simpler and she had been younger and she'd dreamed of him with the unbridled fervor of a willful child who'd always been pampered, a pleasant side effect of her defect. And she still wanted him just as badly, even though she knew she shouldn't.

She laid down the pencil and looked at her notebook, a blank page, always a challenge, even to an experienced writer. It seemed an unreasoning and unreasonable fate to be so much in love and so attracted and have to take such a desperate gamble just to test some doctor's predictions. "Did you ever worry that you might hurt me?"

"When we made love?"

"When you taught me to ride."

"No." He tossed the harmonica in the bed's corner, pushed off the mattress, and strode to the table. "Though I probably should have." He posted himself behind the chair, watching her closely, distracting her with his arresting presence. "But perhaps I was lucky."

"How so?"

"I'd grown up in a world without limits." He pulled up the second chair, sat down beside her, and toyed with her tendrils, the little stray curls at her neckline. "A little king, or at least a princeling. Everything I surveyed belonged to my father—the land and the trees and the cattle." He rested a hand on her shoulder, stroking her curls between thumb and forefinger. "Even the people in many ways,"

"You didn't own the vaqueros."

"True." Reaching forward, he unfastened the ribbon

of the eiderdown kimono she wore to keep warm while she was writing. "They were not literally chattel. But still . . ." He removed the light covering from her. She shivered, though perhaps not from the dampness. "It was a childhood so perfectly privileged that I had no idea I could not have what I wanted. I lifted you out of that wicker wheelchair and onto the back of a spirited mustang and never once worried about it."

"I'm glad you didn't."

"So am I, Bet." He tugged on the ivory combs holding her hair. "So why can't we be lovers? I'm not used to waiting. Not since my engagement. You'll just drive me to the arms of another."

Her hair had tumbled down over her shoulders, releasing its warmth and flowery scent. "That's not like you, Jesse. You've always been patient. Besides"—she tossed back her curls and giggled lightly—"there aren't any others between here and Skagway. I'm the only woman on board."

"True." He kissed her, briefly and softly, in the crook of the neck, between earlobe and shoulder. "But there will be women in Skagway, I'll wager."

She shivered. "Jesse, don't be crude. There'll be only fallen women in Skagway."

"So?"

"I would think you'd believe them beneath you."

"Think again, Bet. Perhaps I've not been so patient as you've imagined, but only looked elsewhere for my satisfaction."

She snatched back her comb, fluffed up her hair, and twisted its wavy mass into a coil. "Is that all I am to you now? Someone to service your baser nature?"

"Why should you be anything more?" He stilled her hand, his dark eyes liquid. "Were you anything more to the poet?"

"At least to him I was worthy of marriage."

He stood up abruptly. "Don't taunt me with that. You spurned my proposal at Berkeley and spent many years making me suffer. Now you see I'm engaged to another, and suddenly we have 'an arrangement.' "

She pushed the ivory comb in slowly, considering the truth of his observations. "I've never wanted to hurt you."

"Then what do you call all those years of waiting?"

"I called them a friendship. And thought they were valued. I see now perhaps they weren't."

He returned to the bed and threw himself on it, stuffing the harmonica into his pocket. "It's not that I didn't value your friendship, but somewhere beneath it there was always this cruel streak. I see it in your jealous reaction. You only want me when you can't have me."

She snatched back her kimono and tied it on firmly. "Is that why you came? Do you want to hurt me? Is this a vengeance, making me want you? Insisting I take you into my body and risk getting pregnant by becoming your lover?"

He stared at her from beneath lowered lashes. For a moment, she thought he might hurt her, so dark and forbidding was his expression. "No. Not exactly."

"Then what is it, Jesse?" She picked up her pencil and started scribbling, not words, not pictures, just aimless drawing. "Why won't you stay within my limits? And why are you taking me to Zack English? And will you return to Christine when I find him?" She tossed down her special utensil, ignoring the clatter of enamel on wood. "And why can't we go back to our friendship, with the exception of these little adjustments? Because I've loved you always and I think you know that. And I've never, ever hurt you on purpose. And it's you, not me, with a bit of a cruel streak, trying to go beyond these boundaries when you know that your actions will only bring heartache."

"Is that what you think?" He launched off the bed, his expression determined.

He wanted to hurt her, at least a little. He was tired of their friendship. Tired of patience. Tired of waiting

for her to come to her senses. He'd always been handicapped by his shyness, as crippling to him as the worst
of her defects. He was determined to be far more aggressive, even if he risked losing her always, for they
had only one more day until Skagway, and he'd lose her
for sure if he didn't seduce her, for in that cold seaport
they might find the poet. He reached for her, lifting her
up by the shoulders. "Undo that blouse and take off that
damned corset."

"Jesse, you have to listen."

"I'm through listening to your excuses." He pulled
the comb back out of her hair, which came tumbling
down over her shoulders. "I'm going to shake you down
to your toes. Better than that son-of-a-bitch poet. He
described it quite well, but I know I can beat him." He
tossed the comb on the table and undid her scarflike lace
collar. "He didn't listen to your maidenly protests, and
I don't intend to either."

She gripped his wrists. He ignored the burning,
though he knew it was his own flesh tearing.

"You promised at least you'd take precautions." Her
voice was soft as a whisper.

"Hang precaution. Your precious poet did not take
precautions."

"I told you—"

"I know. Artistic license. We'll see how this fits in
your poet's musings."

He kissed her, far more urgently than he'd done before, crushing her to him so she could feel his hardness,
his muscles and tautness, and all those years of pent-up
emotion. He'd be damned if he'd lose her to that son-
of-a-bitch, so skilled at description, so devoid of feeling.
He was filled with wildness and darkness and longing
and he was in no mood for precautions. He was tired of
being treated as if his feelings were baubles, childish
amusements she could still toy with. "We're going to
make love like a married couple. With all the risk those
actions imply."

"Jesse."

"Unbutton the blouse."

She followed his order, though she seemed frightened. He didn't know why she looked so hunted, and for a moment considered giving up on this aggressive tactic, but her blouse fell open to the curve of her bosom, and nineteen years of patience gave way to a demon.

"Why?" He pressed her head backward, kissing the curve made by the upward lift of the corset. "Why would you give yourself to that bastard? You deserve so much better. I know I can please you. I've pleased dozens of women, some quite demanding." He nuzzled her earlobe. She gasped. He nipped her, tugging flesh with his teeth. She let out a small squeal, and he stopped, crooning gently. "I'm the man who taught you to ride. Why couldn't I have taught you this other?"

He kept up the soft serenade, boasting quietly of his prowess, easing her blouse over her shoulders. These were outrageous lies at this point, except for the business about riding. He'd had only one consistent lover, the widow of another ranchero, with whom he'd had a number of trysts. They'd kept their relationship quiet, however. The provincial nature of ranchero morals didn't allow for an open affair, even in the case of willing widows. There'd been bordellos in San Francisco, an experience he'd found depressing, as fine wine and elegant trappings still couldn't disguise the despair of the harlots. He pushed the blouse out of the way. He'd reached the corset, that damned stiff device that cinched her. Slowly he unlaced the stays.

"I love your waist," he said as he tugged, "but I sure hate this corset. I don't know why you lace it so tightly. You're tiny without it. I'm sure you don't need it." She didn't answer, but her breathing grew deeper. She remained still as he unhooked it. "It's as if you punished yourself with this ribbing." He pushed his thumb into the cleft between corset and flesh. "Look how it hurts you."

He removed the odd, torturous device, and her eyes widened as she breathed freely. His heart constricted. He rubbed a red welt the steel ribbing created, and an odd sensation stirred deep in his chest. They moved him, these welts. He found them erotic, though why this should be so, he could not fathom, but there was something about her painful confinement that moved him to both pity and fury and made him want to hold her forever.

He kissed her. And hotly. She moaned through her trembling. He could feel her beneath him, half dressed, not naked. He had a sense of her wanting and passion, not just in the sound, but also in the smell of her, the feel of her, the depth of her breathing; the taste of her mouth, hot and accepting. Still, she was frightened. He could feel that, too, in her trembling, not the languid shudder of delicious contentment, or the tiny quiver of expectation, but genuine fear mixed in her passion. He had a sudden urge to hit something.

He pushed away, but kept hold of her shoulders. "Look at me, Bet."

She did as he asked, her expression a question.

"I don't want to play silly games."

"I understand that."

"Then why are you shaking?"

There was fear in her eyes. No, more than fear, terror. He found himself torn between ardor and fury.

He pulled her to him, close to his chest. "I've waited forever."

She nodded. He couldn't see the gesture, could only feel the slight spray of curls on his cheek, but she nodded.

He closed his hand over the back of her neck. "More than forever. Perhaps I'm not a suitable husband, but at least let us see what we're missing."

She simply kept trembling, all curls, lace, and ribbon in those Gypsy-like clothes she affected. He resisted the urge to smash the table. "Has he hurt you?"

"No."

He was pressing her a little too closely. He could see the fear in her eyes. "Because if I ever find out he hurt you, I'll kill him."

"He didn't hurt me. He . . ."

"Yes?"

She wriggled out of his grasp, rubbing her shoulder. "He didn't love me. Not really."

"Then why are you chasing him to the Yukon?"

"Because"—she was trying to rebutton her blouse, but her hands were shaking so badly, her fingers kept slipping—"because . . ." She seemed abstracted and tense, flush, wayward, and rosy, and he wanted desperately to kiss her nipples, which were puckered and upright in spite of the corset.

"Why?" He stilled her hands, suppressing his urge to take her, or at the very least suckle those nipples. "Why are you chasing him? I know damned well you're lying in some way. So tell me."

She looked for a moment as if she would bolt; but she couldn't do it in her current state, with no place to go except a public hallway. He pushed her against the table, letting her feel his maleness and hardness. "For once in your life, be honest with me. Why are you chasing him to the Yukon?"

She balanced herself with one hand behind her, holding her blouse with the other. Her eyes were wild, her ringlets still trembling. She looked disheveled, frightened, and fetching. He felt himself tighten and harden even more. He batted her hand away from her breast, and now she was half reclining beneath him, vulnerable, half naked, pressed tightly beneath him, her eyes filled with longing and terror.

"Because, Jesse"—her voice sounded breathy, husky, and frightened—"I've married Zack English."

"Damn you."

He shook, his whole body full of rage. He was tumbling her backward, his hand moving over her bosom, pulling her blouse out of her waistband.

"Jesse." She wanted him to believe her. She'd prayed desperately he would, for if he didn't stop, she would be doomed. She'd always been a skillful liar, but for the first time her life depended on getting Jesse to believe a fabrication. "Jesse."

He kissed her, pushing her over the table, his thigh planted in an intimate place, completely ignoring her pleas. "Jesse. Stop. Don't you believe me?"

He did as she asked, his eyes dark, his breathing uneven. "And if I believed you, do you think that would stop me?"

Suddenly she knew she was doomed. He did believe her, but the effect was the opposite of what she intended. "You're jealous." She tried to dodge him, but he resisted, locking her between his hard thighs.

"You're damned right I am."

He bunched her skirt up around her waist. The table cut across her buttocks, but she scarcely felt the sharp edge or pressure. The pressure instead came from inside her, a desperate tightness, an awful tension. But she knew she would let him do what he wanted. Not because she couldn't resist him. Not because of the longing or pressure. But because this was her demon, the darkness she'd feared since the doctors had told her that sex would be painful, childbirth fatal. And it was also her only chance to be normal.

She kissed him. She didn't want to. Believed she shouldn't. Wouldn't even die happy, for she wanted love, not just lovemaking, and knew that in the seeds of their childhood friendship lay a deeper, more enduring emotion, which would likely never come to fruition unless the doctors had been completely wrong. None of that mattered.

She kissed him because she wanted this knowledge. She'd wanted it for as long as she'd known him. And he had been right about her short stories. It was he she'd dreamed of, he she had feared. He she'd ridden and always conquered in all those childhood daydreams, extended into adulthood by the twinge in her back, by doctors' predictions. Now it was he who was doing the riding, his hips pressing her, a rhythmic pressure, the fine wool of his pants rasping slightly, a shape and a hardness and a heat beneath them. And she had gone soft, as if her bones had melted, including that crooked, despicable backbone, whose stitch had melted into this passion. For that, if for no other sensation, she kissed him.

He drew back, and she unbuttoned his jacket. She loved the look of his chest, brown and flat and totally hairless, his nipples puckered and a dusky rose color, and a long torso leading into a waistband that right at this moment he was unfastening.

He released himself with an easy movement, and this time she knew she wouldn't escape him. He was guiding himself between her thighs, paused, then coaxed with murmurs and heat, wetness, and caresses, nuzzling kisses against her throat while stroking down lower. Suddenly he was tugging her pantalets down, then forcing an entrance, her mind and her body a conflicting jumble, telling herself to relax; those childhood fears abuzz within her, she wondered desperately when this would hurt her, but Jesse's attention was riveted to her, and he simply kept pressing into her until she realized with a deep sense of amazement that the doctors had been wrong about walking.

And the doctors had been wrong about sex.

This didn't hurt. Not really. She was frightened, and that made her tense, but Jesse was making her feel so delicious that she relaxed and he entered slightly, causing her no pain whatsoever.

He paused, obviously puzzled. "You damned little liar." He frowned. She realized, with a sharp stab of panic, that he'd reached the barrier that gave lie to her story. And not just her story, but to all of Zack's poems as well. The hymen surprised her, for given her riding, she thought she might not be a virgin exactly, but evidently she'd lost this gamble, for she could see his surprise in his expression.

She gave a deep shuddering gasp. He frowned more deeply, his eyes a question, and for the first time in her life she could read his expression. He was glad this had happened. The idea unnerved her, for she thought deflowering a barbaric notion, but she could see in his eyes a brief gleam of triumph, and if she'd thought he would stop, she'd been completely deluded.

He didn't. He pushed into the tightness, bracing himself on the table. The pain didn't bother her much. She concentrated instead on the fullness. He fit her. And she wasn't crooked, the way she'd always expected. Her hips took his weight quite easily, though she was helped in this by their position and the fact that he was pretty much standing.

"Can we lie down?" she asked, nodding at the bed.

"Have I hurt you?"

"No," she answered quickly. "It just seems more normal. To lie in a bed."

He didn't ease out as she expected, but held her pinned there, splayed on the table. "So they were lies. Every word in that volume."

"No." She couldn't explain this, not in this time and place, perhaps not in any place ever. "They were the truth to Zack English."

"Why didn't you tell me?"

"Do we need to have this conversation right now?"

He smiled, then kissed her, pressing more tightly, and something inside her relaxed more fully. Perhaps the table wasn't normal exactly, but it was certainly thrilling, even poetic, to be taken half naked in such wild abandon. She scooted up closer, and he began a rhythm that scraped the table back toward the door. She giggled. He kissed her, murmuring softly, his hands and mouth exploring gently, his hips keeping a movement that bumped them backward by inches until they reached the wall of the cabin.

"The bed?" she asked, laughing gently.

"Forget it. I'm not leaving until we've finished."

He kissed her again, more deeply, more fully, his elbows braced now on the table, and she realized now she could drown in this pleasure, that every bit of this experience was lovely, his soft mouth on hers, the heat of his body, the scent of lovemaking made pungent by citrus. Rose scent and citrus mingled together, made denser, more musky, by the heat of their bodies. Most of all she loved the closeness, the feeling of being so open, a form of expression where she couldn't lie, her body sending its signals and all her clever words pointless, reduced to the simplest truth in the world. A thrill spiraled through her, not sexual entirely, but a deeper thrill of pleasure and triumph.

This is what it meant to be normal.

Nine

The doctors had been wrong about walking. But had they been wrong about childbearing? Bet asked herself that question when she awoke the next morning, the steamer's boilers chugging beneath her, deep in the bowels of the laboring conveyance. Her back didn't ache, though it seldom did at this time of day. Jesse had spent the night snuggled behind her, his arms wrapped tightly around her waist, like a boy with a blanket, old and familiar, he wanted to cradle forever.

Or perhaps, Bet thought as she tried to escape and he pulled her more closely, like a spoiled brat with a new possession.

She sighed, savoring the warmth of his breath on her neck. They'd fallen asleep right after lovemaking, but she'd awakened first, a lucky event since it gave her a chance to assess the lies she'd been telling. She ought to confess. She knew she should. Her deceptions were getting her in so much trouble. She'd hurt Jesse and risked losing his friendship. Heaven only knew what she'd done to his engagement.

Turning over, she examined the face of her old friend

and newly found lover. He remained unreadable even in sleep, all power and beauty, mystery and enigma, the long, smooth line of his cheekbone accented by a sweep of eyelashes so long and thick they actually tangled, the one vulnerable aspect of an otherwise aristocratic demeanor.

She nestled more deeply under the covers. She ought to tell him, but realized she wouldn't. She didn't know how he'd react, especially about the library problem. Jesse wasn't normally a violent man, but he'd beat up that football player in college and for a far smaller offense to her honor than stealing money with which she'd been entrusted.

Jesse stirred. She pulled the sheet over his shoulder, but he lifted himself, his chest brushing her arm as he propped himself on his elbow. "Good morning."

"Good morning."

He stroked her curls lightly, his caress almost reverent. "How are you feeling?"

She took a moment to answer the question. Not that she hurt anyplace really, but she needed a moment to compose herself. "I'm fine."

"Are you sore?"

"Meaning angry?"

"No. Meaning tender."

She paused again, to prolong the effect. She wasn't sore, but her nerves still felt jangled and she needed a moment. A tiny white lie might be in order. "Maybe a little."

He frowned, his black hair disheveled, a shaft of sunlight falling over his eyes, highlighting the latent brown in the blackness. "I would have gone slower, but the poetry fooled me."

"Jesse, you were lovely."

He pulled her in closer, tucked his arm under her neck, reached up, and opened the porthole. The sea air rushed in, bringing the high, lonesome cry of the seagulls and the salt-laden tang of the ocean. "Why did you lie about you and Zack English?"

She sat up abruptly, gathering the covers around her. They'd slept skin to skin, a warm arrangement, but the cold air hit her the moment she slipped out from the multiple layers of soft woolen blankets. "How about if we talk about that at breakfast?"

He nodded, then swung his leg over, wrapping one sheet around him as he tramped off to the small water closet adjoining the suite. She listened briefly to the running water, staring anxiously out of the round window. What should she tell him? Betraying Zack still didn't seem right, but beneath that worry another thought caught her. What would Jesse think of the risk she had taken? What would he say if he knew she'd been foolish, had once again taken a gamble and once again outwitted the doctors' predictions?

And what if the doctors were wrong about babies?

She leaned back into the pillows, picking a bit of lint from the blanket. The line of thought made her head ache. In the bright light of morning, she tried to think through the problem. What had the doctors told her exactly? That sex would be painful. They had been wrong about that. But she already knew from the business of walking that medical thinking sometimes involved guesswork. In the case of her back, how much of the doctors' predictions were accurate science? How much fear and superstition?

This much she knew: In infancy, her lower back had been fractured, and it hadn't healed right. Her gait wasn't normal. She needed the corset. Standing and running, even riding, still hurt her. The doctors had been wrong about walking and sex, but that did not make them wrong about childbearing.

She worried the ball in her fingers. Still, she'd beat their predictions twice in her life, mostly because they didn't consider that an injured person could make compensations. The bones of her back might be crooked, but the rest of her was stronger than normal. Ever since Jesse had taught her to ride, she had exercised as much as she could, partly to allay the terror that someday her walking abilities might somehow desert her.

But childbirth?

Tossing the little ball to the floor, she wrapped the soft wool blanket around her, eased out of the bed, retrieved a small hairbrush, then returned to the porthole, all of the world she'd seen lately as she hadn't ventured out much from this cabin. She peered out, hoping to catch a glimpse of the dolphins, and ran the brush through her tangled curls. A small sound behind her caught her attention. Jesse came out of the water closet, his white shirt unbuttoned, socks tossed over his shoulder, running one hand through his hair. She smiled, for he looked so disheveled, so careless, so easy, and so quintessentially male that immediately she wanted to hug him.

"What are you grinning about?" he asked.

She attacked her curls with vigor, leaning forward slightly, for she liked to get good circulation. "I'm happy."

He sat down at the little mahogany table. "Does it make you glad, what happened between us?"

"Oh, yes."

He lifted his eyebrow, a hint of expression she took to mean he didn't believe her.

She straightened. "Really."

He tossed his socks on the chair, strolled to the bed, and sat down beside her. Gently he pulled her to him, closing his muscular arms around her, snuggling her to his smooth chest, rubbing his cheek in her still-tangled hair. "Truly?"

"Oh, yes." Warmth shimmered through her, and she felt content. She'd known Jesse forever, and their friendship had been largely delightful, but nothing that had gone on in the past had given her this sense of rightness. "Probably happier than you can imagine."

"Better than when I taught you to ride?"

"Much better."

He tweaked her earlobe and chuckled. "Better than those days on the rancho when we'd ride through those hot golden hills, you on Firestriker and me on one of the cow ponies?"

She giggled. "Well, maybe." He was feathering kisses over her neck. "I mean, riding was different." Her muscles tightened. She felt a rise in her wanting and tension. "No. Maybe not." Her mind sifted through the memory he'd evoked. Her body was already responding, and she wanted to turn around and kiss him, take him into her arms and make love again. "I don't know, Jesse. You're asking me to compare apples and oranges."

He nipped at her flesh. "So—metaphorically speaking—which of us is the orange, me or Firestriker?"

She swatted him lightly. "You're the orange, silly. I am the apple. Poor Firestriker. He's just guarding the virgin."

He drew her close, cupping her breast. "A virgin no longer."

"No." She pushed his hand down. She'd better come to her senses. She'd die if the doctors were right about babies. She leaned her head into his chest. "Jesse."

"Yes."

"We need to be careful."

"Meaning . . . ?"

"We shouldn't go any farther without taking precautions."

He loosened his grip, bolted off the bed, and strode to a high-back mahogany chair. "Is that what you did with the poet? Observe the limits you proposed to me?"

"You're changing the subject. That's none of your business. No matter what went on between me and Zack English, you and I need to be careful."

"That's fair."

"You think so?"

"Of course." He picked his jacket up off the floor, reached into its pocket, and pulled out a small bag of black velvet. Returning, he tossed the package to her. "I'll have to teach you how to use it."

She stared, surprised, at the small object she'd caught. "What is it?"

"A precaution," he said, his voice even, his expression guarded.

She took the neat little bundle and examined it closely. It was a small velvet bag, held by a drawstring, containing a snippet of silk almost as soft as the material that held it. Bet knew what the device was, though she'd never seen one. They were banned in most places, but she'd heard them referred to, especially when she'd been at Berkeley. Sewn into a sheath and covered with oil, the silk was supposed to protect her while also giving her pleasure. "You brought this?"

"Of course."

"Where did you get it?"

"In San Francisco, before we departed."

She held her hands steady, though she wanted to giggle as she unrolled the material into a loose pouch. She did blush, in spite of her best efforts and her conviction that she was too worldly for maidenly shyness. Its shape conveyed its purpose so clearly. "Did you mean to seduce me?"

"What else?"

"I see."

He touched her chin lightly. "Does it disturb you?"

"No. Though it does feel peculiar." The thing felt soft, but odd and unnatural, and she already wondered what it would feel like to use it. "Why didn't you give this to me last night?"

"The poems gave the impression you were too much a free spirit for this much caution."

"So why did you bring it at all?"

"Because you said not to trust Zack's descriptions exactly."

"That's true."

He leaned against the wall and smiled. "That's a severe understatement."

She laughed, feeling slightly embarrassed. What must he think of the lie she'd been caught in? "I'd say."

"Come on." Gently he took back the sheath and tucked it into its velvet container. "I can see I've unnerved you. Let's eat. You can tell me about you and Zack English."

Jesse walked to the door. He'd been paying the steward to leave them breakfast, an arrangement that suited his shyness. True to plan, a covered tray waited, along with a pot full of coffee. Jesse picked up the food and laid it on the small mahogany table. As he did, Bet swathed herself in the sheets, tripped to the water closet, and retrieved her eiderdown kimono.

Jesse buttoned his shirt and sat down. He poured out the coffee and buttered some toast, laid it out on a plate, and began peeling an apple with a small paring knife left by the crystal fruit bowl. "Now what's going on between you and Zack English? Why are you chasing him to the Yukon, and why does he write those poems about you?"

She sat down, her appetite fleeing. "I told you before. I'm his mentor in writing. That's pretty much all there is to it."

"That's it?" He pared in a smooth motion that left the peel in one long red spiral. "It seems like such a peculiar arrangement. Obviously you've never been lovers, but are you engaged to be married? Do you have any idea what you've gotten into? Even assuming we get over the mountains, it's hundreds of miles by river to Dawson. Strong men die in the Yukon. If you're not madly in love with this poet, why are you taking such terrible risks?"

She sucked in her breath, fingering the coffee cup handle of white stoneware china. "Okay. We've never been lovers. And we're not exactly engaged to be married."

His paring knife clinked against his saucer. He regarded her across the table. She sucked in another deep breath and continued. This lie had better be true in its essence. "But in our own way, we do love each other. I critiqued his poems; he read my stories. It's hard to explain to a nonwriter, but in its own way that's a shared passion."

Jesse stared at her, his expression impassive, his long brown fingers steady.

"Truly." She picked up her cup and sipped the coffee. "He's a great poet, but bent on destruction. He drinks too much and is full of braggadocio, as reading the poems attests. They're completely false on a certain level, but we really are close, though not in the ways you imagine."

Deftly Jesse quartered the apple, then sliced the seeds from its heart. "And that's all you want? To save a great poet?"

"That's no small ambition."

He quirked his eyebrow, heartbreakingly handsome. "That I'd agree with."

She replaced the cup in the saucer. "It's not so odd as you're thinking, what's gone on—or not gone on—between Zack and me."

"It seems very peculiar to me." He toyed with the apple, staring intently at her. "Did you read those poems? They're extremely explicit. Why did he write them if you were never his lover? And, more important, why did you let him?"

"Why would I stop him? It's just his nature. Those poems are true on a spiritual level."

He arranged the four quarters on the plate before him, then picked up an orange, pushed his thumb beneath its thick skin, and peeled it. "That might be fine between two artists, but why do you let other people believe them?"

"Because they're so lovely. Would you disavow them? If someone wrote you a tribute like that, would you stand up and say you didn't deserve it?"

He laughed, dividing the orange in half. "Maybe not, at least not to the public. But why would you be so cruel to me?"

He handed a portion to her. The scent of citrus tickled her nose. She missed California already. This trek to the Yukon seemed suddenly foolish. She wondered why she'd done it, considering what her quest had precipitated with Jesse. "I wasn't cruel, silly. I pretty much told you not to believe them. I didn't know they'd make you so crazy."

"It wouldn't be normal, no matter how modern our friendship, for me to love you and not be jealous."

She removed the fruit's white spidery membrane, then bit into its succulent flesh. A tangy liquid flooded her mouth, tart and delicious, cool as the morning, one of life's truly wonderful flavors. Sucking her orange, she watched Jesse for a moment. He fiddled with the apple quarters. "*Do* you love me?" she asked.

"Now you're the one who's being silly."

"I don't think so." She chewed the portion left after her sucking. "I haven't known how you felt since you left Berkeley. You didn't speak to me for three years. I would have said those feelings had died."

"Evidently they hadn't."

"No. I suppose not."

His face had gone flinty. How this had happened, she wasn't certain. Smooth-skinned and high-cheekboned, his face had a structure that was naturally haughty. His eyes were so dark they concealed his pupils, and his facial muscles pulled so taut they translated no motion. Still, she could read him, at least a little, and she could tell he had hardened in some manner toward her.

"But don't mistake what's gone on between us," he said. "This doesn't mean we're going to be married."

"I wasn't assuming—"

"I didn't say you were." Carefully he divided the orange into sections and arranged each of those between the apple pieces. His effort made a red and orange starburst, rather pretty, though not necessarily tasty, considering the textures, an odd combination. "But I wanted to be clear on that point. No matter your situation with Zack, I am engaged to another woman."

"Of course." She leaned into the high-back chair, her appetite gone, her back aching slightly.

He continued to toy with his impromptu salad, arranging the pieces into a circle. "Because one thing the poems did make me see is that you and Christine are very different."

"Christine's very pretty."

"I'm not talking about looks."

"And she's a fine rider."

"I'm not talking about riding, either."

She poked an orange slice with a flatware fork. "Was I so much of a disappointment?"

"No." He shifted his gaze to the volume of poems, still carelessly dumped on the floor. "You were all I imagined, and very much more."

The words stole her breath and she trembled. "Then why would you prefer her to me?"

"Because, my dear little liar—Christine is lovely, but superficial. A fine rider, but not in my style. And a cold woman who's after my rancho, but there's one compliment I'll have to pay her."

"Which is?"

"Christine, my dear Bet, is honest."

Ten

In his three years as a miner, Jesse had seen many a mountain, but neither the gentle foothills of El Dorado nor the more tortured landscapes of Nevada's Comstock had prepared him for the scale, the grandeur, or the unearthly beauty that greeted them as the ship steamed into Skagway. He hadn't spent much time on deck, but he had had glimpses of the Inside Passage. For hundreds of miles the ship had been sheltered by a long string of islands, creating a landscape so lovely it left even the most gold-crazed prospector breathless. Emerald slopes rose out of water so placid it reflected the green back toward the sky. Clouds drank the light as they traveled inland, their shadows hurrying over water and mountain, as if they wished to take their squalls inland and leave this magical corridor peaceful. A few small towns dotted the inlets, forlorn reminders of more civilized pleasures and ever more tattered precursors of Skagway, the already fabled gateway to the Yukon.

Jesse already knew from his days as a miner that the boomtown would be chaos incarnate, a ragtag beacon for the world's hopeful, driven by demons or a sense of adventure, to the tiny town at the end of the passage that sheltered this coast from the sea.

"Ah, Jesse, it's gorgeous." Bet clutched his arm as she stood on the deck, staring out at the grand enclosure of mountains, ignoring the town with its slow-moving mass of human flotsam crowding among unpainted wood buildings. His stomach burned, but he held Bet steady. The water was calm, the day cool and breezy, but Jesse knew the tranquil scenery concealed formidable obstacles. The scenery was wondrous both summer and winter, but there was no good season for crossing these passes. Snow capped the mountains in the warm season, making avalanches a danger.

"Gorgeous," he said softly. He was already glad he'd come with her. "But I'd like to strangle that poet. You'd be dead in a minute if I hadn't come with you."

She didn't argue, though she didn't look daunted by either the height of the mountains or the meager collection of false-fronted buildings wandering back from the wide expanse of the mud flats. How they'd cross either, Jesse couldn't imagine. He didn't see signs of the proposed railroad. The scene looked so forbidding, in fact, he had the brief wild thought he should kidnap Bet Goldman, shut her up in the steamer, and force her back to the rancho, the place where she really belonged.

"Come on." Hand on her back, he shepherded her down the rickety gangplank onto one of the newly built wharves. Most of the passengers had already departed, their piles of supplies strewing the beaches as the miners streamed into the town, looking for ways to drink in some courage. There were only a few rules in the Yukon, and Jesse already knew the most important. A miner must pack his own provisions—one thousand pounds of supplies exactly—which had to be transported either over Chilkoot Pass, a steep trail of thirty-three miles, or White Pass, which was longer but less of a vertical climb. White Pass started near Skagway; Chilkoot Pass from Dyea, a bit farther north. Jesse wasn't sure why Bet had chosen this route, or how she planned to get over. He'd wondered about it for most the voyage; but he hadn't said a word on the subject, hampered by his own innate shyness and the wild, impractical hope that she might not have planned well enough, and her long trek after Zack English would be stopped here at the foot of the mountains, stymied by the lack of supplies.

So his heart sank when they trooped down the wharf, through the mucky expanse of the mud flats to a neatly stacked miniature mountain a few hundred feet back from the steamer.

"What do you think?" she asked. "Not bad for a complete beginner."

"Not bad."

And it wasn't. He could see at a glance she'd done proper research. There were bags of flour and cornmeal, beans and coffee, and boxes of hardtack. And even the packs with which they could be carried. For the first time in his life, he looked at her back and seriously considered its meaning and limits. He assumed she'd brought money for porters, but she'd still have to get over that pass, a four-thousand-foot rise better done in the winter, when rain and mud didn't hamper the footing.

He moved his hand to her elbow. "We'll be all right once we reach Lake Tagish, but it'll be plenty tough getting over those mountains."

She stiffened. She couldn't straighten—that was one of her problems—but she could give herself a more haughty posture, and she did exactly that at this moment. "I'll manage," she said, "if I have to carry the whole load myself."

"I see," he lied as his conscience protested. She'd kill herself getting over those mountains. Strong men died from avalanches, falls, and exhaustion. Very few women made it at all, and probably never a woman like Bet. He didn't argue, however. He, after all, had created this monster, a woman who rarely acknowledged her limits, who lived in her head and told beautiful stories and refused to acknowledge the longest of odds. If she sometimes confused truth and fiction, at least she never backed down from a challenge, never used her gifts for any more venal purpose than making a cruel world more pretty.

"Did you bring supplies also?" she asked.

"Of course." He nodded toward his own miniature mountain, stacked a few hundred feet down the mud flat. "Come on." He steadied her by the small of her back, guiding her through the mud toward the wooden walkways. He'd always admired her courage and daring, not just her skill as a horsewoman, but also the little girl who'd never been daunted by a sentence of life in a wheelchair. He sighed to himself as he searched the mountains for the killer pass known as the "Dead Horse." His stomach knotted as his gaze wandered over the snowcapped peaks. His heart faltered, its rhythm uncertain. He couldn't refuse her. To do that required him to point out her limits, and his admiration for her grit recoiled from that task.

He loved her always. He'd love her forever. He might never forgive her baffling deception, her rejection at Berkeley, or her chasing Zack English. But he would get her over those mountains. Someday she'd pick him over that poet. And he, Jesse, had better watch what he wished for. Because if she were free to be proposed to, he would be left with a difficult choice. He could spend his life with a woman who suited him, but whose presence ignited no passion. Or he could propose to this baffling liar, whose beauty stirred him more deeply than fabulous riches, wondrous mountains, or any other woman he'd known.

They set up a tent on the edge of the mud flats. Jesse would have preferred a hotel, but they had no luck finding a room. Like every boomtown he'd ever been in, Skagway teemed with more people than it could hold.

Moreover, the place was even more crowded than usual as one of those strange little wars had erupted in which western towns settled the question of justice. All the miners had come in from the goldfields, attracted by the shooting of some guy named Soapy, a local con man of some repute who'd been running the town like a robber baron. In a city with only a small number of hotels on a good day, there were no private rooms to be had. Jesse didn't like the idea of sharing, of course, so they made up their minds to set up the tent he'd brought.

"Can you believe it?" Bet pounded a stake into the soft ground, muttering in frustration as the mud spattered the hem of her calf-length corduroy skirt. "I know we'll be camping along the way, but it would have been nice to start a bit cleaner."

"True." Ignoring her trials, Jesse fitted the heavy wood tent poles together, using metal sleeves to join the pieces, and made them the right length to hold up a wall tent.

"Why are all these miners upset anyway?" Bet asked.

"Things like this happen." He poked the end of the pole into a corner, then stepped inside and pushed. The canvas flapped upward, settled back down, then closed in around him. Musk and mildew assailed him. He choked, pushing harder, trying to find the far corner. He hated the task of erecting a wall tent, no matter how often he'd done it. There was something so amorphous about the stiff canvas, so stifling, frustrating, and re-quiring such patience. He'd far rather sleep in the open. That wasn't an option with Bet along, however. "I've been around a couple of vigilance committees. They're common in boomtowns. Mining camps are founded by drifters. Sooner or later, if the location prospers, there will be a fight between the lawless and lawful."

"Did you ever participate in a hanging?" she asked as she continued pounding.

"Sure."

"How did you tell which side to choose?"

"Sometimes it's tough." He knew that was a rather vague answer, but deliberately chose to answer equivocally. She'd always been curious about his life as a miner, but he rarely talked about that time with her. He didn't like revealing that darkness, admitting how much he'd missed her.

As he pushed into the canvas, he could hear her putting her weight on the tent stakes. He admired this about her, her stubbornness in the face of reverses, but he still wasn't sure he could forgive her for lying to him about Zack English. He'd forgiven her for turning down his marriage proposal. Why should he forgive her this latest transgression?

He felt for the seam, the part of the tent where ceiling and walls joined. She claimed to love the son-of-a-bitch, but Jesse didn't believe that claim for a minute. If she loved the poet, why were the poems fiction? She'd never been a cold-fish type woman and she'd certainly responded to him in the steamer. Part of him loved that she'd been a virgin, but part of him felt uneasy, suspicious. She'd always been such a free spirit. So why hadn't she slept with that poet? How could she claim she loved him? But if she didn't, why was she chasing him to the Yukon?

Jesse shoved in the stick and poked it into a round metal eyelet. He let go, and the side he'd been holding flopped over. He knew it would, because that was the damnable thing about wall tents. You had to struggle inside this soft structure, with somebody tussling with the rope on the outside, until all the individual parts fit together and the whole damned thing went up all at once. "Could you hand me the other pole?" he asked.

She didn't answer, but handed it in. He fought his way back through the hot canvas. She resumed her pounding. But even through the thin wall of cloth he could sense her thinking, working on a way to get back to the subject of what he'd done in his time as a miner.

"How do you choose which side to fight on?" she asked finally.

He shoved the stick up, catching the corner and wedging the pole in the ground. "You try to decide which men are decent, hardworking, and honest. Who's trying to build a civilization and who's just out for personal riches."

"What did you think of that poster we saw? The one that bans confidence men?"

"Typical. If you want to settle a town, you've got to drive out all the cheaters and keep the ones who make their own fate by hard work and rising to the challenge of making a life in a new place." The two ends of the tent were now standing, but the middle still sagged all around him, and he could still scarcely breathe, so close was the canvas. "Tie off those ropes, will you? The ones on the end."

"Like this?" One wall splayed out, creating a hint of a breeze. He held onto the pole, adjusting it slightly as the tent listed inward a little. "Yes. That's better. Now let's do the other side."

He couldn't hear her, but she must have moved quickly. Within a few seconds, the other side lifted. "Do you think that order would have encompassed Zack English?"

"Probably." He wedged the other pole in its place. "He's oily enough."

Bet's laugh drifted in, a subtle sound, rich, full, and throaty. "I give that little street urchin credit. He's pretty resourceful. That poor cheated miner resorted to killing. With Zack, Soapy Smith just got outwitted."

Jesse fell silent. She been right about the ne'er-do-well poet, as they found out quickly at the local hotels. Zack had spent much of the winter in Skagway, having been fleeced of considerable money by one of the minions of Soapy. True to Bet's assumption, however, the poet had turned out to be pretty resourceful. He'd earned back his stake by writing letters for itinerant miners, reciting ballads in bars and bordellos, and finally conning the con man into giving him back some of his money. "He turned out to be quite a liar," Jesse said.

"All poets are liars." Her voice still sounded breathless. "As are most writers."

Jesse wedged the long stick in more tightly and waited. He could tell from the jiggle of canvas that she was fiddling with one rope after another. She must have been pulling, though he couldn't see her. All around him the canvas walls lifted, her work on the ropes dragging them outward.

As the tent fell into a rectangle, he tied off the poles with canvas ribbons, thinking about her comments on writers. She certainly had Zack English pegged. Stranded in Skagway, he had written a ballad dedicated to Bet, then made up an outrageous story about how she had spurned him because he lacked money.

Soapy, the con man, turned out to have a vulnerable side. He admired Zack's poem so profusely that he financed a trip to the goldfields, an act of kindness that gained him no quarter when the irrepressible con man fleeced a miner few weeks later. Zack, however, had already bought his supplies and paid porters to carry them over White Pass. The proposed railway had not been completed, so if the poet hadn't drowned in the Yukon, he'd presumably sailed the rest of the way to the goldfields.

Jesse squared off the last of the inside poles, the tent having been raised around him. The poet's success left Jesse deflated. Until this evening, he'd hoped Bet would be spared the trip to Dawson, a grueling business for even a strong man, much worse for a tiny, slender half-cripple with a bad back and a soft spot for horses. "But who would have thought he could outwit such a skilled con man with nothing more than a heartrending tale?" he asked.

"That doesn't surprise me."

"No?" He stepped outside to face her. She looked

disheveled and pretty, her face flushed with the effort, her brown corduroy suit splattered by mud.

She pushed a fawn-colored curl off her forehead. ''If a poet has the soul of a con man, why wouldn't a con man have the soul of a poet?''

Twilight came late in the Yukon and lingered, the northern sun hanging low in the sky, turning the blue mountains azure, the green meadows purple, and streaking the horizon with silver. Jesse couldn't enjoy the beauty, however, as these long days reminded him that the winter nights would be equally endless. Under his breath, he cursed the poet, tore his gaze off the unnatural sunset, and ducked into the tent he and Bet had erected. She had fitted it out with two cots, complaining the whole time that she'd prefer to spend the night in a bed with a mattress. Then she'd gone back to her stack of supplies to retrieve a few items, determined to make this temporary home a place of comfort.

Jesse picked up his kerosene lamp. It was still light outside but dusky in here, and he wanted to make the place look warmer. He placed the lamp on a camp table and lit it. The flame flared up. He turned the wick, the dancing flame subsiding into a steady blue one. He missed Bet already. He had liked being with her on that long voyage. He'd never thought of his childhood as lonely, having many friends among cowboys and horses. But he had no friendships with other children, and his friendship with Bet had improved his boyhood immensely.

He threw himself on his cot. The sharp smell of kerosene tickled his nose. She'd always laughed. He'd loved that about her. She'd chattered away, ignoring his shyness, and never seemed blue about that damned wheelchair. And he'd adored teaching her to ride. In a childhood that seemed perfectly privileged, he discovered he needed someone to talk to, the other ranches being too distant, the cowboys being too generally quiet, and the children of his father's workers being too frightened of his haughty demeanor. He'd loved those long rides with Bet and eventually come to love her. She'd taught him the meaning of friendship, the pleasure of a day spent in leisure. So he took no satisfaction in her present discomfort. Perhaps she'd call off this harebrained adventure.

Besides, he thought as he glared at her cot, neatly made up with wool blankets and flanking the other side of the wall tent, he wouldn't mind a soft bed himself, preferably one she'd have to share. She owed him, he thought, for the years of frustration, the three long years in the goldfields, and the years after that at the rancho, when he'd kept up the pretense of a friendship, too proud to admit he still loved her, but also too proud to pursue the woman who'd rejected his proposal at Berkeley.

He was contemplating his prospects for seduction when three shadows appeared on the wall of the canvas.

"Hallo," a deep voice called.

Jesse lifted himself off the cot and ducked under the flap. Hank, Hal, and Handsome stood in the silver gleam of the twilight, puffed into roundness by green and orange mackinaw coats, their jaunty black-and-white houndstooth pants sticking out from beneath them. Jesse stifled a sigh of impatience and stepped out into the cool air of evening.

Hank held his hat in his hand, an absurd fur hat, completely suitable for the Yukon but totally ludicrous topping those pants. "We wondered if we could ask you a favor."

"Hello." Bet trooped up behind them, heavy duck satchel in hand. The three gamblers turned and lifted their fuzzy hats in one grand and coordinated gesture.

"Jesse?" She looked questioningly at him.

He introduced the dandies who'd shared his stall in the steamer. He rather liked them, largely because he'd hardly seen them, but he never enjoyed the presence of strangers, and their sudden appearance made him uneasy. Bet squashed forward through the mud. The three gamblers bowed in a chorus, bending from the waist as they did.

To Jesse's dismay, Bet smiled graciously, indicating the tent. "Won't you come in?"

Jesse wanted to protest the invitation, but Handsome tipped his furry headpiece. The formality made him look so ingratiatingly helpless, Jesse stifled his sense of dissent. The three brothers filed into the shelter, lining up, hats in hand, next to Bet's cot. Jesse watched them closely, feeling both hunted and wary. Cigarette scent and whiskey had wafted in with them, though they did not seem to have been drinking or smoking. Jesse knew their type well from his days as a miner. Probably harmless, but not to be trusted.

Bet smiled, her light brown curls falling over her shoulders, looking vulnerable, female, dreamy, and poetic. Far too pretty to be soiled by these lowlifes. She gestured again, this time toward the cot. "Gentlemen."

The three gamblers sat down in one motion. The canvas cot creaked on its wooden legs. Bet sat down next, making no sound. Jesse remained standing, feeling uneasy. He lifted the hood on the lamp, and the yellow light grew suddenly brighter. He doubted the gamblers would hurt anyone really, but he didn't know why they'd come here, although he was beginning to have his suspicions.

Hank, the tallest, darkest, and oldest, cleared his throat and looked gravely at Bet. "We need to ask you a favor."

"Certainly."

"We suppose you've heard about Soapy."

Bet nodded. Jesse scowled, his suspicions growing.

"Good." The gambler held his hat loosely, deceptively casual considering what pressed him to approach two near-strangers and brave the wrath of a former shipmate who'd never been especially friendly. "Then you might have guessed the nature of our problem.''

Bet nodded again.

''We don't want to impose.'' All three brothers stared down at the toes of their matching patent leather oxfords. ''But we're not provisioned to brave the Yukon. And there's no work in Skagway for men of our talents. We thought perhaps we could make ourselves useful by providing amusement.''

Jesse set the lamp down with a clunk. Hank shifted his hat to the other hand, staring at Jesse with dark blue eyes. ''And seeing as how you were our roommate—''

Jesse shoved his hands in his pants pocket. ''We shared a horse stall. That hardly means I owe you refuge, especially from occupational hazards that professional gamblers ought to have predicted. Do yourselves a favor and get back on that steamer before you're run out of town by the vigilance committee.''

''We can't.'' Handsome, the shortest, fairest, and youngest one, spoke. ''We planned on earning our return passage.'' He coughed politely.

''And my brother's a lunger,'' Hal put in quickly. ''He's apt to get sick if we don't find shelter.''

''Damn.'' Jesse stifled an urge to tear down the wall tent and march back to the steamer. ''I hate disorganized greenlings. Whatever possessed you to bring a sick man to the Klondike?''

''Jesse.'' Bet shot him a pleading glance. ''Don't be cruel. Of course we can help them. We're not so provincial as some of these miners. We're fond of gaming.'' She smiled at the gamblers. ''As long as we don't lose money.''

''There's no room,'' Jess said in a low voice.

She didn't argue, just stared at space between the cots, an expanse of floor that might hold two people, though someone would probably end up sleeping on the mud flats. The gamblers said nothing either, just looked drooped and mournful, vulnerable and silly, shoulders slumped, clinging to their fur hats.

Jesse scowled. He didn't want these men as tentmates. He didn't want anyone but Bet as a tentmate, especially not itinerant gamblers, men of almost no morals or virtues. Men who, no matter their reasons, smelled of cigarettes and whiskey, who wore checked pants and funny hats, who might be thought handsome, and who fleeced the innocent of their money.

Men who smiled and lifted those fuzzy, silly hats, looked pleadingly at Bet Goldman, and said: ''We'll earn our keep by providing amusement. But we thought you might give us refuge.''

Eleven

"Did you have to do that?" Jesse glared at the retreating gamblers as they trudged back to the steamer to retrieve the few belongings they'd brought.

"Now, Jesse." Bet rummaged through her satchel. "Don't be silly. I know it's a hardship, but we couldn't reject them. I'd be so dejected if anything happened. They're darling."

Jesse prowled the small floor space of the wall tent, then peered again out of the flap. "You don't even know them."

"But that's just the point." She pulled out her pencil and tablet. "There must be a reason Fate sent them my way."

"I doubt it." He threw himself on the cot. "But there's probably a reason you gave them shelter."

She blushed. She didn't want to, but she couldn't help it. "Don't be so crass. There'll be plenty of time for that on the voyage. I won't try to shirk my obligations."

"To them or to me?"

"To either." She blushed even more deeply, undoubtedly scarlet. "I am well aware of what you're asking.

We made a bargain, and I hold to my word. I will be your mistress with no physical limits until we get to the Klondike. I'm not interested in a proposal of marriage, so you have to take proper precautions, but otherwise we have an arrangement.''

"I don't understand you."

"It's not that difficult, Jesse."

"First Zack English. Now you're helping these low-lifes, who shouldn't even be in the Yukon."

"I like them."

"That doesn't make sense."

She pressed her hand on her lower back. "The young one's a lunger."

He pulled her close, hugging her fiercely. "Is that what it is? You just can't resist another cripple."

She giggled, dodging his kiss. "Jesse, don't be silly. Zack's not a cripple, and neither am I."

He planted a kiss on her forehead. "Then why are you sheltering these gamblers?"

In spite of Jesse's dislike of the gamblers, Bet was glad in a way for their presence. Jesse was partially right in his observations. She didn't want to face him alone, not after the events on the steamer. Jesse's presence still stirred her, now more than ever, but she was also more frightened than she'd been before. She trusted him to use proper precautions, but his dark looks unnerved her, as well as her impression he'd become hardened toward her once he'd discovered she'd never been with Zack English. So it made her happy that he sat on a campstool playing his Jew's harp, pretending to be absorbed in the music, but really watching Hank, Hal, and Handsome play poker on a wooden box of salted crackers they were using as an improvised table.

She'd played for a while, but was out of this hand, having lost almost all the pennies she'd started with. She didn't mind really. She liked watching the gamblers. They hadn't fleeced her of very much money. Not only was their smooth skill a pleasure, but also the game gave her a chance to think about Jesse and doodle a few notes on her pad.

She didn't know what he wanted, whether he'd meant his remarks about no longer being interested in marriage. His comments surprised her. They also changed her opinion. She'd thought she'd lost him in those years after Berkeley, that his love had turned into hatred, finally cooling to civil forgiveness. Their friendship had revived after a time, but it had never occurred to her when mentoring Zack English that the poems could make her old friend jealous. Jesse's anger was flattering, revealing, disturbing. It had never occurred to her, either, that the lies in the poems had been cruel and shortsighted and that Jesse might never forgive the humiliation of having his long-hidden feelings revealed.

She sighed, watching idly as Handsome increased his mountain of pennies. Almost without thinking, she wrote out a sketch, a verbal description of her impressions. Why did Jesse care if she was a virgin? She thought this a silly male obsession, a mystique descended from vestals and pagans. But the other part of his question distressed her. Why had she fooled a friend who adored her? That lie had been cruel, she now saw clearly, and her heart ached as she sensed his alertness, eyeing her from beneath lowered lashes while the three dandified gamblers kept on with their poker.

She shivered, set down her tablet, and shoved her gloved hands into her sealskin coat pocket. She'd wrapped herself in a fur coat for warmth, but his gaze made her tremble. The three raffish gamblers were playing with good-humored grace, considering they were playing only for pennies so as not to fleece her of significant money. She didn't dare gamble for much more than small change. The notion still chilled her—that Jesse might find out that Zack had embezzled the library money. She needed to hire porters to get over that pass. For all her brave words to Jesse, she couldn't carry a ton of supplies. She'd be lucky, in fact, to get herself over. The rest would have to be paid for, and she'd rather not have to explain to Jesse why she was so short of cash.

Inside her coat pocket she clicked the lead back into her mechanical pencil. Jesse's song drifted over, low and brooding. Bet shifted on the canvas campstool, seemingly lost in watching the poker game. She had never thought of herself as a fraud. To the contrary, she'd always been the most straightforward of women, the curve of her spine translating to something quite different when it came to matters of spirit. True, she could lie when it suited her purpose, but her deceptions had always been flimsy and harmless, the gossamer shadings of the naturally sunny who looked at the world through rose-colored glasses. She'd never hurt anyone with her stories. Zack's flight of fancy made her feel embarrassed. Not the intimate subject matter, but that they made her old friend so crazy. There were matters of spirit Jesse did not understand, any more than she would ever reveal why she'd rejected his marriage proposal.

She glanced at the rancher. Her heart constricted as always at the sight of his beauty. His dark curling hair, his long downswooping eyelashes, the aristocratic curve of his cheekbones. Dozens of women had thrown themselves at him. He'd set his sights on the one who didn't. She'd ached with that knowledge all of these years, flattered, annoyed, and always impossibly hopeful that somehow their love could find expression, if only in a durable friendship.

She fiddled with her mechanical pencil, clicking the nib in a rhythm. Now look what had happened. For all the worry they'd caused her, she would never be sorry for those days on the steamer. And she wasn't sorry he'd come with her either. Watching him now, listening to his song, she felt tiny and crippled in the face of those mountains. She was glad Jesse had been her first lover, glad he was here to protect her. She wondered how on earth they'd get up the Yukon and doubted the wisdom of pursuing Zack English. She quaked most of all at the risks she'd be taking if she continued to accept Jesse's lovemaking. Still, life had become more precious than ever. She was glad for the friend who'd always adored her, the brooding loner who'd always intrigued her, and the man whose act of consummate faith had changed her life so completely it still inspired her to write stories and even novels about him.

"You in?" Hank's voice interrupted her brooding.

She glanced at the gambler, nodded, picked up the cards he dealt her, then sighed and frowned behind her fur-lined gloves.

"You've got to learn a poker face, sweetheart." Hal, the middle one, picked up his cards, discarded three, then tapped for some more. The other two quickly adjusted, while Bet made an effort to look more stoic. A small mountain of pennies was piled in front of Handsome, whose pale handlebar mustache did quirk in triumph in spite of his older brother's admonition. Bet had almost run through her stash.

"I can't fool three professional gamblers." She chewed her lip, her gaze fixed on the fan of cards she held. "If I'm very lucky, you'll fleece half of Skagway before you get around to me again."

"I doubt we're staying in Skagway," Hank said. "This town's pretty slim pickin's since they got rid of Soapy."

"Where will you go?" she asked.

"We'd like to get up to Dawson."

Jesse stopped playing abruptly. "That will be tough on your brother, going up that way."

"Not so tough as starvation." Hank picked up one card.

"Maybe not." Bet threw four cards down and signaled for some more. "But it will be rough on a lunger and impossible, really, if you didn't bring the proper supplies."

"True." Hank eyed her closely but made no further comment. Bet straightened abruptly. Hank looked away. "But we're hatching a plan. We're pretty skilled gamblers, if the town would allow us to practice our occupation."

Jesse plucked a few notes on his Jew's harp. "I wouldn't try cheating. Not in the mood the townspeople are in."

"We never cheat." Hank threw his hand in. "We just keep the odds on our side. That's quite a different matter."

"Maybe," Jesse said, then returned to his playing.

Bet looked at the cards she'd been dealt. A pair of twos and a queen. Not enough to justify playing. She sighed, trying to keep her face neutral. When had the odds ever been with her? Was that why she was so fond of Zack English, or of these cardsharps for that matter? Did she love the underdog always? Or were these relationships more like friendships, like the one she'd professed for Jesse?

Did she need to follow Zack to the Yukon?

"I fold." Bet tossed her hand in. She pushed the last of her pennies at Hank's miniature mountain. The brothers looked at one another.

Handsome adjusted his mustache, already more shaggy than the first day on the steamer. "Another?" he asked.

She laughed. "Don't exert yourself on my behalf. I have no more money, not even pennies, that I can afford to lose on gambling."

"I wasn't thinking of a money wager."

"Then what?"

"Are you the Miss Goldman who wrote the horse stories?"

Bet's chin lifted slightly. "Yes."

"The woman in the poems by Zack English?"

The music stopped. The Jew's harp slammed down.

Bet's heartbeat doubled, but her gaze did not waver.

"I'm the woman in the poems by Zack English."

"Those are fiction," Jesse said quietly. Bet could not see him, but she could tell by his tone he was angry.

Handsome raised a palm in conciliation. "Settle down, friend. I happen to like them. We noticed you reading the poems in the horse stall. We noticed the woman you had stashed in the cabin. When you introduced us, it all fell together. You've come to the Yukon to follow Zack English." He gathered the deck into his skilled fingers. "We're great fans of your horse stories, Miss Goldman. And we liked the poems." He shoved the mountain of pennies forward. "I'd bet the whole pile here against a reading."

Bet hesitated. She'd never considered this problem, how Jesse would react to her public persona as the notorious mistress of a famous poet. The mining camp seemed such an uncivilized place, it surprised her to find her fame had spread here. Nevertheless, she knew from experience in California it did no good to back down from these questions.

"I'd be very happy to do a reading." Jesse started to rise, but she waved him backward. "But that doesn't seem like a fair subject for a wager." She held out her hand toward the glowering rancher. "I don't have a copy of my horse stories with me, but it would be my honor to read from the poems."

Jesse shot to his feet, hand at his breast. He moved between Bet and the gamblers, his expression so grim and foreboding Bet wondered briefly if he were armed and if there were a gun, not poems, in that pocket. Hal and Hank moved to the side of their brother, their postures that of casual menace. Bet suddenly noticed that young men's muscles, sinewy and tough, showed beneath those absurd trousers.

Hank touched the sleeve of his brother's mackinaw jacket. "Slow down, fellas. If we wanted to fight, we could have stayed in Skagway. Look here"—he nodded at Jesse—"we admire the lady. We don't want to cheat

her. We could trade a poetry reading in return for helping her move her supplies to the foot of White Pass.''

Bet glanced at Jess. His eyes had gone hard, dark, and
glittery. Even beneath those downswooping eyelashes
she could see the fury in their expression.

"I could use their help, Jesse. I don't have that much
money."

Jesse's grip tightened over the lapels of his black
chinchilla greatcoat. Bet ignored his gesture and turned
to the oldest brother. ''Do you read many poems?'' she
asked.

"Not many, but I like the ones about you plenty."

"You do?"

"I thought they were ... pretty. . . . And meeting
you, I can see what inspired them."

Jesse cleared his throat. Bet tried to ignore him, which
wasn't easy. He glowered so darkly he looked as if he
wanted to strangle all three of the gamblers. She wasn't
sure what she thought of his outrage. She thought it odd
he'd still be jealous, though reading Zack's poems in
public was always peculiar, not because of the deception
involved but because of the intimate subject matter.

She shoved her gloved hands into her coat pocket.
Handsome wore an avid expression. His brothers didn't
look quite so lustful, but Bet could imagine their faces
when she read the more graphic descriptions. She shivered, but not from the cold. Rage shimmered from
Jesse's direction, leaving no room for quick thinking.

"Could I speak to Miss Goldman alone?" Jesse's
voice sounded odd, husky, and angry.

Handsome shrugged, his pale eyes laughing. ''The
tent is yours. We've got all of Skagway.''

Jesse didn't seem to notice the offer. He tugged Bet
outside, his hand on her elbow, and stomped through the
soft mud of the flats to a private place by her ton of
supplies. ''What are you doing?''

"What's wrong?"

"Can't you see what he's after? The next thing you know he'll be making advances."

"Jesse, I don't think so. He's a fan of the poems."

"The poems aren't the question. He's an outrageous bounder and not even a slick one."

"He likes the short stories. Didn't you hear him say it?"

"Oh, sure. And do you know what will go on in his mind while you're reading about how you and Zack did it?"

"We didn't do it. You know that now. Does it really matter that they'll think we did?"

"Of course it does. Those poems give the wrong impression completely." He grabbed her fiercely, touching her neck. He looked as though he'd like to wring it, though his touch was so gentle she could hardly feel it. "Ah, Bet. Why do you hide behind this pose? I know you're an artist, but you're also a lady. Until yesterday, you were even a virgin. Why would you let anyone think badly of you?"

She jerked back, annoyed. "What's my virginity have to do with this subject? What kind of a male quirk is that? I'm only important if I'm a virgin?"

"No. Of course not."

"Then what? What did you think before yesterday?"

Jesse scowled. He shoved his hands into the pockets of his chinchilla greatcoat. He must have had the Jew's harp in there, for its tinny strings murmured in protest. "I tried not to think about it too closely."

"Don't lie to me. I'd be willing to bet you had misconceptions. Most men do because I'm an artist."

"All right. I'll admit it. You did seem kind of freethinking."

"Is that why you felt so rejected? You thought others were getting something you weren't?"

"No!" Hands in his pockets, he splayed out his greatcoat, the small harp's strings tittering with the gesture. He seemed genuinely outraged by the comment, his full brown lips turned downward, an expression that made him look far more savage.

She touched his breast, where the poems should be hidden. Sure enough, he still had the volume. "Did your suppositions make you think less of me?"

"No. Not at all."

"In fact, they intrigued you."

He didn't answer.

"Come on, Jesse, be honest."

He pulled out the slim volume, staring thoughtfully at its red binding. "Yes, they intrigued me."

"But did you respect me?"

"More than any woman I'd ever known."

She pulled off one glove and laced her fingers in his. The cold air had nipped his skin frigid. She wondered what drove him to play the music even under such adverse conditions. "Why?"

He slipped out of her grasp. His boots made sucking sounds in the mud as he paced next to the pile of supplies. "I always thought of you as a virgin, if only in spirit. You didn't need me, but you didn't seem to need any other man either." He tucked the poems back into his jacket and rubbed his hands briskly together. "There's always been an innocence to you that didn't depend on physical matters."

"Then let me handle this, Jesse. I've had some experience of these requests already. They're usually issued as kind of a challenge, but I always accept because hiding's an error. It's shame and fear that make lovemaking seem dirty. I've done readings before. I've never had anyone give me trouble."

"I don't believe that for one minute."

"Honestly, Jesse. Would I lie on that subject?"

He glanced at his breast pocket. "I love you dearly. I value our friendship. But I have no idea when you're lying and when you're telling the truth. And to be honest, I'm not even sure you do."

She turned back the lapel of his coat, gave him her

best look of exasperation, and patted the place where he'd secreted the volume. Her hands remained on his wide chest, and she could feel his heart booming through the soft material. "Honestly, Jesse."

He twitched back, his expression rigid. "All right. You're probably lying." She started to protest, but he ignored her. "Even if you're telling the truth, you weren't in a mining camp when you did your last reading. If it goes around this town that you're 'that' kind of woman, do you know what kind of trouble you could be in?"

She leaned back into her corset, her back aching badly. "I can't control their reading habits. Evidently I'm already famous. These miners can read the poems without me. Apparently the gamblers have already done so."

"You're not reading those poems out loud."

"Jesse, this is pointless. That genie's already out of the bottle."

"Then we'll just have to pop it back in."

"How? I doubt that the Yukon has any censors."

"Be serious, Bet. You can see for yourself this place is lawless. No one's going to censor the poems. And no one's going to help you if you get in trouble."

"I have confidence in you. I know you'll protect me."

"Fine. But it's a long way to Dawson. Men die on that trail. Though I intend to survive it, you don't need to make a hard journey harder."

"So make a suggestion."

"I'm thinking." He paced the ragged pile of supplies. Darkness was not even falling, although it had to be almost midnight. Bet had to admit she was a bit worried. She'd probably been conned already when she agreed to take in the gamblers. They'd seemed so hapless when Jesse had protested, and she had objected. The gamblers had then moved so quickly they'd brought in their satchels before Jesse could eject them. She could see now that their pose was deceptive. They probably had some purpose in mind.

Jesse stopped, staring at her. "We could disguise you."

"Don't be silly."

"I'm not." He plucked at the fur of her coatsleeve. "You're a little too obviously female for us to do this with clothing, but you do have one quality in your favor."

"Oh?"

"You're an oh-so-consummate liar. You're going to tell those gamblers a tale."

She went back in and explained that she was Bet Goldman, but not the woman described in the poems. Handsome didn't believe her completely and questioned her closely, ruffling the cards through his hands as he did. "Why did you say so if you weren't that lady?"

"I thought I could fool you and maybe make a bit of a profit." She kept her face straight, her expression impassive, almost as impassive as Jesse's.

"How could you profit from poetry readings?" the pale gambler asked.

"You were willing to pay a few minutes ago."

"I heard the poet came through here last winter. The barkeep told me about it."

"I heard it, too. That's what gave me the idea. A good con, after all, has some truth in it."

"Then why are you confessing your ruse?"

She glanced at Jesse, who was watching her from beneath those silky eyelashes. "My friend doesn't like it."

"And what's with you two? Are you two married?"

"Engaged." Jesse stepped between them. "But that's none of your business." He fixed each of the brothers with a look that would have frightened a savage. "You can stay as our guests, but there's a condition. You have to keep quiet about the poems. Do you understand?"

The three brothers nodded, though Handsome looked

a little bit sulky. Hank stepped forward, however, and took the cards from his younger brother. "We're guests with a proposition, though." He turned and faced Bet. "Have you ever worked as a fortune teller?"

She straightened, pressing her hand against her corset, still surprised by Jesse's last announcement. "Of course not."

"You'd be pretty good at it. You look like a Gypsy. And your . . . fiancé . . . here"—he gestured toward Jesse—"is really exotic."

"Why would I want to tell fortunes?"

"How much money you got?"

She didn't answer. She couldn't. They'd made brief inquiries about the cost of porters, and she already guessed she was in trouble.

"That I suspected." The dark-haired gambler flipped the cards through his fingers. "You get here and things are pretty expensive."

Jesse took Bet's elbow, gripping it tightly. "Your point exactly."

"We'd like to get over that pass ourselves." The cards whirred smoothly as the tall gambler fanned them. "Skagway's not going to be healthy for men of our talents. We don't have supplies and we don't have money, and we can't work as gamblers to earn them. But"—he sat down on the cot and divided the deck on the cracker box—"you two need porters. We'd rather use our brains than our backbones, but a man's got to do what he has to."

"We have enough money," Jesse said.

"Speak for yourself." Bet wriggled out of Jesse's grasp and sat on the cot across from the gambler. "What are you proposing?"

"Bet." Jesse plucked at her elbow, but she drew back.

"Quiet. Let's listen. I can see some possibilities in this proposition."

"I don't like it." Jesse glared at the gambler.

"You don't have to like it, just listen," she said.

Hank laid out a solitaire hand. "It will take more than a week to move those supplies, assuming Hal and I move them. If you could set up the tent to tell fortunes, you ought to earn quite a bit of money. Every one of these miners is a fortune hunter. Seems to me there's a need for that service."

"I don't know." Bet watched, fascinated, as he laid out his hand, seeming to play the game without thinking. "I could get run out of town as a bunco artist."

"Naw. These miners would not hurt a woman."

"Then what would happen?" Bet asked.

"You'd pay us the money you earned telling fortunes, and we'd use it to buy our own supplies."

Bet looked at the three brothers. She did not especially like trusting gamblers, especially ones who'd already fooled her about what they'd guessed about her past. Still, they seemed honest, at least honest enough for gamblers, and their bargain would save her a great deal of money as well as get her closer to Dawson. She looked at Jesse. "What do you think?"

"I think I'd like to strangle a poet."

"Why did you tell them we were engaged to be married?" Bet asked as she tied a scarf on her head.

"Why are you being so frugal? Don't you have money to pay for porters? And why are you indulging these gamblers? You don't owe them a thing because of their plight."

"Don't change the subject. I told you before they'd serve some purpose. What's wrong with getting over the pass cheaply? I'd have to wait for paid porters, too. Why not spend those days telling fortunes?"

"You could get in trouble with the vigilance committee. You could spend the time on your novel."

"I doubt the vigilance committee will hurt me; and it will be an experience I can put in my novel. Now go back to the subject. Why did you say we were engaged to be married?"

He shoved his fists into his greatcoat pockets. The strings on his Jew's harp twittered a little. "It seemed more convenient."

"It's not true."

"It is after a fashion."

"What fashion?"

He threw himself back on a cot and pulled the poems out of his breast pocket. "We have an arrangement, at least, you and I. I thought our intimacy would seem less peculiar if people thought we were engaged to be married."

"And how will you explain that lie to Christine?"

"I don't plan on making an explanation. I told you before, she and I have our own arrangement. We're faithful enough when we're together, but we don't honor those vows during long separations."

"Did she really consent to such a cold-blooded bargain?"

He riffled through the red-leather-bound volume. "I told you before, that's none of your business."

"She makes a great fortune teller," Handsome said as he tossed a sack of cornmeal onto the wagon. Jesse glanced at Bet as she emerged from the tent to greet the first in a long line of men ranged outside it. "I knew she would," the short, blond gambler continued. He threw leather sashes over the bag, his arm muscles bulging beneath a newly purchased shirt of warm flannel. "Where'd she learn tarot?"

"Berkeley. She went to school there."

"What did she study?"

"Painting," Jesse lied as he tied down the cornmeal.

"Doesn't surprise me. She has the skills of an artist. Great intuition. A gift for stories. And the kind of insight into human nature that allows her to sense her customer's feelings."

"Sure." Jesse hefted a sack of beans. He didn't enjoy the lies he was telling, but he was determined to keep up the deception Bet had begun with her story. To his surprise, the gamblers had stuck by their side of the bargain. They toiled every day on the mountain. Hank and Hal attacked White Pass. Handsome stayed behind and did the packing. They tackled their chore with amazing vigor, considering Bet had forbidden harming the horses she'd bought. Another fight that had happened between Bet and Jesse, as she had bought a pitiful lot, assuming they'd be better treated with her than if they were bought by anyone else. Probably true, but also quite foolish, considering the pass's vicious reputation.

The gamblers seemed undaunted by her foibles, however. They used the nags to ferry her ton of supplies, along with those Jesse had brought for himself. Every evening, after Bet paid them, they had scavenged, traded, and bargained a growing pile of supplies for themselves.

Still, Jesse didn't trust them. They didn't bring up the poems again. Jesse strongly suspected they knew he was lying, but had their own motives for accepting the story. They never mentioned Zack English again. Jesse was glad for the silence. He didn't like strangers, especially gamblers, but their tact was helpful in a tough situation.

He glanced at the tent. Bet had gone inside with one of the miners.

"You keep a close eye on her, don't you?" the pale young gambler asked.

"Of course."

"Are you worried she'll throw you over? She doesn't seem like that type to me."

"No."

"Then why don't you ever come up the mountain? We'd get over faster." He loaded on another sack. "You're good with the horses. You're wealthy, I know, but I see your muscles. You don't seem frightened of manual labor."

"I don't like to leave her. In some people's view, a fortune teller's not far from a con man."

"I don't think you have to worry. The vigilantes accept her. She's got a good reputation and doesn't charge much for the fortunes."

Jesse checked the harness on the lead horse, a white, swaybacked nag whose knees knocked together. "Her rate is quite cheap until you consider her product is worthless."

Handsome petted another, a brown and white pony that looked to be in pretty good shape. The gamblers were surprisingly good with these creatures, a relief to Jesse, as many animals died on the pass. "Don't be so narrow-minded. This is a town full of desperate men. She understands what they want exactly. She makes her predictions hopeful and detailed. From their point of view, her talents are priceless."

Jesse gave him a look of exasperation. He wondered about him. The boy still wore the fuzzy hat, still seemed remarkably perky, considering the desperate fix he was in.

He caught Jesse's glance and smiled back. "Okay. Maybe not priceless, but they sure are a bargain."

Jesse took the bait. He didn't want to, but he needed to know. Where did that cheerfulness come from? And what did Bet see in this pale young miner that made her shelter him in that way? "How do you know the value of a prediction until you know if it's come true?"

"You don't." The boy drew pieces of sugar out of his pocket and fed each of the horses as they waited. "But the customer gets to spend time with a woman. Look what you'd pay to do that in Skagway."

"She's not a whore."

"I'm not implying she is. But you pay a percentage girl just for dancing, and Miss Goldman does something better."

Jesse felt a tic in his jaw. He'd never entered the tent when she told fortunes, but she'd assured him there had been no misbehavior, and he'd heard not a whisper to contradict her. "Like what?"

"She's good to talk to."

He glanced at the long line of men, a steady stream that had not diminished since Bet began her predictions. "You think conversation is what they're after?"

"No, not exactly." Handsome gave one last scratch to the lead horse's chin, then returned to check on the lashes. The air was cold, the day crisp and breezy. "But conversation is what they're getting, and after they've got it they're glad to have it."

Jesse could smell the snow in the passes. "Does she seem so easy?"

"She seems kind of free on the surface, but they all know she's a respectable woman."

"Then why do you think they line up like that? They look hungry as dogs waiting for dinner."

"Wait just a minute." Handsome had gone down the line of horses, whispering to each and checking their cinches. When he finished, he retrieved a cup of coffee from the small campfire they'd built, sat down on a sack of flour, and sipped the hot liquid. Jesse busied himself with the packing, shifting supplies so the wagon would be more balanced, but all the while wondering. What did Bet see in this young gambler? Clearly she adored him, giving him shelter, though Jesse could not understand why exactly. She treated all the miners with patience, adopting them as if they were children. She lent the gamblers the floor of the tent, a fact Jesse accepted with extremely poor grace, as it kept him from private moments with her, as well as imposing three total strangers on him, if you counted Hank, who slept on the mud flats. And the miners adored her. They'd come in droves for her fortunes. Almost as if they'd read the poems, though Jesse didn't hear any more about them from either the gamblers or other miners. That still didn't explain her devotion, however. "What—"

"Wait." Handsome held up his hand. "Look."

Jesse glanced at the tent. Bet had emerged, giving a sisterly hug to the departing miner. He trudged off with a backward glance as Bet turned to face the latest arrival. "Look . . . look at her face," Handsome said.

Jesse did as he asked. Bet was smiling, of course. She smiled always, a sunny expression surrounded by curls and accented by ribbons. It was odd how she always gave that impression—light, color, and movement, the fripperies of a natural-born Gypsy, the subtle glow of her honey-colored lighting.

"What do you see?" the boy asked.

"Nothing. She's smiling, that's all."

"She's smiling." He tipped his coffee mug in that direction. "And what do you think that means to a miner? A man who's going to spend the winter in darkness? Who's going to gamble life and limb on a long shot?"

"A lot, I suppose."

" 'A lot.' That's all you say for it? She's tiny and pretty and crippled, living in a tent at the foot of a mountain, about to tackle a monstrous pass, surrounded by men at their most grizzled, dependent on a snobbish rancher who's wildly protective and irrationally jealous and three seedy gamblers she scarcely knows." The boy's chuckle reached him, deep for his youth. " 'A lot' doesn't begin to describe it. That woman has courage, and she's always hopeful. Those are qualities any sensible man would sell his soul for."

Twelve

Bet would never forget the plight of the horses, not for as long as she lived. Their corpses strewed the length of the pass. They broke their legs on the boulders, sank in the bogs, collapsed from exhaustion, and died of starvation. Far more disturbing, however, was the cruelty of the men who drove them.

Kind men shot their mounts when they were injured. The cruel left them to scream out their terror. Jesse killed at least three that had been abandoned that way. The truly depraved took out their frustrations by beating the beasts to death for their failure. Jesse marched Bet past these scenes, grim-faced and disturbed, but never interfered with the whipping. Bet's heart went out to him each time he did this, and she regretted what she'd gotten him into. No pretty story or lover's embrace would wipe those sights from Jesse's mind either.

It had taken two weeks for Hank, Hal, and Handsome, supplanted by porters, to move their supplies to Lake Bennett and for her to earn the money to pay them. Then she and Jesse had gone over White Pass by themselves, agreeing to join the gamblers in Dawson. Jesse hadn't liked that idea, but she and the trio had formed a friendship. She didn't like the idea of parting forever, especially here in the wild Yukon where she had no friends really and was totally dependent on Jesse.

She'd hiked the pass, refusing to burden a horse. Jesse had not even tried to dissuade her, sharing both her sense of compassion and her view that she could succeed at the challenge as long as she had proper support.

And he had been supportive, taking ten days to get over the trail, shielding her where he could from the sight of the horses, guiding her gently, massaging her back to keep it from aching. He never brought up the subject of lovemaking, probably because they were both so distressed, but also, she suspected, because he was thinking about their relationship's meaning. She didn't believe his excuses that he'd be content with an arrangement that simply sated his masculine ardor.

She'd known Jesse all of her life, and he'd never been ruled by that kind of passion. His strongest feelings had been for the rancho, and he'd be thinking now about its best interest, and what to make of the lies she had told him and what to do about the two women he was nominally engaged to. But she knew he would bring up the subject because of how long she'd known him and also because, no matter how gruesome the trail, there was something in the way he touched her, the way he kept looking at her calf-length hem, that let her know he hadn't forgotten, but was simply waiting for the right moment. That moment came on the edge of Lake Tagish.

They'd set up a tent at the end of the lake, as far as possible from the other stampeders, whose tents created a small, white-walled city. Canvas flapped in the wind. Its soft sound whispered beneath the happy song of the birds and the harsher music of hammer and saw. Crossing the pass, she and Jesse had used a small shelter, as it was far more easily erected than the unwieldy wall tent. They were using the same tent this evening. As she finished the dishes, Bet looked at the triangular shape with foreboding. It had been an exciting, frustrating experience, sleeping so close to Jesse, having him touch her, but proceeding no farther with their lovemaking.

Jesse had made a dinner of trout, as Bet was a marginal cook on a good day and had no skill whatsoever with cooking and camping. They'd taken the day to design a raft to take them by river to Dawson. At home with both camping and boating, Jesse had looked forward to this part of the voyage. She felt unsettled and useless, but glad to be done with the walking, the part of the voyage that made her back hurt most.

She also felt frightened, for she'd made up her mind to tell him the truth, or if not the whole truth exactly, at least a portion.

She began right after dinner, as they were sitting by the shore of Lake Tagish drinking their chocolate, a little fire dancing before them and a cold wind whisking over the water.

"Jesse."

"Yes?"

"You know I love you."

He took a long sip of his chocolate, eyes dark and brooding in the waning daylight. "I believe you've mentioned that fact."

"I know it's frustrating, sharing that tent."

He did not comment. The days had started to shorten. The water was almost as dark as his eyes, but the horizon glinted with silver, a northern phenomenon really, as the light at home always seemed golden. This was the hard part. She really did love him, now more than ever, but she needed to explain some of her limits, to quash his hope for a genuine engagement.

She clutched the spatterware cup in her hands. "I assume you're expecting we'll resume . . . well . . . you know . . . where we left off in the steamer."

He didn't answer, and his expression didn't give away his emotions. She took another sip of the dark chocolate.

Jesse had tossed a bit of cinnamon in, a Mexican custom left over from childhood. The spice made the sweet liquid exotic. It also made Bet feel homesick.

Tears pricked her eyes, but she suppressed them. She knew underneath what she wanted. She also knew she couldn't have it. Eleven years in a wheelchair had taught her that dreams sometimes came true through action. They never came true from mere dreaming.

"I don't think it's such a good idea to go back to . . . you know . . . whatever you want to call it."

He blew a breath over the top, making a curl of steam on the surface. "Why not?"

The cold seeped under her sealskin jacket. She shivered and took another sip of the chocolate. "I don't want to be your mistress."

"What's wrong with being my mistress? You've turned down my marriage proposal. I'm not asking you to give up your writing or come and live with me on the rancho."

"You're engaged to another woman."

"Don't be provincial."

"I'm not."

He stood. For a moment she thought he was angry, but he moved away from the campfire, sat down in the dark, and pulled out his Jew's harp. He played a ditty, nothing sad, but a seafaring chanty, the kind that keeps up the spirits. She waited. She knew this was one of this habits, to pour his feelings into his music.

When the music ended, he turned, his gaze dark, his expression impassive. "I told you before. I'm not the boy you rejected at Berkeley. Christine and I have an understanding."

"And what if I said I didn't believe you?"

"We're friends, and I'll love you always, but that doesn't mean I share your defects. You might have lied about the poet—"

"But that's just the point. I'm not engaged to Zack English. You don't need to be jealous. He's a friend.

Just the way you are. It would be too . . . hollow . . . being your mistress . . . simply to service a primitive need.''

"Do you want me to tell you I love you?"

"Not if you're lying."

Another song, this time more mournful. He looked so beautiful really, a dark and elegant shadow, the moonlight painting his lithe form in silver, the wind ruffling through black, curly hair. She longed for him, ached for him, wanted him badly. She also wanted to live.

The music stopped, and he stood up again, secreting the instrument in his pocket. "This is not a debating society, Bet. You see that lake?"

Bet nodded. She saw it. Deep and cold and so long she could not see across it.

"Do you know how to sail it?"

She shook her head, not needing to answer. He knew perfectly what she'd answer. He closed the small space between them, took the cup from her hand, set it down on a rock, helped her stand up, tilted her face toward his, and placed both his hands on the side of her head. "I could cross this lake with my eyes shut. I don't expect very much from you, but if you expect help getting over, you'll service—as you put it—my primitive needs." The pressure of his touch increased, though he did not hurt her, simply framed her temples and cheekbones. "Do you understand?"

She nodded, her heart squeezing smaller, her stomach lurching. She had no more excuses, no more wild stories. "We couldn't . . . I don't know . . . go a little bit backward? Perhaps like those first days on the steamer?"

He shook his head. She eased out of his grip, and he let her. She moved to the edge of the water, bent down, and doused her face, trying hard to regain her sense of composure. Her heart boomed, and her hair ribbons fluttered, the one feminine touch she hadn't abandoned. She ought to confess. She knew she ought to. It only made sense, but she couldn't.

She stared out at the lake, dark and foreboding. The wind whipped her cheeks until they burned. Her hands froze inside her coat pockets, and she desperately missed warm California and those long-ago days on the rancho. Why couldn't she tell him? Was she so much the liar? Did she need to see herself as normal? She glared at the distant horizon, lost now in the inky blackness, the first leg of a journey she finally realized she couldn't take without Jesse's help.

She could sense him behind her, waiting with patience, his anger leashed but not discarded. She rubbed her temple, then picked up a stone and threw it. It disappeared into the lake with a plunk. She ought to give up her quest for the poet. But she couldn't. She wasn't a quitter. She didn't like being cheated. She needed to get the library funds.

She picked up another small stone. No, that wasn't true. She needed to get the library funds, but that wasn't the problem. Behind her, Jesse resumed playing the Jew's harp. She listened. He plinked the strings gently, his soul in the song. Its mournful notes made her heart ache, brought back those summers long ago on the rancho, the long rides in the hot golden hills, afternoons spent walking on beaches, and cool evenings singing by campfires. She wanted them, longed for them, was ready to—what?

She curled her fingers over the pebble and turned to look at the shadowy figure behind her. The darkness made a sketch of his beauty, blue-black hair made silver by moonlight, his face a high-cheekboned unreadable cipher, long, blunt-tipped fingers playing that Jew's harp, and a slender elegant body whose warmth and texture had imprinted itself so strongly that she could sense them through both chill and distance. In that moment she discovered a harrowing truth. She wanted to live, but this wasn't living, this lying, deceit, and pretending. Maybe she wasn't normal exactly, but she wasn't the Gypsy Jesse thought her to be. She did feel cheated, but

not by Zack English. She felt cheated by those doctors'
predictions.

She had loved Jesse always and for this reason: He
had taught her to beat the long odds she'd been handed.
And if she confessed, he'd never touch her. She'd be
trapped forever in the lie of all these years' making.
Because he loved her, too, at least on a certain level, but
he wasn't the boy who'd taught her to ride. True, he was
still patient and gentle, but the man he'd become—
shrewd, calculating, and cautious—the man who wanted
an heir to his rancho, who spent three years mining for
copper, who watched and sheltered his clever investment, who'd marry a woman who didn't love him to
guarantee that rancho a future, would never risk all he
had worked for on the fragile faith of a deformed writer
who believed sincerely, though possibly wrongly, that
once again the doctors were wrong.

And it would be over, the dream she'd nurtured,
which hadn't died, though it certainly should have, that
someday her life would be normal, that she'd marry
Jesse Wheeler and bear his children, pass on the childhood they'd shared on the rancho.

Turning, she tossed the pebble into the water. "But
you'll use the . . . device . . . you brought from San Francisco."

"Certainly, though if anything happened—"

"Oh, Jesse, don't say it."

His boots crunched on the pebbles. Citrus and chocolate. Cinnamon and mohair. She smelled him, sensed
him, ached with her wanting.

"Is that why you're frightened?" he asked. "Does it
worry you that you might get pregnant?"

"A little."

"You know I'd take care of you always."

"You're engaged to Christine."

"An arrangement, I told you, that I'd throw over if
only . . ."

He placed his arm over her shoulder, a gesture of

comfort, not of seduction. He ran his hand down her spine, the slight curve the corset did not straighten. She stiffened, or tried to, though she couldn't truly.

"Has someone told you stories about childbirth?"

"No." She could feel his touch, a steady pressure, even through her sealskin jacket. She ought to tell him. She knew she should. She couldn't. That was all there was to it. "Nothing frightens me since the wheelchair. It's just—"

"Because I'd never hurt you. Not for the world."

"I know that." She kept her voice low, her face angled away. Pulling her hand out of her pocket, she laced her fingers in his. "I don't know how you can stand playing that Jew's harp when it makes your fingers so cold."

"I'd never hurt you. Do you understand that? I'd die before I'd let anyone hurt you, and I'd never do so myself."

Her breath left her body. He was speaking the truth, which was the problem exactly. He'd never approve of the risk she was taking. And she intended to take it. She'd beaten the doctors twice in her life. Both times with the help of Jesse Wheeler. The odds were against her succeeding again. But they were her odds—this was her hand—and she was going to play it.

"I trust you, Jesse, but we're a long way from California. This"—she gestured at the black-shouldered mountains, the dark pines sighing beneath them, and the white-tipped waves and inky black water, the beautiful, cruel, and encompassing landscape that seemed to embody the Yukon—"would be a terrible place to be pregnant." She smiled and batted his sleeve. "And besides, you're engaged to another woman. It was never my intention to spoil your engagement."

He smiled. "I don't believe *that* for a moment." His expression grew serious, and he drew her closer. Even here, close to the Arctic, he smelled of citrus, of home, of California. "We don't have to go on playacting about this."

She didn't know which he referred to, his tenuous engagement to Christine Deutch or her own hopeless quest after Zack English. She decided he meant the latter. "Yes, Jesse, we do. Because I'm still after the poet. You'll just have to trust me. I don't want to discuss it, but it's important to find him."

He lifted her chin, his expression shuttered. "Give me one reason why I should trust you."

"There isn't one, but I know you will." She touched his curls, his proud, high cheekbones, the questioning lines of his dark eyebrows. "For the sake of our friendship."

"True." He nuzzled her earlobe, under her ringlets. "Too true, but there's still one condition. I'll do my best to protect you, one way or another, but for the duration, you must act as my mistress, and by the time all this is over we'll have discussed both our engagements, mine to Christine and yours to Zack English."

They made love that evening and every evening thereafter for the two weeks it took them to get to Dawson. Bet thought about that as she stared at the canvas above her, the first rays of morning turning the stiff material to the color of linen. She and Jesse were cocooned in the softest of shelters: a small canvas tent, its floor lined with pine boughs, fur robes for a mattress, flannel sheets and wool blankets above that, though neither fur nor wool equaled the warmth of their naked bodies.

They slept without clothes at Jesse's insistence, and to Bet's shock she found it lovely—warmer than she'd thought it would be, heady, erotic, and totally natural.

Jesse was happy, Bet knew. She was happy also. The journey downriver had been thrilling and jaunty. She'd never been frightened shooting the rapids. Perhaps she should have, but Jesse loved boats the way he loved horses and handled them nearly as well. Every evening he recommended their lovemaking. He used the protection assiduously, which made her feel equal parts treasured and frustrated.

She turned slightly toward his sleeping figure. She didn't know much about the silk sheath, how well it worked or how badly. Half of her wished she would get pregnant, while the other half regarded that outcome with terror. Outside, the birds were singing. There wasn't a proper sunrise exactly, but the northern birds had not lost their morning habits. She glanced briefly at Jesse, hoping their songs wouldn't wake him. Down the lake, men were stirring. Many had risen. She could tell by the clink of ladle on skillet, the pungent scent of frying bacon. She sighed, wishing the trip downriver could have lasted longer.

He stirred, and she snuggled backward. She wished this moment could last forever, though she did not like the sheath, nor her reason to need it, nor the desperate lies she told.

"Jesse?"

"Yes?"

"Was it . . . like . . . this . . . with Christine?"

"No." He kissed her earlobe. "She doesn't like tents."

"Be serious."

"I am."

She turned away, pulling the blanket over her shoulder, fighting a sense of despair.

"Don't be jealous," he murmured, stroking her lightly.

"I don't like to be provincial, but it's hard to envision you getting married to someone who couldn't share moments like this."

Jesse reached under the blanket and pulled out a blue flannel shirt and a pair of long johns. He struggled briefly with each of the garments, but managed to get himself into his clothes without leaving the warmth of the blankets.

Propping himself on his elbow, he pulled her toward him and planted a brief kiss on her nose. "Don't be provincial and don't make me discuss this. I'm reasonably sure you'd feel cheated if we got into a truthful discussion."

"Did you try to control . . . conception . . . with her?"

"Bet!"

"I'm sorry." She ducked under the covers, sucked in a deep breath, then popped her head out from beneath the fur robes. "But I wondered if you had any experience . . ." She blushed, seeking to recast the question. "I mean . . . do these really work?"

"I hope this doesn't make me sound like too much the rustic, but I'm not like your poet. I never discuss what goes on in the bedroom with you or Christine or anyone else."

Bet looked pointedly at the canvas walls. "I'd hardly call this a bedroom."

He laughed. "Tents either." He tugged one of her ringlets. "Now up you go, lady. I know this was lovely, but it can't last forever. We've a poet to find in Dawson."

September 1898
Dawson, Canada

Bet bent over the inert figure, wrinkling her nose against the smell of saloon and the odor of a half-open whiskey bottle. "Zack." She shook his limp body. "Wake up. We've come to help you."

"Bet?" The poet lifted his head, hair disheveled, eyes bleary.

Even through the effects of dissipation, Jesse could see why a woman might love him. Though a little smaller than Jesse expected, the infamous poet was a fine specimen of male beauty. His leonine head topped a sinewy body. He was a bit barrel-chested with the hands of a workman, but had luminous eyes and a sonorous voice that probably carried when he recited.

"Bet?" He grabbed the half-finished bottle and swigged it. "Ah, my Betsy, have you come for the money?"

"What money?" Jesse asked.

"Shush." Bet bent toward the poet, plucking the sleeve of his brown corduroy jacket. "We've come to help you. We'll talk money later."

"Don't have it." He wagged his head slowly, his thick brown hair falling over one eye. He was pale, his gums were bleeding a little, and Jesse suspected he had a touch of the scurvy. "Don't have it. I tried." He sighed, then laid his head on the table. "I tried . . . but this land is a killer."

"Quiet." She struggled to lift him, nodding at Jesse. "Help me, will you?"

Jesse did as she asked, hating this task. So this was the man she'd chased to the Yukon. He seemed unworthy, a dissolute wreck, all the more undeserving because it was clear in those eyes, in the fine youthful body, and, Jesse hated to admit, in the poems he had written, that this man had the potential for greatness. Right at the moment, however, his strong hands were trembling. The smell of whiskey clouded his breath. His dark brown jacket was frayed at the sleeves, and his hobnail boots were scuffed almost useless. Stifling an impulse to hit him, Jesse hefted the man half onto his shoulders.

"Wait." The grubby poet grabbed up the half-filled whiskey bottle.

"Zack!" Bet punched his arm, but he ignored her, leaning on Jesse and cradling the amber-colored liquid.

"Fine, take me." He lolled heavily. "Just let's not forget this bit of comfort."

Bet sighed visibly, then posted herself on the other side, contributing more balance than carry as she and

Jesse, working together, guided the wobbly young man through the saloon door.

"Where shall we take him?" Jesse asked, his stomach revolting against the smell of the whiskey.

"Our place," she answered, by which Jesse knew she meant the wall tent they'd pitched at the edge of Dawson. As they turned in that direction, the poet sagged heavily, but the cool air must have hit him.

He lifted his head, looking at Bet. "Betsy. . . . Betsy . . . ah, sweet Bettina . . . she's come." His voice rolled over the mud-crusted street. "You hear that, you mountains? You men of the mountains! She's come!"

"Zack," Bet whispered, making a shushing motion. As usual, the streets were crowded with miners, and the poet's pronouncements were attracting attention.

"She came for me, my proud, lilting lady, goddess and icon; delta of Venus—"

"Don't . . ." Jesse jerked the poet out of Bet's grasp and plowed him against the wooden saloon wall. His chin snapped up, his head splintering a board. Jesse ignored the sound of its impact. "Don't start with that. I know all about the lies you've been telling."

In spite of the rough stuff, perhaps *because* of the rough stuff, the poet's gaze cleared, his expression becoming alert as a husky's. "Who's this?"

"This is Jesse Wheeler," Bet answered. "He's the friend I told you about."

The whiskey-scented bard placed his hands on Jesse's forearm, holding the bottle suspiciously steady in light of his previous behavior. "A rival?"

"No," Bet said.

"Yes," Jesse responded.

"Not exactly," she said.

"Exactly," Jesse countered.

The poet fixed his gaze on Jesse and held it. His eyes were tawny, clear, not bloodshot, and he didn't seem frightened of Jesse. "Let go of me, please."

Jesse did as he asked. The two men squared off. Jesse

wasn't frightened of the poet either, though physically they were an even contest. Bet had told the truth in her description of Zack English—a soulful gaze backed by workingman's muscles—his life on the streets not far behind him.

Pulling back, the poet assessed Jesse with grim confidence. "A nabob," he said to Bet. "You've done well for yourself."

"Zack."

"Smart of you to find a man with money."

"You're being foolish. . . ."

Jesse touched Bet's elbow, frightened for her. Clearly she had told the truth to this level. For all that the poems were full of braggadocio, there must have been some love between her and the poet. He could see the fear in her expression, sense the tension flowing between her and Zack English.

"I suppose you told him you'd been swindled," the poet said slowly.

"I haven't told him a thing."

"Swindled?" Jesse swiveled his gaze back to the wretch crouched against the wall.

He met Jesse's gaze and held it. "Then what lies is he speaking about?"

Jesse pulled the poems out of his vest pocket and slammed the barrel-chested boy into the wall. The poet didn't try to escape, though he didn't fight either, simply clung to the bottle, glaring at Jesse.

"I know about these." Jesse held the small volume in front of the sun-weathered face, even with the blood-flecked mouth. "I know that you've never been lovers, that you don't have a civilized bone in your body to write lies like this about a lady."

Zack English glanced between Jesse and Bet, then slowly took a swig from the bottle. Surprisingly steady, he contemplated the red leather binding. "And how do you know those are lies?"

Jesse didn't answer. He didn't have to. As the poet

gazed between him and Bet, the truth came in a current, strong as that carried by copper, a palpable feeling flowing between them—he and Bet—Bet and the poet.

"I see," Zack English said.

But Jesse thought he didn't. His mind caught on a word. He felt a brief swell of disgust. "Swindle?"

"A mere expression."

Jesse grabbed his shirt collar again. "Don't lie to me, lowlife. You might be drunk, but you're also a writer. You never use a careless expression."

The poet drew himself up, removing Jesse's hand with a delicate gesture. "I suppose there's no harm in telling."

"Zack!" Bet tried to move closer, but Jesse restrained her.

The poet straightened his drooping coat collar. "I admire you, dear, for trying to protect me, but the race is run, I can see that." He glanced around at the crowd the fracas had attracted. "Perhaps we can discuss this someplace more private."

"Fine." Bet picked up her short skirt and flounced off, tossing her parting words over her shoulder. "But whatever your fate, just remember you brought it on yourself with your drunken revels. I would have merely told him a story."

Zack watched her stomp off. Jesse watched her, too, her bicycle boots sinking into the mud, her short skirt swaying against the upper curve of her ankles. He wanted to follow, but remained with Zack English, determined to get to the truth of this matter.

As she reached the end of the street, he turned back to the poet, still huddled against the wooden saloon wall. "Swindle?"

"Well, not a swindle exactly. . . ."

"Then what?"

"I borrowed some money. . . ."

"From her?"

"Not only from her."

Jesse glanced at Bet's receding figure. It began to make sense. So this was why she gambled for pennies, yet risked her life in this long trek to the Yukon.

The poet, as if sensing a weakness, held out the bottle. "What has she told you?"

Jesse slapped back the offering. "Don't try to con me." He tucked the volume of poems back in his breast pocket. "I'll find out the truth if I have to break your fool neck to do it."

"Ah, a straightforward fellow."

"You bet." He took Zack English by the elbow and guided him into the muddy street. The crowd of miners receded before them, men brown and grizzled, already marked by this land's beauty and harshness. "Now, who did you swindle?"

"No one. I merely borrowed some money. . . ."

"From whom?"

"From library patrons."

"How much?"

"Twenty thousand dollars."

Jesse took a minute to absorb the number. The amount shocked him. He didn't know how much Bet made from writing, but he knew her stories had not made her wealthy. She pretended, of course. Her works were quite famous, but very few authors lived solely on writing, and Bet wasn't one of the privileged few. She'd worked in libraries always, as well as raised money to start them. This embezzlement would be a disaster on both counts. Though no western jury would ever convict her of theft, because of both her sex and fine reputation, the poet's indiscretion could cost her dearly, both in terms of her job and her fame as a writer. "Let me get this straight. You were starting a library together?"

"Yes."

"And you borrowed this money to come to the Yukon—"

"Very smart."

"Don't be so smug." He grabbed the whiskey bottle

and took a drink from it, hating the taste of the poet's lips on it but needing a bit of strength from it. "I'd like to kill you, but I probably won't, mostly because I think she loves you."

"I had the best of intentions. . . ."

"I'm sure."

"I did. What better place than the Yukon to parlay a stake into a fortune?"

"Do you have any left?"

The poet fell silent. He shoved his hands in his pockets and hunched up his shoulders, protecting his head against the strong wind. Jesse took another swig of the whiskey. Twenty thousand dollars. Considerable money, even for him. He could buy her way out of this problem, but why should he do that for the sake of a friendship, even for the sake of a mistress, especially one who did not trust him enough to share her dilemma with him?

"So you lost the money?"

"Yes."

"Damn." Jesse launched the bottle against the closest saloon wall. It shattered, scattering glass shards into the sodden ground. "What kind of idiot are you, to hare off like that with someone else's money?"

The poet paused, staring thoughtfully at the puddle made by the liquid. "The same kind of fool as Bet. Always hopeful. Always willing to bet on a long shot."

Jesse scowled, grabbing the smaller man by the elbow, stepping over the whiskey pool in the mud.

The poet followed, looking mournfully at the receding puddle. "It's not so crazy as it might seem. There are plenty of men who've made their fortunes in the Yukon."

"That's not really true." Jesse glanced at the still-steady poet. The drunkenness must have been a bit of a fraud, because he walked evenly now, almost as though he were sober. "Some make a fortune, but not very many. And those who do generally earn it."

"You sound so world-weary." The poet gave Jesse a

look, amused and disdainful, as if Jesse were the youth and he were the one who was older and wiser.

"I am," Jesse said, drained of his anger but still curiously jealous. "And also experienced. I know about fortune-hunting because I've done it. Successfully, I might add."

"Really?" Zack English took a silver metal flask out of his pocket and screwed the top open. "How?"

"I have a college degree in mining." Jesse borrowed the bottle and took another swig of it. Excellent whiskey. The poet knew his liquor. "And I never succumbed to gold fever. I kept in mind always: Gold is the ultimate swindle. It has no intrinsic use whatsoever, only the value we all assign it."

"And that helped you find it?"

"No. It helped me know better. I invested in copper. A far better value."

"But far less romantic."

"Maybe. But it's supported my rancho for years."

The poet borrowed the silver flask back and took another swig of the whiskey. "But where is the beauty in searching for copper? Now gold, there's a quest for a poet."

"Hogwash."

They'd reached the end of the town. Bet had disappeared into the large tent city that climbed up the slopes and surrounded the more permanent buildings. Jesse headed off in the general direction she'd taken, toward the small wall tent they were sharing.

The poet followed, slogging along in the mud. Even here they were jostled by miners, mud-covered mostly and awfully grubby. Jesse could barely contain his irritation. She'd lied once again to protect this unworthy poet. He thought it a sign of her innate perverseness. Almost as foolish as these grubby miners. These camps were teeming with people looking for flakes of one precious metal while completely ignoring the riches around them, land and trees and game for the taking. Bet had in him a man of real value, but seemed blinded by the poet's pretensions. If he ever got her back to the rancho, he thought it would be a long time before he let her off his private domain.

They'd picked their way through about half the tent city before the poet spoke up again. "I don't think it's hogwash, mining for gold. Copper has value to our generation, but gold's had value for ages."

"Hogwash also. Any fool can be dazzled by gold's color and beauty. Give me a metal with practical uses."

"Then why are you so devoted to Bet? She's hardly a practical wife for a rancher."

Jesse glanced back at the poet, who seemed notably sober and was staring at him with brown eyes so pale the Yukon light caught them, making his expression transparent. Jesse halted, staring at his grubby rival, then glanced down at his own jacket. As always, he was impeccably tailored, but even his chinchilla greatcoat had taken a beating coming down the Yukon. He drew himself up to his full height, almost six inches taller than the compactly built poet, deeply regretting the exotic coloring that sometimes fooled people about his status. "I am not a *peón*. I don't require a practical wife. Bet is pretty and worldly. She'd make a good mother—"

The poet choked on his whiskey.

Jesse tensed. "What?"

"Nothing." The poet's gaze shuttered, and Jesse couldn't read it, but he knew in some way he'd just been cheated. "A mere observation. I assume you know all writers are useless. We're much too self-absorbed to be parents."

Jesse gave him a glare. "Is that why you never . . . why the poems are fiction?"

"Not exactly." Zack pulled up his shirt collar. "The poems are fiction because I really love her. I might dishonor her in my fiction, but I'd never defile her in person."

•   •   •

They found Bet in the tent, furiously writing. She'd decorated the place to make it homey, a talent Jesse noticed
on the trip to Dawson. Like a true Gypsy, like a real
poet, she carried her world around with her, taking com-
mand of every new space, rearranging it with the subtlest
touches, flowers and ribbons, even small objects, like
those she'd collected on the camp table, a few rounded
rocks, a piece of driftwood, a long stick chewed clean
by a beaver.

She was working on the new novel. Jesse could tell
by the stack of loosely bound tablets. She didn't look
up when he and Zack entered, though they paused and
waited for her glance. She ignored them. Her mechanical
pencil scratched the tan paper, its soft sound filling the
silence as she covered the blank page with her tiny,
flowing, elegant writing and the God-given gift Jesse
had always admired of getting her dreams onto those
pages. Zack shrugged and sat down on one of the cots.
Jesse waited longer, but she ignored him also, so he
planted himself in front of the small camp table, facing
her squarely.

He touched the volume of poems in his breast pocket.
"He's told me."

She didn't look up, just kept writing. "Told you
what?"

"Don't be coy. About the swindle. About why you
followed him to the Yukon."

She lifted her eyes from the rapidly filling pages and
turned her frank gaze on the poet. Never before had
Jesse been so struck by how honest she looked, how
clear-browed her expression, and how that beauty concealed her deception because in her heart she was so
much the artist, so naive, hopeful, and well-intentioned,
she didn't know when she was lying. "I didn't tattle."

"I know," Zack said. "I did."

"Why?" she asked.

"Why did you come?" The poet dangled the bottle

between his fingers, his expression sharp, his jaw pugnacious. "Did you really come all the way for the money?"

"That and to save you." She lifted one of the pages. "I'm writing better than I have in ages. For that I have to thank you. The horse stories are selling. The poems made them famous. I'm a hundred pages into my novel, and that wouldn't have happened if you hadn't pushed me to make my writing a little more risky."

"And him?" Zack nodded at Jesse. "What's he got to do with your writing?"

"He helped me find you."

"Because?"

"We've been friends forever."

"No." Jesse paced to the door, looked out at Dawson, his fingers drumming over his breast pocket. "I hate speeches." He glanced at the poet, then pulled out the volume of poems. "I hate conversation, though I generally don't feel that way with Bet. But I'll never compete with two famous writers, so I'd appreciate it if you'd both just listen."

Bet put down her pencil, staring, astonished at him. The poet leaned back on an elbow, a Roman, slightly saturnine posture, and held his palms open, a gesture of friendship. "Go ahead. Speak. I won't interrupt you."

Jesse unfolded the paper. He'd written this out on the steamer, uncertain of what he would blurt out when demanding she choose between him and the poet. He didn't look up as he spoke, but kept his gaze on the words he had written.

"I love you," he said. "And not just 'in certain ways.' I love you completely. I always have. I probably always will. I asked you to marry me before, and your refusal almost killed me. It's taken me years to get up the courage to ask you this question again." He wasn't trembling, which made him happy. Perhaps he should have done this in private, but he wanted the poet to hear this. "I'd like to get married. But I have some condi-

tions. You have to give up the your friendship with
Zack, both in real life and as his inspiration. You have
to agree to live on the rancho. You can keep up your
writing, including your novel. We'll travel sometimes to
San Francisco. But mostly I'd like to live on the rancho.
I still believe you could be happy there, both as a woman
and as an artist. You spent much of your childhood
there.'' He steeled himself, because this part did make
him tremble. ''I always believed you were happy. I
was.''

At the end of his speech, he looked up. Bet had paled,
white as the snow on the mountains around them. He
waited. He couldn't read her expression. At least she was
trembling. That made him happy. He didn't know what
she'd think of his proposal. He scarcely knew what he
thought of it himself. The poet was right. He was taking
a terrible gamble. She wasn't a practical wife for a
rancher. Flighty, artistic, a terrible liar. And God only
knew why she loved this poet.

Jesse didn't care. He assessed this tiny, unpredictable
Gypsy and for all he was taking a gamble, he knew right
away he'd made the right decision. She moved him on
a physical level, but most of all he loved her spirit. She
moved him with all those ribbons and ringlets, the swirl
of her shawl, the back kept straight by the corset. He'd
been happy during those days on the steamer. He'd been
happy on the trip down the Yukon. He'd been happy
when they were children together. He believed in his
heart he'd be happy always, if only she'd accept his
proposal.

She stood, using the table to steady herself. ''What
about Zack? If he gives back the money, will you let
him come with us?''

''The money's gone,'' Jesse said quietly.

She looked at the youth lounging on the cot. ''Is that
true?''

He nodded.

''Twenty thousand dollars?''

He nodded again.

"Every last cent?"

Even Zack English did not have the heart to acknowledge his sin with a gesture.

She sank back into the chair, her shawl and hair ribbons trembling. "What will I do? You know I'll be ruined. I can't go back until I've reearned it."

Jesse bent down and gripped the table. "You're not staying the winter. That's not under discussion."

"Jesse, I have to. My life will be over. Everyone will think I'm a thief."

"Accept my proposal, and I'll repay the money."

"Oh, no. That wouldn't be fair. And what about Zack? You know I can't leave him."

"Why do you care about that swindler?" He gripped the table more tightly, afraid he might hurt her, so foolish did he think this question. "He's worse than a thief," he said in a voice low as a whisper. "He tells you he loves you at the same time he robs you."

"We're kindred spirits."

"I don't believe that." He folded his speech back into the volume, then shoved it into his pocket. He took one step to the side of the tent, then picked Zack English up by the shirt collar. "I shouldn't allow this, but you can come with us to San Francisco. If you so much as look at her sideways, I'll kill you. And we part when we reach the city. That's the last you'll ever see her again."

The poet didn't respond, though he didn't seem frightened.

Bet remained fixed behind the table. "Do you think that's reasonable, Jesse?"

"Reasonable, no." He flung the little coward down on the cot. "I'd like to kill him, and he'd deserve it. He robbed you blind, and you can't see it because you're so taken with the lies in his writing."

The poet straightened his collar, assessing Jesse with those luminous eyes. Ignoring the look, he turned back to Bet Goldman. She'd turned even paler, if that could happen. She twisted the nib on the pencil she held. A corkscrew curl fell over her shoulder, accented by a slender red ribbon. "And Christine?"

"Christine will accept whatever happens. With her it's a matter of money."

"Will you continue to see her?"

"It's a small valley. I'll have to be civil."

Her eyes flared in anger. She glanced at the poet.

"Fine. Then not for years. Maybe not ever. Maybe we'll trade—when I see Christine, you see the poet."

Zack tugged on the sleeve of his frayed jacket, the silver flask dangling between his fingers. "Do I get to plead for myself?"

"No," Bet and Jesse said in concert.

Still trembling, she moved away from the table. She looked pale, even nervous. A light sheen misted her forehead. All the playful quality had gone out of her movements. In spite of her obvious discomfort, she straightened so stiffly her corset protested. She glanced fearfully between him and the poet. "I'd like to speak to Zack by myself."

Thirteen

"You're not going to marry that yokel?"

"No." Her hands were shaking. She felt sick to her stomach. "I don't know." She couldn't believe Jesse had proposed. "Believe me, I'd love to."

"You've never told him?" Zack unfolded himself out of the cot.

"Told him what?" Bet stared at the young poet. He looked both darker and lighter than when she'd last seen him. Life outdoors had bronzed his complexion to swarthy, but gilded his naturally tawny hair.

"That you can't have children."

She sat down abruptly and folded her hands. "Who told you I can't have children?"

"No one." Zack walked to the table. He picked up a pile of pages from Bet's looseleaf notebook. "But I'd rather deduced it."

"I wouldn't advertise your deductions. For all you know they are falsehoods."

"Are they?" He glanced sharply at her, sat back down on the cot, and leafed through the pages.

"I don't have to answer that question."

"Not to me you don't. But you ought to tell that love-sotted rancher." He paused, scanning the papers. "How much of a risk are you taking? You must be sleeping together. Does that fool know he might kill you?"

"That's none of your business."

"Ordinarily not." He turned another page over, perusing it quickly. "But he's made it my business. You've been my meal ticket for ages." He prowled the tent, riffling the notebooks. "Does he know who he's talking to? My poems have been published in *Atlantic Monthly*. What makes him think he can dictate who's to inspire me?"

"Zack." Bet got up from the campstool, pressing her hand to the small of her back. "Just slow down, will you? You don't know what that proposal cost him. I turned him down when we were at Berkeley. I thought I'd lost him. . . ."

"You aren't going to accept?

"I'm not sure." She moved to the cot, bent at the knees, her stiff corset creaking, and balanced herself on the edge. "Don't you want to get out of the Yukon?"

"I don't know." He looked over, his gaze surprisingly sober considering how much he'd been drinking. "This wilderness suits me."

"I don't believe that for a moment." Standing beside him, she touched the shabby sleeve of his coat, his lip flecked with blood, likely the beginnings of scurvy. "You look like it's going to kill you."

"A poet's stock increases if he dies early."

"Zack, don't be silly."

"I'm not." He pulled the silver flask out of his pocket, unscrewed the cap, and took a swift swallow. "I've been writing so beautifully here."

"You can't stay in a place so savage just because it inspires you."

"Why not?"

"Because. You said it yourself—this land is a killer.

Immortality's a wonderful goal, but you have to be dead to achieve it.''

He gave her a look, sharp and insightful, the kind a lead husky might give its master. He screwed the top back on the bottle, then caressed the ringlet dangling over her shoulder. ''Would it make you sad if you lost me?''

''Of course.''

''It really would make you immortal if I managed an end that was perfectly tragic.''

She clasped his hands tightly. They were rough, still the hands of a workman. She felt a sharp stab of terror and pity. She understood a little too clearly what drove him. ''Listen to me. You might fool everyone else, but you don't fool me and you shouldn't lie to yourself. Don't let those romantic notions seduce you. That's the ultimate swindle: to let someone else get rich off your suffering. That's what happens to most of these poor prospectors.''

''But isn't that what everyone wants from an artist? To live like a wild man; to flirt with destruction?''

''Some do, it's true. But you don't have to give people what they want exactly.''

''Some of us do.''

''True.'' She kissed the tips of his fingers, tobacco-stained and smelling like whiskey. ''That's why you'll be immortal, and I'll just be a writer of children's horse stories.'' She squeezed a little more tightly. ''But couldn't you die in California?'' She smiled and chucked his chin with a knuckle. ''It's warmer.''

He threw back his head and chuckled. ''So you do love me.''

''You know I do.''

He pulled her close and kissed her—lightly, though, and on the forehead—then tugged playfully on her scarlet hair ribbon. ''Enough to turn down that yokel?''

•   •   •

Bet called Jesse into the tent late that evening. A kerosene light reflected off the canvas wall, lending a golden
glow to her fawn-colored curls. She sat in the back, behind the camp table, wearing her shawl over her elabo-
rately figured eiderdown kimono and swaddled in
several layers of blankets. They'd slept separately, the
cots being narrow, though the little beds had sufficed for
their lovemaking. Jesse had wooed her the whole length
of the Yukon River, taking immoderate pleasure in her
seduction, making use of the sheath part of their pleasure, though he longed for the days when he would not
have to use it, both because the device seemed unnatural
and because he liked the idea of children. He didn't
know what multiple layers of clothing meant, but he
suspected they didn't bode well for her answer. She patted the cot, motioning for him to sit close to the table.

He remained standing, hands in his pocket. He could
feel both his Jew's harp and the paper on which he'd
written his speech.

"What is your answer?" he asked.

She moved onto the cot, dropping the blankets. "My
back aches. Do you think you could rub it?"

He stood there, unmoving, hands in his pockets. "I
want my answer."

"I don't have one yet." She removed her fur mittens,
her shawl and kimono, dropping them one by one on
the camp chair. "I need some time to think this over."

"What's there to think over? You've had eight years
to consider this question."

"That's not accurate, Jesse." It was cold in the tent,
but she ignored it. She tugged the ribbons out of her
hair. "I didn't know I could reconsider until a couple
of hours ago."

He moved forward, stilling her hand. "It hasn't intrigued you all of these years?"

"Of course it's intrigued me."

"So answer."

"I can't. Not here, not in the Yukon."

"Why not?"

"It's too . . . cold . . . in this place. I can't think right in such a cruel and beautiful landscape."

"Hogwash." He ran his fingers through one of her ringlets, all gilded by moonlight into silver and silk. "The cold hasn't kept you from chasing the poet. You're going to choose between him and me."

"I will." She slipped out of her corduroy skirt. Her strong calves disappeared into white pantalets. He felt himself tighten and harden. "But not until you take us to San Francisco. I don't trust you." She touched the top of her blouse. He stopped her, suddenly conscious of what she was doing. She meant to seduce him. "You'd like to leave Zack to die in the Yukon. How do I know you won't do it once I give you an answer?"

He took her by the chin, holding it tightly. She smelled like soap, old roses, and almonds. She meant to use his own weakness against him. To use her feminine wiles to get him to waver. He didn't care. The passion they felt was her weakness also. It held them together. "Why would you try to protect him? He deserves to be left. At the very least, he deserves a good beating."

"I don't know." She trembled but did not try to escape him. "Because I have to." The absence of ribbons made her seem paler, more natural, and somehow more pretty. She unbuttoned the top of her blouse. "Because he helped with my writing. Because we share a friendship, and I owe him a debt I haven't repaid."

"Do you think he'll be safer? I really would like to kill him, and not just because of the swindle. If he touches you ever—"

"Shush." She kissed him firmly and drew him to her, pushing back the lapels of his black chinchilla coat. He let her strip off his top layer, remove the red volume from his breast pocket. He hadn't come to this conversation frightened, but realized as he watched her the risk he had taken. She might turn down his second proposal. She might even turn down being his mistress. He didn't know why she would do that, but from the beginning she'd been a puzzle, and he'd never been able to predict her reactions. He took her into his arms and kissed her, determined to show her what she'd be missing if she were to leave him.

She kissed him back roughly, all passion and hunger. He had a surge of anger at Zack. Somehow her reaction had to do with the poet. He did not understand her motives exactly, but he knew she was angling to protect that swindler. He pushed her away, looking down at lips reddened by kisses. "I mean it, you know. I really would like to kill him. I can't promise he'd be safer with me."

She stilled her hands on his belt. "I understand that, but he'll die for sure if we leave him. Sometimes he exaggerates the effects of his drinking. But every so often, he doesn't. He has squandered every bit of his money. He has gone so hungry he's developing scurvy. He'll freeze to death if he stays the winter."

He didn't touch her, though his muscles were aching, the rest of him straining to finish what the kisses had started. "What do you care? He stole from innocent people. And if you don't pay them back, he's going to ruin you also."

She turned her clear gaze on him, her brow, so childlike, framed by those tendrils that always made her seem so disarming. Jesse thought this tactic the rankest blackmail, her standing there hand on his pants placket, gaze full of pleading for that dissolute poet. He kissed her again, this time more roughly. He ought to kill that damnable poet; such a fate would be justice. Only his love for her stopped him. He took out his anger in passion instead, pushing her down against the small bed, grinding his hips against the thin cotton of the flimsy pantalets she was wearing. Her blood salted his mouth, but he didn't care. It was nothing compared to how she'd hurt him.

"Ouch." She twisted away. "Do you have to hurt me?"

He didn't answer, simply kept her pinned under his body.

She must have read his thoughts in his expression. "When have I ever abandoned a friend?"

"Last time you rejected my proposal of marriage."

"*Touché*. And if I turn you down now, will you leave me again?"

"*Touché* also." He centered himself over her body. "But you're not going to turn me down this time. I have you right where I want you. We're going to be married. You're accepting the money. You're leaving the poet here in the Yukon. You're coming with me. You're having my babies. And you're spending the rest of your life on my rancho."

They lay in the cot snuggled together, having made love more passionately than they ever had in the past. Zack English had spent the night in Dawson. And in the aftermath of their lovemaking, Bet had gotten Jesse to relent on his demand that they leave Zack behind in the Yukon. She promised to remain Jesse's mistress, to respond to his proposal in San Francisco, and to not so much as look sideways at Zack.

She had a plan. Perhaps not a good one, but the best she could think of. She wanted to see if she could get pregnant. If she didn't, she'd assume her condition had made her barren. She would turn Jesse down on those grounds. She'd even be truthful about why she'd done it. She hoped the truth wouldn't hurt him, especially considering how she'd deceived him. She hoped her deception wouldn't cost her their friendship, but she'd wanted this one little chance, one time in her life when she could be hopeful, one shot at being normal. Of course she'd have to do something about the sheath.

"Jesse."

He stirred behind her, drawing her close.

She cocooned more deeply into the blankets. "I hope you don't feel bad about our bargain. After all"—she laced her fingers in his—"I could have lied and said I accepted, then changed my mind in San Francisco."

"No more lies." He turned her over onto her back and propped himself up on his elbow. "This is the rest of our lives we're discussing. We want to be happy. I'm sure we can do it, but you have to promise to be more truthful."

"I'll do the best I can."

She touched his high cheekbone. He looked gorgeous as always, sleepy-eyed and disheveled, with tousled black curls and tangled eyelashes. She wondered if she'd ever tire of his beauty.

"I'm serious."

"I'm serious, too. The truth is not so simple as some people think, especially through the eyes of an artist. To us, truth and beauty are the same things, and truth's not always found on the surface."

"More hogwash." He pushed the tendrils off her forehead. "Even an artist should be able to tell a lie from a fact."

"Not true at all." She sat up, indignant that a man so clever would not understand the point she was making. "I spent eleven years in a wheelchair because some doctor thought he knew what the truth was. I don't trust predictions and I never confuse truth with the facts."

He pushed out of the bed and began to dress in his long johns. It made her cold just to watch the way his skin puckered, though she loved the long, pagan line of his thighs, his tapering waist, and his sculptured shoulders as he slipped them into the worsted white cotton. Ignoring her comments, he rustled through her duck satchel, retrieved her tortoiseshell brush, and returned to the cot. "Does that pretty speech about truth and beauty mean you're going to turn down my marriage proposal?"

"No, not at all. I just wanted to wait until San Francisco."

"Turn around," he said.

She did as he asked, though she never liked revealing

her back. He draped the blankets off her shoulder slightly, lifted her hair, and began to brush it. The attention felt lovely, his touch gentle and tender. She remembered how he used to groom the horses. "I'll tell you this much. You can feel hopeful. I'm thinking I miss life on the rancho. It would be a good place to write a novel."

His hand stilled. "Do we still have to take Zack to San Francisco?"

"Yes. That's my condition. I know he doesn't deserve it, but he is a friend, and I owe him."

He began brushing, this time with more vigor, though he didn't jar her or hurt her. "How will you pay back the money he swindled?"

"I don't know exactly, and it wasn't a swindle. I'm thinking I'll pay the money back with proceeds from the novel I'm writing."

"A long shot."

"My whole life's been a long shot. Why should this be any different?"

He laid the brush down on the cot, having done with untangling her hair. He cuddled his arms tightly around her and gently nuzzled her earlobe. "He's not sharing even a minute in our steamer cabin. I don't care if the scoundrel sleeps with the horses."

"Of course."

"Because if this trip is our last time together, I want it to be a time we'll remember."

A thrill of terror shot through her. What if the doctors were right? She pushed the thought out of her mind. It was too sad to consider, dying in childbirth. Surely the gods could not be that cruel. She turned around quickly. "Jesse?"

"Yes?"

"What were you thinking that day on the rancho when you put me on Firestriker and let me ride him?"

He smiled. "How pretty you were. How much I liked

you. How hard it must be to be trapped in that wheel-chair.''

"Did you think you might hurt me?''

"No. Never. I'd spent all my life around horses. Fire-striker is a wonderful creature. I knew I could control him.''

"But you didn't think it would hurt me? The riding itself?''

"No. Why should it have? I could see that sometimes your back hurt you, but riding's good for the muscles. It's good for the psyche. I didn't see how it could harm you.'' He placed one hand on her shoulder, pushing her curls back off her forehead with the other. "Why do you ask?''

"No reason. It puzzles me that no one else tried it, that even the doctors didn't have that much insight.''

He wrapped himself in the blanket, strode to his coat, pulled out his Jew's harp, returned to the cot, and sat down. He put the harp in his mouth and plucked it, a low, mournful ditty but somehow uplifting.

She put her head in his lap and listened, remembering those long ago days at the rancho. The fantasy returned with a vengeance, of spending her life with this man. She didn't know if she could do it, but she intended to give herself the chance.

She stroked his thigh beneath the blanket, running her fingers in time with the music. His interest renewed, and she wondered again how to talk him out of using the sheath without revealing the risks she was taking.

"Jesse.''

He stopped his playing. "Yes.'' The sounds of the mining camp wafted into the tent, the low voices of min-ers, the clink and rattle of their equipment.

"If you got married, would you want children?''

"Of course.'' He stilled her hand. "Are you worried about that? We're not so provincial as you might be thinking. I'd get all the best doctors and bring them out to the rancho—''

"I'm not worried," she lied, taken aback by his insight. She could see right away this tack would not work. Any more questions would arouse his suspicions. She knew perfectly well she was his blind spot, the one part of his life where his shrewdness deserted him. It wouldn't do to push too hard on that limit. "I just wondered what you thought about having children."

"I'd like to have one heir at least. My family's been on that rancho for four generations."

She sat back up, scooting toward the corner, the small of her back suddenly aching. "You don't need extras, just in case—you know—something happens?"

"I'll take my chances." He reached out and tugged at the edge of the blanket. "I don't need a litter. I don't even care if it's a son or a daughter." He flipped up the blanket and kissed the inside of her knee, then rubbed his cheek on the tender flesh. "See how forward-thinking I am?"

"Be serious."

"I am." He straightened. "I know writing's important to you." He kissed her again. "Promise one baby, and I'll be happy."

She grimaced, withdrawing farther into the corner. "No woman can promise conception, not even Christine Deutch."

"True." He kissed her forehead, then drew her into his chest in spite of her struggles to remain in the corner. "But every woman can promise to try."

Fourteen

"Are you alone?" Zack asked, poking his head into the cabin of the steamer they'd used to leave Dawson, having reluctantly borrowed their passage from Jesse.

Bet shoved her hands into her lap. "Yes, I'm alone."

"At last." The youthful poet entered the cabin. Bet was sitting next to a small mahogany table, a silver hatpin poised in one hand and the black velvet pouch in the other. Beneath the concealing top of the table, she shoved the needle through the thick material. Her hands were shaking, but she concealed that also as she avoided the gaze of the poet. "I'd leave the door open if I were you. He's taken a walk because I asked him, but he doesn't much like this arrangement."

Zack slammed the door behind him, strode to the table, and tossed the manuscript on its surface. "Doesn't he ever leave you?"

"Not very often."

"What's he afraid of?"

"He isn't frightened." She stared pointedly at the door he'd just shut. "He doesn't like strangers."

"Well, it rankles my pride to ask his permission just to speak to a fellow artist."

"You should be flattered. He's very reclusive, not to mention jealous. He's walking the deck to give us a conference, a considerable concession for a man of his nature. So"—she glanced at the stack of tablets he'd brought—"what do you think?"

"You little fool." He gave her a look, both shrewd and suspicious. "Don't even think you're going to marry that yokel. Because this is the best thing you've ever written." He pulled up a matching mahogany chair and pulled it close to the table. "It's brilliant." He flung one arm over her shoulder. For once, he did not smell like whiskey. "I'm sure that rancher has money, but marriage is always death to an artist and a bet with the devil for a woman with your particular—shall we say?—limits."

She tried to pull out of his grasp, but he tightened his hold, holding his face too close for comfort. She fiddled with the bag in her lap. "You know nothing about my particular limits."

"Are you going to deny them?"

"I'm not going to discuss them. But if you want to get out of the Yukon, you'll keep your thoughts to yourself."

He laughed, ruffling the manuscript pages. "Are you going to have me thrown overboard?"

She didn't respond with her usual giggle, only clutched the bag a little more tightly. "I can have you put off in one of the ports. And don't think Jesse wouldn't do it. He'd have sooner killed you than pay your passage. I wouldn't push my luck on this subject."

"Too true." He let go abruptly and glanced at the bag, which she'd tried to conceal beneath the table but which he could see when sitting this closely. "But I think you're a fool to settle for marriage." Rising, he paced the small suite, similar to the one on the steamer to Skagway. Hands in his pockets, he stared out the porthole. "I've been reading the novel. It's the best thing you've written."

"You think so?"

"I know so." Returning, he stared once more at the little black bag. "That's why I think it heartbreaking that you'd even consider his marriage proposal." He gripped the edge of the table. "Does poverty frighten you so?"

"Poverty frightens me plenty." She knotted the string holding the velvet. Zack was funny in certain ways. Sometimes he could be oblivious, other times almost preternaturally insightful. "But I'm not considering it because of the money."

"Then what? I thought our . . . arrangement . . . worked very well."

"I'm sure you would." This time she laughed. "You swindled my money and ran off to the Yukon, nearly getting yourself killed in the process."

"An error in judgment."

"Be serious, Zack."

"I am being serious." He sat down again, bringing his face close, his expression hungry. "I'm sorry I hurt you, but if I frightened you into an attack of convention, it's me—not that yokel—you ought to marry."

She rose, still clutching the bag. She wished she had pockets, but she didn't use them. She hid the pouch in her skirt folds instead. "Give me one reason why I should marry a man who has defiled me on paper, swindled my money, and is bent on destruction, not only of me, but of himself as well."

"Here's one." He picked up the first page of the manuscript tablet. "You'll never do this with him as a husband. I may push you hard as an artist, but I accept all your womanly limits."

Her fingers curled over the pouch. The sharp needle poked her finger and pricked it. She dropped the bag with a mild cry. Zack dove toward her feet and retrieved it.

"Thank you." Bet's heart skipped a beat. A small wound bloomed on her finger. Ignoring the blood, she held out her hand for the bag. Zack returned to the chair,

eyes assessing her shrewdly. Bet's heartbeat quickened.
"As for my limits, I told you before, you're making
assumptions."

"Perhaps." He kept the bag clutched in his hand.
"But I think you're gambling, and in the worst way. I
might be an unusual husband, but I do have certain virtues. Do you think you'd have produced this novel without me?"

"Probably not, but I wouldn't have produced it without Jesse either. After all, he inspired it. He encouraged
it. He gave me the time and the quiet to try it."

"I know." He fiddled with the string on the end of
the bag. "I'm jealous."

"Zack, don't pretend. I know why you haunted those
library stacks."

"A boyish diversion—outgrown, I assure you."

"Suppressed, maybe, but never outgrown."

"Now you're the one who's making assumptions."
He ran his fingers over the cloth, a delicate gesture but
sly and assessing. "Because I never did . . . touch . . .
anyone really. Not in the way you're thinking. I save
that energy for my poems. I was as much a virgin as
you were before you gave in to this yokel."

"I understand your poems very well."

His hands stilled. "Understand what?"

"I know who's being described in those poems."

He turned, his brown eyes penetrating. She met his
gaze and held it. That was one of the things that kept
her and Zack balanced. They each had their secrets.
Their admiration—artist to artist. Their understanding—
outcast to outcast. He dropped his gaze and studied the
pouch, examined the knot, then felt the contents. Bet
held her breath.

"Ouch." A red spot bloomed on his finger, an identical match to the wound she'd sustained. He shoved the
finger into his mouth and sucked for a moment. "Sew-
ing?" Removing his finger, he arched one eyebrow, his
expression a question.

"Give me that, Zack." She held out her hand.

He held on to the pouch. "Who do you think I wrote those poems for?"

"For yourself." The room was hot, warmed by the engine chugging beneath her. A bead of sweat trailed down Bet's forehead. "For the innocent boy you lost so early."

His eyes narrowed. "A pretty theory."

"It's the truth, and you know it. Both characters come from you really—the ravenous poet, but also the virgin. That's true of all artists. We plunder ourselves, our own crippled spirits, far more than we steal from those around us."

His fingers relaxed. He hefted the bag, perusing the knot. Her breath left her, the room growing hotter. He assessed her shrewdly, then tossed the pouch to her. "And you think *I'm* making assumptions."

Bet hated to do this, but she couldn't figure out how else to fool Jesse. She opened the string on the black velvet bag and took out the silk sheath. She'd come to know this peculiar device almost as well as she knew Jesse himself, even come to think of it as a friend, for so far it had offered protection. But she no longer wanted its help.

Hands trembling, she pulled out the silver hatpin. It seemed risky to do this, not just the chance of pregnancy, but also the risk that Jesse might discover this new deception. It also seemed rather immoral. This was far more serious than a little white lie. This was more than a lie altogether. This was an action, a deliberate effort to cheat him, to take a gamble he wouldn't approve of and see if she could get pregnant. She shouldn't do it. And if she were a better woman, she wouldn't. But she couldn't confide in Jesse any further. Their last conversation convinced her. Had he understood the risks she was taking, he wouldn't allow her to take them.

She froze, suddenly aware that someone was watching.

"What are you doing?" Returning, Zack had opened the door of the cabin, but so quietly she had not heard him.

"Nothing." She shoved the pin back into the bag, but he strode across the small suite and grabbed her.

He pulled out the hatpin and looked shrewdly at her. He picked up the silk sheath, pushed the silver lance through it, and laughed. "If you think this is love, you're fooling yourself. No woman in love resorts to these measures."

"Give that to me." She made a swipe at the pin.

"And don't tell me you're that maternal. You don't need children. Why are you taking such risks?"

She sat down in the chair and dropped her head into her hands. She didn't know what Zack would do now. Not that he minded lying. He could be the prince of liars, if that's what he wanted, but she had to give him a reason. "I don't know what I'm doing. I thought I knew, for most of my life, but lately . . . it's all gotten confusing. He wants to get married. I don't know what to tell him."

"Just tell him you're not a whole woman. Any fool can see what a baby might cost you."

"But what if it doesn't? What if it's all unproven assumptions, stuffy doctors being provincial? I spent eleven years in a wheelchair because I didn't question their first prediction. And they told me . . . well . . ." She picked up the sheath, the tiny hole he'd made barely visible in it. "Never mind what they told me. They've been wrong in other predictions."

"Now you listen, Bet. I know you think I'm a swindler, and I certainly am on some levels. But you've done your best to save me, and while you haven't reformed me entirely, you have convinced me I'm worth saving."

"What are you saying?"

"You don't want children. Your books are your ba-

bies. You're in love with Jesse Wheeler, and I don't
suppose I can blame you, but you have to stop this self-
deception. You've come to the point where you might
lose him and can't bring yourself to accept that."

"No. It's not true."

"Don't be foolish, Bet." He secreted the pin in his
pants pocket. "Look at yourself. You're a clever woman
in many ways, and I have to admire what you've accomplished, but any fool can see what childbirth might
cost you. Your back is all crooked. If you look so odd
on the outside, what must your insides be like?"

She stiffened, or tried to, though she'd never really
managed that posture. "Jesse doesn't see me as you do.
He's never looked at me as a cripple. He taught me to
walk when we were children."

"What's that got to do with having his baby?"

"He'll help me. I know he will once I get pregnant.
I might go to my grave, but I'll go trying. All these years
I've lived in terror. My whole childhood is gone, and I
can't get it back. I gave the first part of my life to those
doctors' assumptions. I'm not going to give up the rest
of my life without even trying."

"If you really believe he'd help you, why don't you
just tell him?"

"Because I don't even know if I can get pregnant. If
we did this the conventional way, he'd have to gamble
my life and his rancho. That's not fair to ask of a husband."

"True. At least you're lucid on certain levels." He
returned to the table, pulled up a chair, and sat, knee to
knee, straight across from her. "Now let me be clear. I
don't love you, not the way he does. But I do care." He
took both her hands in his. His calluses scratched her,
but she found his touch gentle. He was a beautiful man
in his own way, with his tawny hair and golden complexion, his workman's hands and prophet's expression.
"He taught you to walk. You taught me to read—as
liberating to me as riding that horse was to the girl con-

fined in the wheelchair. If it's marriage you want, I'll
make you that offer." He squeezed her fingers. She
winced, though not from his touch, only from the words
he was saying. "I know you're frightened of the life of
a writer. I'll agree the work isn't steady, but it's a lot
less risky than being an oyster pirate." He grinned,
touched her cheek, and pushed back her tendrils, a gesture oddly reminiscent of Jess. "And for you, my dear
little liar, it's a lot less risky than conventional wifedom.
Turn down that yokel. Don't give him a reason. Forget
living on in a baby. You'll live on in my poems and in
your own novel. Perhaps that's not the best arrangement,
but it's the best two cripples can hope for."

Heart booming, she tried to wriggle out of his grasp,
but he held her firmly, his gaze thoughtful and earnest.
His proposal surprised her. She thought him a genius,
but she'd never known what to make of his friendship.
He'd always been the consummate artist, risking everything for the sake of his legend. She'd never thought of
him as a husband. "I'm surprised at you, Zack." She
smiled and straightened the lapel of his jacket. "Think
of the ballad. You don't think dying in childbirth would
be rather dramatic?"

He smiled, kissing her forehead. "Dramatic, yes. But
far too shortsighted. I much prefer a living meal ticket."

"He's drunk." Jesse stormed into the cabin a few hours
later. "And he's reciting. You'd better go and collect
him if you don't want me to kill him."

Bet hustled down the long center hall of the steamer,
its strong engine churning beneath her, the smell of sea
air in her nostrils. Jesse followed behind her, bootheels
echoing on the wooden flooring. He stopped at the door
of the men's smoking salon. "You're not really supposed to be in here and I hate for you to even hear the
drivel he's reciting, but if you don't stop him, I may
have to kill him."

She brushed past him, ignoring his threat. "For

heaven's sake, Jesse, I inspired that drivel.''

"I'm glad you think so.'' He opened the door. "I think he's got a pact with the devil. I wouldn't mind sending him back to his master, but I didn't know how to stop him without starting a riot. He's got the whole salon captivated.''

She paused in the doorway. Zack sat in the center of a small circle of miners, a small tablet lifted before him, having enraptured about a dozen failed prospectors, all just as tattered as he. " 'Her eyes flashed, the northern lights in them, and she came to me threadbare—' ''

"Stop!'' Jesse charged into the room, the muscle in his lower jaw ticking. "This party's over.''

"Hey!'' One of the miners stood up, his chair banging behind him. "We was just getting started.''

Jesse grabbed Zack by the collar of a frayed corduroy coat not a bit improved by its life on the ocean. He swiped at the tablet. Zack clutched it tightly.

"Where *do* you get this stuff from?'' Jesse asked the poet. "It's fiction!'' he shouted to the little circle of men, some of them toothless, all hairy, wind-chapped, and bedraggled. "It's all an illusion. The product of a warped imagination. He's maligning a lady.''

A few of the miners stood up. They looked reckless and brutal, and Bet suddenly feared them. These were men who'd been disappointed, men who'd gambled their lives in the Yukon and come out of the place with nothing, with less than nothing, having lost their health to fevers and scurvy.

"Jesse.'' Bet tugged on the sleeve of his black velvet jacket. "Zack.'' She touched the brown corduroy coat. "Come away with me. Now.'' She turned to the muttering miners. "The recital is over.''

In spite of their toughness, perhaps *because of* their toughness, the sourdoughs settled at the sound of her voice. Jesse pulled Zack toward the side of the room, but he broke away with surprising swiftness.

"No!'' He broke a beer bottle on the top of the oak,

claw-footed table. His eyes were bloodshot, red-rimmed, and crazy. Bet could tell he wasn't fooling. He jumped to the top of one of the tables. His nostrils distended, bottleneck in his hand, the jagged edge dripping the poison that fueled the fits that came upon him. Waving the tablet as well as the dark brown bottle, he turned his glazed gaze on Jesse. "You're not going to take her! I won't let you do it!"

Jesse held his palms up, hands steady, though his expression was hooded, serious, and deadly. "Don't be melodramatic. You don't love this woman." He nodded gently in Bettina's direction. "You're in love with a wholly fictional creature, a figment of your own imagination."

"You"—he jabbed the bottle at Jesse, the gesture making him totter wildly—"are in a poor position to talk."

"Zack." Bet sprang forward, barely missing the glass shards on the floor. "You promised." She tugged on his pants leg and smiled sweetly. "Please."

He sat down cross-legged on top of the table, reached forward, and swayed into Bet's shoulder. "Ah, pretty lady." He smelled of whiskey and smoke, the rot of his scurvy. "Don't make me beg."

"Don't make me beg either," she said softly. "Come back to the cabin with Jesse and me."

The three of them returned to the cabin. Jesse dumped Zack on the floor in the corner. "Sleep it off there. I won't give you the satisfaction of having a place on the bed."

Zack gave him a lopsided smile and fell over. Jesse slipped the tablet out of his hand, but Zack did not even notice.

Jesse scowled, flipping through the tablet. "I don't see how you can like him, much less love him. He doesn't deserve even your friendship, and how you can abide those recitations—"

"Shush." Bet bent down and felt Zack's forehead. He smelled like something retrieved from a graveyard. She sighed. He'd seemed almost lucid when he'd made his proposal. "Have you never loved someone unworthy? What about your dear Christine?"

"Christine understands her half of the bargain. She's just after my money." He held out the tablet. "Do you know he's writing more of these about you?"

"I can't stop him." She shrugged, unbuttoning the top of Zack's shirt collar. "It's what he does for a living."

He flapped the tablet against his thigh. "I don't see how you can abide it. Christine doesn't love me, but she'd never embarrass me in that way. Never make a fool of herself in public."

"Be quiet. He's sleeping." She rose to retrieve a cloth from the water closet.

"I see that." Jesse threw the notebook of poems in the corner. "And I don't care if he drowns in his vomit. He's not staying with us in this cabin."

Fifteen

Jesse stayed awake until late in the evening, the poet tucked into the bed that he ought to be sharing with Bet. She watched his unconscious figure. Jesse watched her watch. She sat by the the damned scoundrel's side for most of the night, caring for him with such tenderness that Jesse realized, with some sense of heartache, that she did have some love for this damnable poet, though why this should be so, he couldn't fathom. Perhaps it had to do with her childhood sufferings. Or the complex camaraderie of two artists. Or maybe it had to do with something only the poet could give her, though what this was Jesse could not fathom either.

He'd loved her always and with total devotion, complete respect. And he had money. She didn't need to give up her novels. He didn't care if she was an artist. All he wanted was her company and someday an heir for his rancho. But women, Jesse knew, were mysterious creatures. Look at his mother. She'd married a sailor on the assumption that he'd take her away from that beautiful rancho, and never, not in forty years, had she forgiven his failure to do that. Jesse would go to his grave without understanding his mother's bitterness at his father's deception. The rancho was lovely, but not what she wanted. But why, Jesse had wondered all of his life, if she couldn't have what she wanted, couldn't she be happy with what she'd been given?

The poet stirred in the bed. Bet touched his forehead. Jesse shifted in a mahogany chair. The poet opened his eyes and moaned softly. He peered at Jesse through eyes turned to fire by the demons that consumed him, by the pale blue flame of the gaslight. "I hate you," he said to Jesse. "You're going to kill her."

"Be quiet." Bet pressed a cloth to his forehead. "You're running a fever."

"No." His sore mouth looked bloody. "He accuses me of hallucination, but you're far more a creation of his imagination than any poem I've ever written."

"Zack." There was an edge in her voice, a hint of desperation. "I thought we agreed we'd stay off this subject."

"What subject?" Jesse asked.

"The poems," she said. "Their interpretation." She glowered at Zack. "Who they're written for and why he wrote them."

"Hang your assumptions." The poet sat up, rising unsteadily from beneath the thick layer of blankets. "I don't care what you tell him. I'm not going to let him get away with your murder."

"Zack—"

"Here." He pushed at her shoulder. Jesse shot out of the chair. Rising from the bed, the shirtless poet tossed a silver object down on the table. It fell with a thin sound, like distant laughter. "Look what she's doing," he said.

Jesse picked up the pearl-topped hatpin. He blinked, looked at Bet, then at the poet.

"You've been using a sheath," Zack said drunkenly. Jesse shoved the pin into his thumb. He winced, but not from the pain. He didn't want to believe what he was hearing.

"Go get it," the poet said.

Jesse hesitated, glanced once at Bet, then held out his hand. She retrieved it from a box in the water closet.

"Hold it up to the light." This from the poet.

Jesse gazed for a moment at Bet. She looked pale and frightened. Her ribbons were trembling. He held the silk sheath up to the lamp. A pinprick of light stabbed through the membrane.

"What do you see?" the poet asked.

"A hole," Jesse said calmly.

"Do you see what she's doing?"

"She's trying to get pregnant." He looked at Bet, who'd sunk down in the chair and sat there, hands folded, ribbons still trembling. He stilled his own hands. He did not know why she would do this, but he'd be damned if he'd admit that to the poet.

"She's trying to fool you." The poet sank back down on the bed.

"Why should I care?" Jesse said. "If she succeeds, we'll just hurry the wedding."

"You don't wonder why she'd want to deceive you?"

"No," Jesse lied. "I trust her completely. This"—he held up the damaged sheath—"is an unorthodox way to start a family, but I'm sure she knows what she's doing."

"She's gambling her life. That's what she's doing."

"Bastard." Jesse bolted across the room. He jerked the poet out of the bed and held him so close his nose almost touched him. "Are you the reason she's been so frightened? What kind of lies have you been telling?"

"No lies." The poet touched Jesse with a delicate gesture. "I've given her nothing but friendship. It's you who are lying."

"I've never told a lie in my life."

"Perhaps not to another person, but you've lied about her to yourself for years."

Jesse let go of the collar, staring surprised into those luminous eyes. From one side he heard Bet's sound of distress. He ignored it. "Go on."

The poet bent down and picked up the tablet, pressing the cheap paper with care. "You're like Pygmalion. You know the story?"

Jesse nodded.

"Wise ones, those Greeks. What incredible insight into human nature."

Jesse could not see Bet, but he could hear her breathing, hear the rise and fall of her stiff corset.

The poet hugged the new poem to his bare chest, pale and lightly sprinkled with hair. "You've fallen in love with your own creation."

"That's true enough," Jesse said. "But what's that have to do with the story?"

"Because you're so proud of her transformation that you can't see the miracle's limits. Look at her, rancher. Look at that back. Do you really think she can have children?"

Jesse slugged him. The poet crumpled forward.

"Zack!" Bet jumped between them. Jesse let her. Pain flared to his elbow and with it a memory, the buckle of teeth beneath his knuckles. Blood and sweat misted toward Bet. Jesse drew back farther, shocked by the damage. In the rage of the moment, he'd forgotten the havoc already wreaked by the scurvy.

Bet knelt beside the bleeding poet, using her skirt to stanch the red fluid. "Oh, Zack . . ." As she lifted the material off his mouth, two teeth appeared in the little cradle she made, "You're so bent on destruction. I could have told you he wouldn't believe you."

"Believe what?" Jesse asked.

"He thinks I can't have babies."

"Can you?"

"Yes."

He looked steadily at her.

"Maybe." She returned his gaze with a clear-browed

expression. "I'm not positive really. But no woman is positive really."

Zack lifted himself on his elbow. "Don't believe her for a minute. Look at her back—"

"Watch your mouth." Jesse lifted his arm as if to backhand the poet.

English cringed and spat out a wide glob of blood. "All right. Don't believe me. But at least ask yourself questions. Why are the poems works of fiction? Why has she never been married? How does a woman so pretty get to be a thirty-year-old virgin?"

"The writing," Jesse said. "Perhaps she didn't have many suitors."

"She had two for certain."

Jesse gazed at Bet. For the first time in his life he looked, really looked, at her back. It was true it was crooked, though he seldom noticed. She concealed her posture with artful dress, though he had always been aware of the corset, of the slight disruption of her fluid movements whenever she had to go someplace fast. He studied her expression, her paisley shawl, her fripperies and ribbons. He'd never looked at her clothes as deceptions, though he'd been vaguely aware they concealed her shortcomings. Mostly he considered his blind spot. It was true, what the poet had said. He'd never considered that Bet might have limits. She'd always seemed such a transcendent creature. The little girl confined to the wheelchair whose faith and courage had outwitted the doctors. The woman whose wit and worldly laughter had eased the loneliness of life on the rancho. His view of her had never been well balanced. He'd been so much in awe of all she'd accomplished, he'd never considered its actual meaning. In some ways and on certain levels, this woman was a professional liar.

He stood. She was pale, trembling, all fringe, ringlets, and ribbons. He threw down the sheath and took her face in his hands. "So soft," he said, "and so pretty. He watched you closely, to write those poems, but not more closely than I.'' He kissed her and murmured, ''And if truth really were beauty, this would be life's truest moment.'' He broke off the kiss. ''He's right, isn't he?''

''Jesse.''

''That's the reason you turned down my proposal. It's been the reason always. I was just too blind to see it.''

She trembled. ''I love you.''

''I know that.''

''I'll love you forever.''

''I know that, too, but you'll never be Mrs. Jesse Wheeler.'' She said nothing, but he knew what she was thinking. ''Not because you can't have babies. I wouldn't care if you couldn't have children. I love you more than that damned old rancho. But we'll never be married''—he steeled himself from trembling, forced himself to look at the tablet—''because I can't trust you. I understand now what you see in this poet. Scratch the surface and you're perfect soulmates, not artists, but gamblers and con men, who wouldn't know the truth if it came up and bit them and for whom life is not exciting unless it's got a bit of risk to it.'' He tossed the sheath on the table and strode to the door. ''I love you. I'll miss you forever. Don't bother turning down my proposal.''

He slammed the door behind him.

''Where are you going?'' she asked the next morning as the ship steamed into St. Michael.

Jesse looked exotic and brooding, swathed top to toe in black—leather boots, wool pants, bareheaded, hair tousled, chinchilla greatcoat revealing a velvet-trimmed jacket. The outfit reflected his mood, no doubt, and the gray sky created a dramatic backdrop. She wanted to kiss him. He looked so troubled. The light in his dark eyes warned her not to.

''I'm getting off here,'' he said.

She gripped the handrail and straightened inside her

stiff corset. "I'm sorry," she said. "I should have told you."

"It's too late for apologies, Bet."

She pulled her sealskin coat tighter and tugged on one of her scarlet ribbons. She wanted to believe what he'd said about babies, that he'd love her even if she couldn't have them. She took his departure as a rejection; and her heart cried out that she should remind him that if he really loved her he'd accept her limits, physical and moral also. She didn't. "How will you get back to the rancho?"

"That's none of your business."

"Will you marry Christine now?"

"That's none of your business either."

"Zack doesn't have very much money, and I don't have much to give him."

He touched his breast pocket. "He could sell me the rights to the poems."

"Why would you want to have them?"

"So there'll never be any more published."

"I don't think he'd do that. He's quite proud of them. He'd starve before he'd see them destroyed."

"Then his financial straits are not my problem. I've paid his passage to San Francisco. Don't contact me once you get there."

She gazed out at the harbor. "Can I come this Christmas?"

"Don't bother. I'll make your excuses."

The chill wind lifted her tendril, brought the scent of salt to mix with his citrus. "Will you take care of Firestriker for me?"

He nodded.

· · ·

December 1898
San Francisco, California

"Are you all right?" Zack asked.

Bet nodded. She was trembling, bent over a small chamber pot decorated with roses, chipped on the edges but otherwise pretty. "It's just the oysters. I can't stand the smell."

"You used to like them." The ragged poet trotted to the kitchen of the small flat they had rented. "You used to have a strong stomach. You didn't get seasick on the steamer."

"I know."

He returned with a towel, which he handed to her. Her wave of nausea had produced no result, except a slight relief of her nausea. She wiped her face anyway, comforted by the texture and dampness.

Zack touched her shoulder. "Is something the matter?"

"No." She struggled up from her knees, her discomfort subsiding. "I'm fine," she lied as she took the pot and replaced it next to the bedstead. She wasn't fine, but she didn't want to discuss the reason.

He raked one hand through his tousled hair, then shoved his fists in his pants pockets. He nodded at the thick stack of papers on the battered pine table shoved in the corner. "Maybe you're working too hard."

"No." She sat down, still shaking, and picked up a pencil. "I'm just a bit weak since we came back from the Yukon. I'm sure I'll be better once I get these odd fluxes out of my system."

"We've been back for more than three months."

"I know." She shivered and drew her paisley shawl more closely around her. "But some illnesses hang on for a while, and sometimes it's just hard to recover from a long journey."

Ignoring the obvious omission of Jesse, the boyish

poet sat down in a chair and picked up one of her manuscript pages. He perused it with those luminous eyes,
brown, almost amber, and nearly translucent in the
muted light filtering through the flat's tiny window.

"This is good." He lifted his pen, one of fine black
enamel, and made a small notation on the side of the
grainy paper intended for newsprint, but the cheapest
way of producing drafts. "Great!" He put an exclama-
tion point next to the first paragraph, then coaxed her
with a smile of delight. "Come on. Go back to your
writing. You're awfully good at it. I wish I had such a
gift for a story."

She smiled weakly. "I wish I had your gift of expression."

He bent over the paper, scribbling quickly, his large
scrawl filling the margins. She tried to go back to her
writing, though resuming the novel did not come easily.
She never wrote well when she was sick. She also
missed Jesse, especially now. It seemed a special, hor-
rible torture to write about him after she'd lost him, but
the debt to the library loomed, and she was too far into
the book to change its hero completely.

She pressed her hand to the small of her back. She
enjoyed working with Zack, but their shared artistry
wasn't the same kind of bond she'd enjoyed with the
brooding ranchero. For all the apparent sincerity of his
devotion, and for all the two of them had in common,
there was always a certain tension between them.

She watched as he scrawled over her writing. They
were too much the same, she and Zack, creatures of
spirit and essence, poorly suited for practical matters.
And then there was that little green monster. She feared
and admired his talent, and she suspected he returned
the favor. He lusted for greatness in a way she couldn't;
had a devilish bent for self-destruction that inspired both
terror and envy. Though she didn't know what he loved
in her stories, she suspected he envied her also. They
helped each other, but they were also destructive. Two

childlike creatures, too consumed by their talent.

Reaching over, she picked up the page he had marked. The scene described an afternoon in her childhood, not a time when they'd ridden together, but the winter before, when she'd been in the wheelchair. She'd never written about that time in her life and she found the experience painful—revealing. For months Jesse had carried her around the rancho, down to the stream, into her bedroom, anytime she needed to be moved from the wheelchair, and she'd re-created her helplessness on these pages. Hands shaking, she scanned her words. As happened sometimes, her own writing surprised her. She'd made her old self—her crippled self—come alive on those dingy pages. And she remembered. Where it had come from, this drive to be normal.

She'd learned to lie in those years in the wheelchair, a subtle art, crucial to survival. She charmed those around her into forgetting the cripple, seducing strangers with laughter and beauty, adorning herself with ribbons and colors, fanciful dresses her mother embroidered, distractions from legs that were spindly and useless, from a girl who could not control her own movements. She'd developed her gift for telling stories, for looking at life with grace and good humor, for ignoring the implacable fate that tied her into that wicker chair and escaping her bonds in brief bursts of fancy.

And then had come Jesse. She could almost feel him, his brooding and beauty, his citrus scent and silky eyelashes, the commanding exterior and silent friendship, who'd carried her around without protest, one of the few who'd seen her helpless and liked her. Her eyes burned in their sockets, and she leashed her tears fiercely.

Zack looked up from his writing. "What's the matter now?"

"Nothing."

"Come on." He touched her chin with his pen. "Life's not so bad. The book's half done. Putnam's advanced your living expenses. We're going to sell this for lots of money. By the time anyone comes looking for the library funds, we'll have repaid them completely. Then we'll set up an endowment—"

"Don't." She smacked his arm once, then a second time. "That's what you said about prospecting."

"That"—he waved his pen in the air—"was different."

"How?"

"For one thing, we weren't working together. For another, we weren't trying to sell a novel." He ruffled the thick stack of yellowish pages. "Say what you want about my skill as a miner, but don't malign my skill as a writer."

"I've never underestimated your talent."

"True."

She went back to her work. He didn't. She could feel his gaze, but she ignored it. She started writing on a sheet of blank paper, trying to conjure Jesse on its surface. This was hard to do in front of Zack, though she'd finally learned to ignore his presence. Head down, she reread her last sentence, then returned to the paper's clean surface. This was the hardest challenge in writing, that blank page, pure as a virgin. She'd heard it said sometimes that a woman could not write a great novel, that a woman could not muster sufficient aggression, that female creativity went into children. She wondered briefly if that were true, that if—she brushed the thought out of her mind and pushed down the pencil, marking the surface.

As soon as she started, she knew. She was going to have a few moments of pleasure. The words came quickly. They spilled onto the paper, the pencil lead flowing smoothly, the imagery coming uninterruptedly as she escaped inward and shut the world out. She ignored Zack and focused on Jesse, re-creating both that child creature and the magical, brooding boy who had cured her. Most of all she ignored the critic, the voice that questioned what she created. Later she'd deal with the work's imperfections. For now, she was gambling, pure and simple, letting her thoughts drift onto the paper, with little idea of what she'd conveyed, its quality only to be discovered later, perhaps incoherent or perhaps of great beauty, but always, always, the truth as she knew it.

She was vaguely aware that Zack wasn't writing, but it wasn't until she reached for her fourth piece of paper that she realized he was still poised in the ladder-back chair, staring at her as she poured her thoughts onto the pages.

"You can trust me," he said.

She looked up, surprised. "I never said I didn't trust you."

"We aren't living only on Putnam."

"I know that, Zack."

"I've sold three poems."

"I know—"

"I've cut down on my drinking."

"I appreciate that. Truly I do."

"I haven't set foot in a bordello and I'm not demanding favors from you."

She set down her pencil, a little frustrated at the interruption. "What's the problem? I've never said I was unhappy."

"You're pregnant, aren't you?"

She stood and moved to the stove where his coffeepot simmered. Lately she hadn't been able to stomach that liquid, but she needed a moment to gather her thoughts. "What makes you think so?" she asked.

He nodded in the chamber pot's direction.

She wet her lips. She considered lying but discarded that notion. She was tired of lying, of all those complications. She wasn't, after all, that little cripple who needed to fool all those around her. She could walk, if not normally. Her clothes were only a tiny deception. Jesse had even seen her naked and liked her . . . she cut off that thought. Certainly she couldn't fool Zack, who could read her more clearly than any soothsayer. If truth worked in fiction, perhaps it would work also in living. "I'm still not certain. We used a sheath. . . . I never did . . . trick . . . him the way I considered."

"You ought to be seeing a doctor."

"For what?" She lifted the pot from the burner. "To have him scare me to death? To be told I'm taking a gamble?" She pressed one hand on the small of her back and tried to pour without the other hand shaking. "I already know that."

"Maybe they can help you make it safer. Maybe even get rid of the baby."

In spite of her efforts, her hands were trembling, and she set the coffeepot back on the burner. "I want the baby."

"How are you going to support it?"

"I'll finish the novel, pay back what I owe the library fund, then go back to writing horse stories."

"I'll lose my meal ticket."

She abandoned the stove, returned to the table, sat down in the chair, and took Zack's callused hand in hers. "You don't need me to survive. Look how well you've been doing. You've been selling poems. You haven't been drinking. You even managed to survive the Yukon. Not many writers can claim that distinction."

"I'd have died there without you."

She didn't dispute his assertion, only squeezed his fingers.

He smiled. "I can always go back to smuggling oysters."

She returned the grin, then brushed back the mop of hair falling over his forehead. "Ah, Zach. Don't ever lose that street urchin. It's what makes your writing so touching."

He shied away slightly. "Are you going to tell that yokel what's happened?"

She bolted out of the chair and to the room's window, wrapping her shawl tightly around her. "No. I don't think so.'' On the windowsill she'd placed a jar of wild roses, and the sunlight caught in their petals. The heavy scent roiled her stomach. She struggled for air and braced herself on the worn-out pine counter. ''If he's curious about me, he knows where to find me.''

''Now you're being sulky. You were using the sheath. He has no reason to suspect you're pregnant.''

''I don't care. He's sulking also, and I won't go begging.''

''The two of you have been through this before. The child will be grown before he breaks down.''

She gave Zack a glance. He lounged in the chair, fists stuffed into his corduroy jacket, his prophet's gaze reflecting her doubts as surely as if she looked in a mirror. ''I don't like to see you marry that yokel,'' he said, ''but I wouldn't like to see you die either. He's a wealthy man. He'll get you good doctors. . . .''

''No doctors.''

''Bet.''

''No doctors. I already know what they'll tell me. I'm not going to spend this whole pregnancy frightened. I've beaten their predictions twice in my life. I'll just have to beat them again this time.''

Sixteen

"Everyone will think this baby's mine."

Zack was printing an address on a brown paper package, and it took Bet a moment to realize his comment did not refer to the manuscript they were sending to Putnam but to the child she was carrying.

She frowned, pressing her hand to the small of her back. The fetus had grown into a considerable burden, and she repeated this gesture more often these days. "You think so?"

"I know so." He wrote the addresses out neatly, both their tiny flat in San Francisco and Putnam's offices in New York City. Paper and twine littered the small kitchen table, which had been cleared of all her draft pages. That stack had grown along with the baby. Now the novel was done, and so was the infant, both of them close to delivery. "They'll believe he's mine because of the poems."

She retrieved a small pair of scissors from the kitchen drawer. "I suppose that's true. I've been so busy finishing this one, I hadn't really considered what people would think about the baby."

He looked at her with those luminous eyes. Sometimes she didn't know how he did it, look so much like both a boy and a prophet. She supposed that was the essence of a poet, half child, half wizard; simple on some levels, complex on others. "The novel's gone well, don't you think?"

She nodded agreement, though she wasn't sure. She never knew what she thought of her writing, and the novel had been an all-consuming experience, halfway between flying and drowning. She no longer knew what was in it, much less whether she liked its contents.

He unwound a length of string from a ball. "And the pregnancy?"

She wanted to nod but found she couldn't. There was something about carrying the baby that severely crimped her flair for lying. She'd secluded herself while writing the novel, not only because she wrote better, but also because she didn't like answering questions and could not bring herself to make up a story about Jesse's baby. In seven months of confinement, she hadn't thought what she would say to people, had never considered what the situation would look like. Everyone, perhaps even Jesse, would think her baby belonged to the poet. "I don't know how the pregnancy's going."

He looked at her sharply. "You never complain."

"You never ask."

"I'm asking."

She sat down in the chair and pushed the scissors over. He cut the twine, then wound it around the paper-wrapped package. A thrill went through her, and she forgot his question. She had a sweet sense of satisfaction but also a strong sense of jitters. "Do you think Putnam will like it?"

"They'll love it, but you're avoiding my question. How do you feel the pregnancy's going?"

He crossed the twine, then nodded toward the place where the string crossed. She pressed her finger over the intersection. "It's not going all that well, really. My back's not so bad, but I have trouble breathing. Mostly I'm frightened.''

"Why?" He did not take his eyes from his task.

"What if the doctors are right?"

"They've been wrong twice before." He glanced up quickly. "You told me yourself."

"But what if the third time's a charm?"

"You sound like those gamblers."

"Hank, Hal, and Handsome?" She laughed. She slipped her finger from beneath the knot, and he cinched the brown twine down tightly. "I wish we could help them. They looked so forlorn when they came to visit. They didn't do well in the Yukon."

"They survived it. They should count themselves lucky." He lifted the package, inspecting it closely. "Perhaps we can help, after we've sent this."

She held out her hands. He handed the bundle over, and she took a moment to savor its weight; to use the heft and completeness of it to banish her terror of sending it out. She smiled in spite of her jitters. "Not so heavy perhaps as a baby, but it took almost as long to produce."

"The book's charming, as is this creation. . . ." He patted the high curve of her stomach with a genuine reverence that seemed odd in one who'd always been so self-destructive. But the last few months had changed Zack also. His suntan had faded and with it his scurvy. He'd managed to stay away from his drinking. He didn't look at other women and didn't frequent bordellos. "But I think the book will live longer."

"You think so?"

"Of course. You're a wonderful writer. Your grand-children will read this. With a little luck, they'll even live off its proceeds."

She put the hefty brown bundle back on the table and sank wearily into the ladder-back chair. "I'd just like to pay back the library fund and have enough to support the baby until I can write some more stories."

"You will."

"I suppose so. Oh, Zack, I'm so frightened." She picked at the splintered edge of the table. "Poverty scares me. I don't remember my back getting broken, but my mother told me about it. We lived in a tenement in New York. Terrible place, evidently, probably worse than even this flat." She looked around the small, dark room, smoke from the lamps staining the walls and ceiling. "The roof caved in one winter. My poor father gave up his writing to take care of the child his folly had crippled. I always wanted to make up for that fate. But what if I simply repeat his failures?"

Zack trotted to the knee-high pile of drafts in the corner and picked up another stack of papers, smaller than the one they'd just sent, but also done on creamy bond paper. Returning to the kitchen table, he stood the papers on end and tapped the stack lightly. "Go back to your library work."

She waved at her stomach. "I can't work in this condition."

"We've got enough money until after the baby."

"Not even after. Think of the scandal."

"The poems were scandalous. They didn't hurt you."

"It's not the same." She patted the bulge protectively. "People will forgive paper transgressions. After all, the poems might be fiction."

"They were."

"My point exactly."

She smoothed down the front of her clean white painter's smock, a simple creation and pretty but one that displayed, not disguised, her condition. "But my point is I would not want to do it. An unmarried woman having a baby—what kind of example would I be for the children?"

"Now who's being provincial?" He tugged on one of her ringlets. "Has motherhood given you an attack of convention?"

She smiled. "Perhaps."

"There are always short stories."

"I'll have the same problem. They're *children's* short stories. No one knows yet because of the novel, but when they discover I've had a baby—"

"They'll blame it on your poet-lover." He lay down the smaller stack of white papers. "So marry me, Bet. I can support you. I've been writing these ballads." He gestured at the slim manuscript. "They're hokey, but I'm sure they'll sell well. Mayhem sells even better than eros, and there's a real rage for tales from the Yukon."

She touched his cheek softly. "Ah, Zack. Don't do that—bowdlerize your poems for my sake."

"I'm trying to prove I'd make a good husband."

"Why would you want that? You're such a free spirit. . . ."

"Because I know what it feels like to be abandoned." Jerking away, he picked up a roll of butcher paper and tore it straight across with a slash. "I created this baby in certain ways. And I wouldn't mind being its father. I'll never get children the normal way. . . ."

She centered the poetry manuscript on the brown rectangle of paper. "I suppose that's true. What with your problem—"

"I don't have a problem."

"All right. You're perfectly normal, but that doesn't make you a suitable husband."

He paused, twine in hand, and gazed at her with those luminous eyes. "May I know the reason?"

What could she tell him? Who would make a her suitable husband? She could get pregnant, but she still didn't know if she could deliver. Nor did she know if she wanted more children. All she'd ever wanted besides being a writer was to be Jesse Wheeler's wife and bear him an heir for his rancho. She'd botched that ambition on every level and not only because of her physical defects. "We're too much alike. All feeling and spirit. We'd never balance each other."

"Who needs balance, as long as we're happy?"

"Do you think you'd be happy? Marrying me and pretending to father another man's baby?"

"Of course." He kept that amber gaze fixed on her. It did not give her shivers the way Jesse's would have, and she wondered if that fact was important. "I've adored you since boyhood," he said. "Who else would put up with my foibles?"

She bolted to the room's one tiny window and looked out at the brick wall it faced. It made her feel trapped, this one slice of light, this tiny flat, cramped and cluttered. It wasn't a place for raising children. On the other hand, things might get better. Zack had written some wondrous new poems, on subjects that were not erotic. She'd finished her novel. And who else was standing there offering to support her? Certainly not Jesse, the baby's father. "Don't I have the right to be happy?"

"You won't be happy married to me?"

She wanted to tell him she'd never be happy, that she'd spend the rest of her life pining for Jesse, but it didn't seem fair to saddle him with that burden. She settled on a half-truth instead. "You've forgotten about the green-eyed monster."

"I've never looked at another woman."

"That's not what I mean."

He picked up the pen, pulled up the ladder-back chair, and printed on the package. "I'll always be jealous of that rancher yokel, but it won't affect how I treat the baby."

"I appreciate that. Truly I do. But that's not what I mean either."

"Then what?"

She sat down beside him at the small pine table where he'd created the poems and she'd written the novel. He had his own kind of beauty, childlike and fetching, and she stroked his hair as he wrote out their address. "I'm jealous of you, of your wildness and talent. . . ."

He set the pen down and clasped her wrist tightly.

"You have just as much talent, and as for the wildness
. . . that's more of a myth than a requirement. Look at
Jane Austen."

She drew away quickly and fiddled with her mechanical pencil. "*Look* at Jane Austen. A spinster. Name me
one truly great woman writer who raised a baby, legit-
imate or otherwise."

"Charlotte Brontë."

"Only after she'd written her novels."

"True." He eased his grip a little.

"And she died pregnant."

"Bad example." He shoved his fists in his pants
pocket and stared at the slice of light in the kitchen.
"George Sand."

"I don't live in Europe. And I don't have de Musset
or Chopin for a lover."

"No." He stacked one manuscript on top of the other
and shoved the little stack at her. "You don't have Chopin for a lover, but you do have me, at least after a
fashion, and I'm becoming quite famous, if not as immortal as the composer. Why not let me pose as the
baby's father?"

"I don't want my fame to come through another.
That's something the poetry taught me. I want to earn
my own reputation, not just be known as somebody's
lover." She stared at the packages, their two creations.
She felt a subtle stir in her stomach. "Besides, we'd be
living a lie."

"What does that matter? We're writers. Professional
liars, at least after a fashion."

"I don't know why it matters." She crossed her arms
over the baby, her child and Jesse's. He might not want
it, might not even care about its existence, but that didn't
mean she would give it away, especially not to Zack,
who, much as she loved him, would never make a proper
father. "I just know it does."

"Does that mean you're going to tell that yokel?"

"No." The stir grew to a thrash, then kicked her ribs sharply. She sucked in her breath. "No."

"You're getting down to very few choices."

"I know." She shifted positions, trying to settle her rebellious infant. "I know, but I'll figure it out."

Two weeks later, Bet rose from her writing chair and pressed her hand to the small of her back. "Zack," she called out. The ripples had been increasing all morning, painful spasms that traveled her stomach, coming at first in long intervals, but arriving now every few minutes. A warm liquid dripped between her legs. She had not seen any doctors, but she'd been reading a ladies' medical guide and recognized that her water had broken. "It's started."

He rose from the other side of the table where they'd been working all morning together. "You think so?"

"Near as I can tell from my reading, it doesn't seem to be an exact science, but I'm pretty sure labor is starting."

She'd said nothing about the wavering movements, uncertain whether the sporadic contractions represented true labor or only false symptoms. She knew from her reading, however, that the gush of warmth meant her baby was coming, probably sooner than later, perhaps today, though even that much did not seem to be certain.

A sharp pain stabbed her. She gripped the back of the ladder-back chair for balance. The cramps came in waves and from all directions, a hard clench in her stomach, a sharp stabbing in her lower back, nausea and sweat, self-pity and terror, as a great force seized her and racked her. "Get the doctor."

"Don't panic." Zack dashed to the doorway, stopped, and dashed back. "Don't panic." Gently he patted her shoulder. She glanced at him through the haze of her terror. His hands trembled a little, and he'd turned pale beneath his faded sunburn, but his mouth was set and determined, and the look in his eyes gave her courage.

"Go!" She nodded toward the door, dark green, battered, paint peeling.

He grinned, then ran down the stairs, boots stomping loudly. The moment he left, she panicked.

"Oh, Jesse," she whispered. She looked around wildly, wishing desperately the brooding ranchero were here to help her. After all these years, after all that dreaming, she was finally going to give birth to his baby. For better or worse, he would not be here to see it. Right now, she was sorry for that fact.

She rose from the table, pain-racked and worried. Contrary to her conversations with Zack, and much as the doctors had predicted, the pregnancy had not gone smoothly. She'd remained ill for most of its duration, though not in the ways she'd expected. She didn't have much of a problem with her back, though it ached more than usual. Instead she'd developed severe breathing trouble, as if her lungs were pushing into her shoulders. She felt that now, shortness of breath laced with panic. The cramping subsided, but her dizziness persisted. She staggered to the narrow bed in the corner.

Zack reappeared, hair tousled, corduroy coat even more tattered than usual. "I sent the landlady for the doctor."

Bet attempted to nod, but she could no longer manage. Like a fist just under the surface, a wave of pain washed over her stomach. She tried to hold out her hand.

The ragged young poet knelt down next to the iron bedstead, his gaze frightened and worried, his shirt collar dirty. "Tell me what you want me to do."

"If I die—"

"Don't." Reaching down, he retrieved the quilt folded over the footboard, unfolded it quickly, and settled it over her bulky stomach. "You're not going to die."

"I don't intend to." She thrashed around, pushing back the thin covering, and struggled up, pressing her aching back to the pillow. The effort brought relief to her breathing but increased the cramps and contractions. "But let's not be foolish. Let me give you instructions . . . in case . . ." She bore down, gasping for breath, as another pain rolled over the baby and the burn at the small of her back turned hot and fiery. "In case . . ." She breathed deeply, struggling for air. "In case, for once in my life, those sons-of-bitches are right."

Zack nodded. He clutched the blanket, looking himself like a baby.

She grabbed the sleeves of his threadbare coat. "Remember your childhood. If I die, don't let my baby repeat it. Get hold of Jesse. Don't be foolish and *don't* be jealous. I know he'll take the baby back to the rancho, but you keep track also. Jesse will be a wonderful father, but Christine might be a vindictive stepmother. I don't want my baby poverty-stricken and I don't want him hurt by a vengeful stepmother."

"Do you think they've gotten married?"

"Not until the end of the summer. I've seen the banns in the newspapers."

"You don't think the baby's arrival will change it?"

She turned her face to the dark-colored wall. "I hope not. I don't want to spoil Jesse's marriage. I just want the child to be happy."

Zack put down the blanket and held her hand. His hands were shaking, but he laced his fingers in hers and held on tightly. "You should have told him."

"I couldn't. Not after he walked out that way."

He stroked her forehead, a tender gesture, and she wished it were Jesse who were here to do it. "It would make a great ballad," he said quietly, "but who would believe it? I've never seen two lovers so foolish."

She was panting and sweating, her breath coming deeply as the contractions washed over her stomach and her muscles labored. The pain subsided a little, and she realized that childbirth might be a little like writing. The way to make the process easier was to let the birth happen without trying to control it. She wouldn't worry about her own limits. She'd simply trust nature to help her. She fixed her gaze quickly on Zack. "Recite for me, please."

"What?"

"A poem, maestro."

His hands really did tremble. "I couldn't. Not . . ." He must have caught her expression, for he gripped more tightly and bent down close to her earlobe. "I couldn't recite one of my own, but I have a story that I could tell you."

She nodded, panting, exhausted, but somehow detached from the cramping and muscles. She couldn't have had a better friend than the poet, for she knew this trick, and he knew it, too, the art of escaping from the painful present.

He began in a singsong, his voice low and prophetic. "In the waning days of my childhood, I met a horse with a star on his forehead. . . ."

She smiled, for she knew the story, the first one written about Firestriker, the first tale she'd gotten published.

"Brown, he was, and well muscled. . . ."

"I didn't know you could recite these," she whispered. She knew Zack had read them and admired them, but this display of memory surprised her.

He kissed the palm of her hand, his lips soft and gentle, his amber eyes blazing. "I know this story by heart."

She lurched.

He gripped her more tightly. "How do you think I became a poet? These were the tales I adored so completely. I learned to read so I could get to the endings more quickly. And this is where I learned to love you. And also to be filled with envy. I'll never know why you think you're the lesser talent. These are the stories that will make you immortal."

Panic assailed her, and she wished for a moment that she were not pregnant, that she could undo the whole foolish notion that she could be normal and simply go back to being an artist, content with a life a deferred creation, reaching out to others over a distance, avoiding real life with its complications, and living always in a world that was perfect. She stifled a scream and clutched Zack more tightly as pain sheeted over her lower back. "Help me," she gasped.

Zack dashed to the kitchen, and she grabbed the iron sides of the bedstead. The squeak and slash of the pump distracted her from the sensation of cramping. There were too many feelings now to keep track of, stronger, more consistent contractions, an intense sense of nausea, the pain in her back, and, above it all, more trouble with breathing. Alone she could not divert her attention, and it all came back, the panic and terror. "Help me," she called in her strongest voice, though somehow the cry came out feeble and tiny. Zack scrambled back with a wet washcloth. Kneeling, he placed the textured cloth on her forehead. "Oh, God. I'm sorry."

"For what?" She arched her backbone, wrenched into contortions by the forces of nature driving the baby out of her body. Zack watched, eyes pained and frightened, and held her hand through the process. "More story, please."

"Ah, Bet. I can't." He placed her hand on his cheek. She could feel them there, the salt tears and wetness. "I should have known better than to tell Jesse," he said softly. "If you'd just stayed together, this wouldn't have happened . . . at least not in this place, not so . . . poverty-stricken."

"Don't . . . be . . . silly." She tried to clutch his callused fingers, but her grasp had lost some of its power. She was tiring more quickly than the books said she should be. Suddenly she thought she should talk a bit on this subject before she had no breath left to discuss it. She didn't think she would die, but in case that happened, she didn't want to fuel Zack's already-too-lively sense of destruction. "You're not a prophet. How could you have known Jesse would leave me?"

"I was *trying* to get him to leave you." He was stroking her hair, kissing her forehead. "I might never have been with a woman, but I knew how violated he'd feel."

"Zack, don't be melodramatic. . . ."

"I'm a poet. I'm supposed to be melodramatic."

He rubbed the wet washcloth over her lips. The nubby cloth felt lovely, cool and distracting, if a little rough-textured. She couldn't have had a more soothing comfort. She knew she was approaching exhaustion, because the pain had faded, along with her breath and almost all her sense of terror. She couldn't see Zack terribly well, but she could still hear him.

"I've loved you always, at least after a fashion." He spoke as though he were reciting one of the poems he'd written. "And I really hated that yokel. He was blind to your suffering. He thought you were normal, I knew . . ." His voice dropped away briefly. "I worried about you. I tried to prevent this. But we seal our fate when we try to escape it. I know that quite well. I run from my childhood, but the harder I run, the more it haunts me."

A silly question popped into her head, and she asked it. "Am I dying?"

"No." She could tell he was lying. She tried to smile, but still couldn't see him and didn't know if he'd responded. She tried to curl her fingers in his, but found suddenly she couldn't feel them. He must have had some sense of what she wanted, however. He lifted her into his arms and held her, trembling, in the worn folds of his corduroy jacket. "No. You're not dying. But I am."

Seventeen

"She's done *what*?" Jesse asked. He was pacing the study of his rancho, a far grander place than Zack had imagined. It was homey, rambling, and unpretentious, but it was also clear the rancher was wealthy. A twinge of guilt tugged at the poet's heart. He'd made a mistake in the Yukon. He'd thought Jesse's haughty demeanor the false pride of the Spaniards, but somehow the rancher had avoided the troubles that afflicted so many of California's original settlers. Desperation squeezed in the young poet's chest, and he felt a fillip of grief for his Bet. He had not envisioned the ranchero so prosperous. He should have come for help sooner.

"She's had your baby and she wants you to take it."

"When? Where?" Jaw muscles ticking, hands clenched behind his back, the tall ranchero loped from one side of the room to another. He reached one of the adobe's deep windows and stopped. Light pooled around him. The sepia of the room gave way to gold tones, but the beautiful light did not soften the anger in the rancher's expression. "Why didn't she tell me?"

"Six weeks ago. In San Francisco. She didn't want you to know in case she lost it."

"Is she all right?"

"She's still—weak—but she came through it."

"And the baby?"

"A boy. Dark like his father."

Turning, Jesse leaned his forehead against the sun-washed wall. For the briefest of instants Zack thought he could feel it—the cool interior brick of the house, the fear and despair in his rival's heart. Jesse started, as if the current of sympathy had reached him. He circled the room, fingers skimming the books, as if he sought comfort in the gilt and leather bindings. "Why doesn't she want to raise the babe?"

"She finished the novel. She's had a generous offer from Putnam. They want another, but she doesn't think she can write while raising the baby; doesn't believe she can be both writer and mother."

Jesse's hands clenched behind his back. He paced from one side of the room to another. Zack could sense his torment, his hurt and his anger. He waited. Bettina's fate, the infant's fate, rested on the caprices of this imperious rancher. On Jesse's fourth pass of the bookshelves, he pulled a cue stick off the wall. He eyed Zack from beneath lowered lashes, then placed the stick on the dark green pool table dominating the sunwashed room's center. With calm motions, he reached for another stick and balanced it between the palms of his hands. "Would you like to play?" he asked.

"For money?"

Jesse nodded. Zack picked up the stick from the table, a slight bit of glee running through him. He was good at this game. He'd learned in San Francisco. He never turned down a chance to gamble, especially against a man who had money. He watched Jesse, though, just a bit wary. Though he couldn't read the ranchero's expression, there was something in the flare of the nostrils, in the broody light beneath those silky eyelashes, that let Zack know this man intended to trounce him and would just as soon kill him if he made one false move in this game. With a flare of delight, Zack chalked up the cue stick. "I'll break."

Jesse stepped back, watching intently. "Does Bet know about my engagement?"

"Yes."

"What does she think about that?"

"How much are we playing for?"

Jesse scowled, tapping his fingers on the edge of the cue stick. "One thousand dollars. Do you think you can make that?"

Zack shook his head. "Bet did well selling to Putnam, but we don't have that kind of cash, especially not to waste on a gamble."

"Then I'll help you," Jesse said. "I'll bet the thousand against a particular volume of poems."

"One volume?" Zack cocked his eyebrow. "Just one? Against a thousand dollars?"

"It's a particular volume, yet to be published. And I'll raise the ante so you won't think I'm stingy. Five thousand dollars against every unpublished poem you've written on the subject of you and Bet Goldman and a promise that you won't publish another, at least one in which she's portrayed as your lover."

"Five thousand dollars. Are you still that jealous?" Zack asked.

"I'm protecting the baby. I don't like to think what he'll think of his mother."

"You can't get back what's already been written."

"No, but I can limit the damage."

"Seems kind of silly, but sure." Bending over, Zack broke. The cue ball hit with a smack. The rest careened in all directions, three of them falling into side pockets, giving Zack the choice of stripes or solids. With a grin, Zack straightened, assessing the table, making sure of all the positions. "And as for your previous question, Bet wants you and Christine to be happy. She thinks the horsewoman will be a good mother." He moved to the side and pointed to one of the balls. "Solids."

"She doesn't think she'd be a good mother herself?"

"No." Zack didn't lie in this particular matter. Bet adored the baby. That wasn't the problem. And she thought maybe she could support him, for there had been an offer from Putnam. But she hadn't been able to care for the infant, at least not in a normal manner, and she wasn't sure she'd be well enough, ever.

Jesse loped to one side, watching intently as Zack landed a ball in another pocket. "How do I know this is my baby? We were taking precautions. . . ."

"You would know if you saw him—"

The flap of long fingers caught Zack's attention. He ignored Jesse's drumming. Bending over, he lined up the easiest shot. "If it makes you feel any better, I offered marriage. I even offered to pose as the baby's father." Zack kept his gaze on a ball and far pocket, ignoring the anger, the palpable tension, radiating from Jesse's side of the table. "She didn't accept my offer either."

"But you've been caring for her?"

"Yes."

"And writing about her?" The rancher's voice had a thickness, reflecting his fury, and Zack could sense the heat of anger even at this distance. The musky scent of warmed citrus emanated from the dark ranchero.

For the first time since he'd known him, Zack felt a fear of the rancher. "No. I've given up writing about her." Jesse's jaw muscles slacked slightly. Jesse had probably been more of a threat in the Yukon, but in those days when he flirted with death, Zack hadn't felt much fear of the rancher. He did now, however. This last year had changed him. There'd been something about his stint in the Klondike, the closeness of death, the grit and the darkness, the grandeur of nature and its indifferent beauty, the nine months with Bet and watching her struggle, that made him think closely about the false allure of destruction and gifted him with a desire to live longer. He slapped the ball in, a run of three solids. "I've been writing about my Yukon adventures."

"But people still will believe the baby is yours?"

"Yes." He bent down, lined up his next shot, and missed on purpose. "I suppose so."

"And for the rest of my life I'll wonder."

"Only if you choose self-delusion." He loved the funny, dark-haired baby whose soft black fuzz stuck straight up from his head. Zack didn't know why exactly, but the months with Bet made him feel bonded, as if the child were his, like the poems or the novel. And though he really would like to take him, he could see right away that Jesse would make the far better provider, and probably even a better father, if he could only get the stubborn ranchero to accept the fact that he'd sired a baby. "The child is yours. Any fool can see that quite clearly. I didn't sleep with Bet before you did, you know that yourself, and I didn't sleep with her after. She loves you dearly. Only a blind man would not see that. And you're far worse a madman than I if you don't acknowledge this baby and raise it."

Jesse took his shot and missed it. "If she loves me so much, why doesn't she want me?"

Zack hesitated. He hated this rancher. He'd always hate him, because Bet loved him. Neither did he like Bet's cruel deceptions. In her efforts to avoid this man's censure, she often acted in ways that were brutal and never more so than at this moment. Still, his sympathy for the imperious ranchero was tempered by the knowledge that the man in some ways had brought on his own fate. He'd not even questioned the effects of the child-birth, so stubborn was he in his perception that his little cripple was perfect. "I don't know why she won't have you," Zack lied, ashamed of himself but sorry for Bet and determined to help her. "She's a wonderful artist and a complex woman. I can't say myself I've figured her out."

"But you swear to me that this is my baby?"

"I swear."

"And you swear to me that Bet is all right?"

Zack swallowed. He didn't like lying, even to this rancher. It was one thing to tell a half-truth as a writer, one thing to pose as the baby's father, but another to lie to protect an illusion, to indulge Jesse's fantasy that Bet was normal. "She's weak." This was the truth, though not the whole of it. "But she's come through it."

Jesse bent down and lined up a shot. He sank one stripe, then another, glanced grimly at Zack, then ran the whole table. Straightening, he looked down at the poet and smiled in triumph. "I'll take the baby." He replaced the cue stick. "And the unpublished volume." Turning, he fixed his dark gaze on the poet, his expression suspicious. "But I'll have to talk to Christine about our engagement and make an arrangement for how we'll raise him."

Christine took the news better than Jesse expected. She'd been completely serene since he'd announced their engagement, and she took the news of the child calmly enough. She stroked one of the bays she'd brought to the stable, a Thoroughbred she used in jumping, whom she'd given the stall next to Firestriker.

"He's scruffy," she said, pointing to the mustang. "But I'll take the baby." She ran the brush through the bay's mane. "Actually, I think it rather convenient. The child will relieve me of one of my duties. You'll already have an heir to this rancho. I can pass mine down to one of my nephews. Given the proper infusion of cash, we should be able to put it on a paying basis."

"Don't get your hopes up." He shoved his fists in the pockets of his denim jacket. "Even my rancho doesn't pay for itself. My money comes almost entirely from investments."

She shrugged, her gray riding jacket wrinkling slightly. "Perhaps we can change that. I've always believed these ranches would pay if we had enough money for modern improvements."

Jesse let her comment lie. He knew she was deluding herself. In college he'd made a detailed study of the historic patterns of ranching. Throughout the world, since the Middle Ages, cattle ranching was driven to marginal places, taking place on land with few other uses, a definition that had once fit California but one that was fading as the world expanded. Steam-driven ships made the world smaller. His home, which had once been at the edge of the world, had been forced more and more to the world's center.

He placed his hand on Firestriker's warm neck. This was one of the reasons he'd always liked Bet. For all her Gypsy-like, unpredictable nature, she'd linked him to the world that was coming, a world of tolerant, cosmopolitan people who would value this land for its location and beauty, for its golden hills and exquisite weather, its ports that bound far-distant cultures. Christine was less suitable in that feature. Though she loved the rancho and all that went with it, she did not understand that her way of life was fading. The ranch would be an expensive hobby, at least in this particular location, not a practical way to make money. He squelched the train of that thinking, however. He couldn't have Bet. He'd been rejected and he needed to find a mother for his baby. "You don't want your own children?"

"Not really." She crooned into the Thoroughbred's ear. "These are my babies. I would have obliged you for an heir, of course, but it's rather endearing that she saved me the trouble."

"Do you think you could love him?"

"The child?"

Jesse nodded, still touching the old mustang's neck.

"I won't try to fool you." She put down the brush and picked up the oat bag, sifting the grain through her fingers. "If you bring the child back to the rancho, I'll arrange for an appropriate nanny, but I won't pretend I could love it." She stroked the bay's muzzle, feeding him from the flat of her hand. "I'll teach him to ride. If he likes it, then we'll have that in common. I won't guarantee maternal devotion." She gave him a dazzling smile, her blue eyes frank, her blond hair sunshot with the wonderful sunshine this place produced, the product of sunlight reflected off hot hills. "I'm sure you understand because we're the same in this feature. We like land and horses. We don't much like people. The child will be an unnatural burden, but one I'll oblige in return for my freedom from the wifely duties that would likely produce another."

"That's a straightforward bargain." He stroked Firestriker's mane. "What if I don't like it?"

"Then go back to your little liar. Look at me, Jesse."

He did as she asked, struck once more by her golden beauty.

"I might be cold, but at least I'm honest. A woman who loved you wouldn't make this agreement. She'd reject the baby and probably hate you for cheating. And if I never have my own baby, I'll never be jealous of the son you've been given."

"I suppose that's true enough."

"Good." She wiped her hands on the back of her pants. "Then we have a bargain?"

"Yes, I suppose so."

"I do have one other condition."

"Which is?"

"This nag should go." She nodded in Firestriker's direction. "He's old and he's ugly. He was probably never a very good jumper and has no use now except riding children."

"That's true." He kept stroking the mane of the dark brown horse with the star on his forehead. "But there's nothing wrong with that usage. Bet really loved him. He's the horse in her stories. Perhaps someday Jesse, Jr., will ride him."

"Jesse, Jr.?"

"That's what she's named him, and I think I'll keep it."

"How quaint. How provincial. Are you going to tell Junior about his real mother?"

"Yes." Christine seemed to flinch slightly, so Jesse added quickly, "It's too small a valley to keep the truth a secret. People will ask questions, and I've never made much of a liar."

"He'll believe her a whore."

"Not if we don't present her that way."

"At the very least he'll feel abandoned."

"Yes, I suppose so." He touched Firestriker's soft muzzle. "But I can't change that. At least not unless she reconsiders."

"Are you going to ask her again?"

Jesse didn't answer. He didn't need to. She could see the answer in his expression.

"And if she rejects you?"

He didn't answer that question either.

"Fine, I'll accept whatever happens, but if you return to me with this baby, then you must grant me this foible. I'll raise the child. I'll hire a nanny. Don't make me look at that woman's horseflesh."

Bet looked pale and frightened, her ribbons trembling, and the wild assortment of bright-colored fribbles couldn't disguise her lusterless eyes, her pallid complexion.

Jesse approached her slowly, heartsick and shocked. The poet had said she was weak, but she looked far more ill than he expected. He pulled a chair up to the cot, a slender iron bedstead tucked into the corner of the dingiest flat Jesse had ever been in. "I've seen the baby."

She smiled weakly, but there was joy in her eyes, and that luminescence reminded Jesse with some force of the little cripple he'd taught to ride so long ago, though she was confined to a wheelchair. "He's gorgeous," he said, taking her hand.

"Will Christine take him?" She'd been reading from a stack of bound printed pages, and she dropped them into her lap as she spoke. "At least until I get better?"

"Of course," Jesse lied. Christine had agreed to take the baby forever. They hadn't discussed what might happen if Bet decided to take him later. Still, she was clearly too ill to take care of him now. They'd discuss the rest of their problems later.

Her hands moved over her thin quilt, and he smelled her illness beneath the odor of roses. "I hope it won't spoil your wedding."

He grinned, in spite of himself. "Somehow I don't believe that."

"Honestly, Jesse."

He glanced at the top page of the papers and saw her name on it, evidently a draft sent back from Putnam. He shoved his hands in his pants pockets, resisting the urge to grab the papers and tear them into tiny pieces too small to be read. For the sake of this book, for the sake of the poet, she'd borne his baby in these awful conditions, brought herself to the brink of exhaustion, and had neither the decency nor the good sense to tell him she had conceived a baby, how she was living, or to ask for money. Still, he supposed in some ways he should be grateful. On the Barbary Coast of San Francisco, it was easy enough to get rid of a baby. "You would not reconsider my marriage proposal?"

She paled, almost to white. "Don't—"

He grabbed both her hands. Their frailty hurt him. She'd lost both weight and color, all impression of substance. She was pale as a ghost, far more frail than her beloved mustang. He stifled the impulse to gather her tiny body, bundle it into the threadbare quilt, and carry her off to the rancho. Perhaps if she knew her horse were in danger . . . He squelched that silly train of thought also. That wasn't enough reason to get married. "This is the third request. I won't ask again. You can have babies. You already proved that. I don't know why you didn't tell me. But I'll forgive everything—every rejection—your secrecy and your lies, your foolish illusions—

if you'll give up this poet and come back to the rancho and spend the rest of your life as my wife.''

She tried to draw back, but he held her. He didn't know whether to hold her or crush her. He didn't know why she'd been so foolish. ''You don't have to have more,'' he continued. ''I'll use better protection. . . . For God's sake, Bet, we don't have to have sex, if that's why you're frightened. We could go back to that first arrangement.''

''For the rest of our lives?''

He didn't answer.

''Don't.'' She turned her face to the wall. ''Just don't.''

Letting go, he paced to the room's tiny window. She'd decorated the sill with wild roses deftly arranged in broken crockery. He recognized her aesthetic as clearly as if this were her writing. As she did in her clothes, as she did in her writing, she'd created beauty from scraps and fragments, as if poverty meant nothing, as if his money meant nothing, as if nothing else mattered except the world in her head and her frustrating, admirable gift for translating the world she carried inside her. ''I don't understand you. It's not as if I'll make you do this every year.'' He sat down again and removed one of the ribbons. ''I love you, Bet.'' He didn't know why she'd done this, but they made her look girlish, and it unnerved him to see her dressed in these trifles. He smoothed her hair back as he spoke and continued removing the ribbons. ''I've always loved you. You wrote that novel single and pregnant. You could write another. I could make your life easy. Why can't you just come live on the rancho?''

''What kind of life would that be for the baby?'' She sifted through the bright-colored streamers, her expression sad, almost defeated. ''It takes thousands of hours to write one.''

''Is this it?'' he asked, lifting the paperbound novel.

"Yes." She brightened slightly. "Those are the galleys. I'm making corrections."

"Are you sure you should?" He smoothed her ashy-brown curls again. "In your condition?"

"Oh, yes." She touched the stiff paper with the same reverence as an old woman might touch a communion wafer. "These are all that keep me going. Those and the thought that you've come for Jesse."

"I don't understand your self-imposed choices." He turned the volume over. It was thick and substantial, as if she'd transferred her former self onto this paper. "We have servants, for God's sake. What does it matter? I know you love writing, but you must love the baby. After all, you were trying to have him."

"Jesse." She took the volume out of his hand and grasped his velvet coat sleeve tightly. "Please believe this. I never got to use the trick with the pinprick. Jesse is a product of the love I bear you. He may represent a failure of science, but he's a real triumph of human nature."

"What does that matter?"

"I want you to love him. I want his life to be normal."

"Then give him a mother."

She stiffened. He wasn't sure how she'd done it, for she never straightened, but her whole figure went rigid with some emotion he couldn't quite fathom, maybe anger, maybe even anguish. "His life will never be normal with me as a mother."

"What do you mean?"

"I mean I'm a victim of my own self-deception. I thought I could do this, be domestic and happy. Settle down like other women, but I've realized the truth since I've been pregnant. I can't really love him, not really. I need to live in my world of illusions. Raising a child would not make me happy. I haven't even been able to nurse him."

"You're sick. You're depressed." He ruffled through

the ribbons, the visible signs of her efforts to cheer her-self with something pretty. "Who wouldn't be, lying in this place?" He indicated the window, the tiny kitchen. "Let me take you back to the rancho. I can get you good doctors. . . ."

"No doctors."

"Bet."

She huddled under the quilt and turned toward the wall, crushing her fripperies beneath her, all her laces and ribbons, all the silly disguises he thought she'd abandoned in the days since she was eleven. He picked up the novel and threw it. She ignored the thunk on the wall. "Goddammit, Bet, why won't you let me help you? I don't care if you think I'm provincial. A child should have a father and mother. I don't care if you're domestic or not. . . . Just be there. For him. And for me. Go on writing your novels. Just lend us your presence. We'd look for your smile every evening."

She let out a small whimper. He stopped. For all her faults she never cried, and he knew from the sound that he had hurt her. "I'm sorry." He sat down on the chair. "I didn't mean to be cruel. All my life, you've made me happy. Not the rejection, but your smile and your laughter, the way you look at the world. It was as if you looked right through my shyness, ignoring the height, the darkness, the exotic features. You simply saw a self-conscious boy, took him into your heart, and brought him laughter. That's all that I want. That's all I need from you. That and perhaps a few of your kisses."

Turning, she gazed at him from beneath her drooping tendrils. "Jesse, please don't feel rejected. I don't mean to grieve you. I'm simply not like other women."

"You won't reconsider?"

She did not need to answer and didn't.

Eighteen

"Did you tell him?" Zack asked as he brought Bet a cup of spiced tea. She seemed so forlorn, he was worried. She'd always loved life, had such valiance and courage, but she'd been so ill since the childbirth, seemed so crushed by the results of her gamble. Now that she'd taken care of Jesse, Jr.'s, future, he didn't know whether she'd recover. "Why don't you tell him? Perhaps he could help you."

She accepted the small cup of tea from him. "And spend the rest of my life as the object of his pity? No, thank you."

"How are you going to keep it a secret? He's bound to find out sooner or later."

"No. I don't think so. At least not for a while. A working novelist can be very reclusive."

"So you won't go back to the library work?"

"No." She shook her head for emphasis. She'd taken to wearing four or five ribbons, massed together, their edges zigzagged, all the ribbons in different colors, which made her face gay and full of movement and detracted from her otherwise stillness. "There will still be a scandal. I don't think Jesse intends to lie to most people. I don't think I would want that either. I'll simply have to hope he doesn't come visit. I'm not really worried. I doubt Christine will let him.''

"He'll find out the truth sooner or later."

"Just as long as he finds it after they're married, after Christine's accepted the baby."

She'd finished her tea. He took the cup from her and set it down in the small kitchen. "Do you want to be moved close to the window?"

She glanced at the patch of light on the floor, shimmering through the wild roses she'd placed on the sill. "Sure. It gets hard to read this"—she held up her galleys—"as this place gets darker."

He moved the bed and small table into the sunlight. "I'm going to find a better place for you, now that we've gotten the money from Putnam."

She threw off her covers. He could not see her legs, but he knew they were lifeless, the harrowing result of her desperate gamble. Though he didn't approve of Bet's decision, he could understand why she'd given the baby away. That damnable yokel might well have money, but he had little else to recommend him. He would probably never have married Bet Goldman had he known what had happened when she had the baby.

"This is Firestriker." Jesse chucked Jesse, Jr., on the chin. He already loved him, this little urchin, with hair like his and skin like his mother's. Even Don Wheeler loved him, though the old land baron was deeply suspicious of the reasons why the baby had been abandoned.

"You ought to go get her," he said, referring to Bet in her absence. "Never listen too much to a woman. They don't know what they want anyway." He'd argued long and hard against Jesse's agreement to raise the baby without his real mother. He didn't care that Bet didn't want to be married, contending her point of view did not matter once she'd given birth to the infant. "I don't care if she'll be happy. She has her duty and she oughtn't shirk it. Give Christine some cash for her rancho and go back and retrieve your son's mother. You've created this child together. Now is not the time for silly romantics."

Jesse had ignored his advice, though, and brought only the baby back to the rancho, though he found he missed Bet even more badly than he had after their first two separations.

"Your mother rode him," he said to the child, longing for the day when they'd ride together. "But I suppose you won't." It hurt him to get rid of the mustang, though he supposed it would be a small gesture to indulge Christine in her request to do so. He wouldn't have him destroyed, of course. But he could be sent to another rancho.

Jesse lifted the child to his shoulder. "I know this is not realistic, but I hope you remember him just a little." Jesse nodded at the marvelous mustang. "He's a unique creature really. He inspired the stories that many children have grown up on."

The dark-haired infant gurgled and cooed, barely able to hold his head up, but smiling sweetly at the restless mustang, as if he knew that uneasy creature with the flaring nostrils and still springy canter was something precious, something of beauty. The baby held up one hand and stretched out his fingers, a silly gesture, one Jesse couldn't interpret.

"She was a fine rider, your mother." Jesse held the boy higher. He knew Christine watched from the porch of the rancho. He'd put off the wedding in a fit of self-doubt, and his long-suffering fiancée was becoming impatient. She didn't love the gurgling infant, but true to her promise, she'd hired a nanny and tolerated the infant's presence. She minded, however, that Jesse's reluctance to finally marry had made her the object of pity and gossip, and she pressed him daily and with more insistence that he get rid of this other reminder of the woman he'd loved since his childhood. "She rode these hills with me when we were children. You and I will ride them also. And sometimes you and your step-mother."

The baby cooed, though not in response. In his few short weeks as a father, Jesse had learned that the infant could be quite attentive. He often seemed to be listening and he certainly watched, as if he were waiting for the world to come together inside a brain that could not interpret words, objects, people, or meaning, that could barely get his legs to respond, except to whir wildly in circles. Still, the child's smile was charming. Jesse found it a comfort. For the rest of his life he'd have a reminder that one woman had loved him, that one woman had managed to make him happy. When he felt the sting of her rejection, the smile of this child somehow assuaged it, though he still felt an intense grief and sadness that she rejected both him and the infant he'd fathered.

He tucked the bobbing head close to his shoulder. Jesse, Jr., snuffled against his shirt collar, his little head fitting in tightly. The scent of him, an incredible sweet-ness, made Jesse's chest muscles tighten.

"She loved this cow pony." Jesse watched the old mustang, his russet coat gleaming in the golden sunlight. The sight made him ache for Bet more. "I wish I could hate her. I wish I could tell you she was a monster, inhuman, an impractical fool. But you should have seen her." He watched the old horse circling, circling, as if he were looking for his little Bettina. He clutched the baby more tightly. "And you should have seen what the delivery had cost her. She's frightened." He stroked the soft hair, cooing softly. "It took a great deal of cour-age to bear you, and she gave us both something irre-placeably precious. In your case—life." He kissed tiny fingers curled into the fist of a sleeping infant. "In my case—a child by a woman who loved me, though per-haps not enough to risk her life twice. Still, we ought

to be grateful and try not to judge her now that she's
discovered how much childbirth can cost her.''

Firestriker cantered around the corral, restless, seemingly younger. The sunlight glinted off his brown withers. At the sound of his hooves, a memory came back.
''You should have seen her in that wheelchair.'' He continued stroking the sleeping infant. ''It was metal and
wicker. She lived on the porch all summer. When I carried her, her legs were so withered. But I enjoyed it. She
was light and fragile, soft and full of laughter. You
couldn't believe the small things that pleased her. The
sound of the stream. The feel of the water. The colors
of the flowers around her. It hurt me to see her in that
apartment. Bedridden.'' Firestriker moved past him, the
sound of his hooves a distant reminder. ''I don't imagine
she liked it either. She could not rise to greet me.'' He
clutched his son tighter. ''She didn't rise the whole time
I pleaded. She offered me the same old excuses, the ones
she must have rejected. . . . God, what a fool I've been.''
Jesse pulled back Jesse, Jr., and cradled his head, looking at the dark infant as if this were the first time he'd
seen him. She'd carried this baby, this strong, lusty
baby, and cradled him in that once-broken pelvis. And
he, blind as always, had seen the miracle but not its
limits. ''She was worried about the doctors' predictions.
They told her . . .'' He held his son to his chest, smelling
his softness. ''Never mind what they told her. She never
got out of that bed.''

''How did you know?'' the ragged poet demanded when
Jesse showed up on his doorstep, demanding Bet. ''She
wouldn't let me tell you what had happened.''

''I didn't.'' He pushed back the damnable scoundrel,
more tattered than when he'd first seen him, but also
more healthy-looking. He strode into the dingy flat. ''I
was watching the horse. I finally realized that she was
lying and why.'' He knelt down next to Bet. She was
lying, eyes shut, on a small cot in the far corner, thinner

and paler than when he'd last seen her, and with an ugly rasp to her breathing. He picked up her hand, which was terrifyingly lifeless, and put his other on her cloth-covered forehead. He could feel the heat even through the rough material. "Has she seen a doctor?" he asked.

"Yes," Zack answered. "She doesn't like them, but I insisted. Though it's hard to get good ones on this side of town. We've got enough money, but I've been frightened to move her. . . ." He made a small gesture, uncertain and helpless, then shoved his fists in his pants pockets. Jesse bent down close to Bet's earlobe. She smelled like camphor and roses and illness. For the first time since he'd known her, he felt truly frightened. Her general health had always been good, but she looked so frail, so labored and helpless, it was hard to imagine how she'd pull through this. "Bet, can you hear me?" he whispered.

She didn't respond, but he refused to be daunted. They'd spent all their lives pushing her limits. He wasn't going to give up on her this time. He plucked her up by the shoulders and shook her.

"Hey!" Zack grabbed the sleeve of his jacket.

Jesse shook him off with a furious gesture. "Bet. Listen." He shook her again. "I've come back to help you. I know what happened. You can't walk, can you? You lost that in childbirth. That's why you gave me the baby."

Her eyes fluttered open. "Jesse." For a moment she seemed not to focus, but looked around wildly, confused and panicked. "Jesse."

"Be gentle." Zack plucked Jesse's elbow again, his voice equally frightened. "She didn't want you to know what had happened. It's bad enough that she's been crippled. But now . . ."

Jesse looked from Bet to the poet. They both looked paler than they had in the Yukon, though the poet looked generally better beneath his tattered coat and dirty shirt collar. Bet looked so much worse than she'd been before that Jesse glared at the poet, his gaze both accusation and question. "So tell me why you're standing there healthy and she looks like she's starving, not just crippled, but living in squalor as well."

Zachary English, street urchin and prophet, looked as though he had been punched in the stomach. "Pneumonia. She came down with it after you left." He looked away, tears in his eyes. "I didn't think anything could be worse than my childhood. Then I went to the Yukon. It was grim enough to sober me up, but this . . ." He indicated Bet's small, blanket-wrapped figure "This is so painful I don't think I can bear it."

Jesse scowled and turned away from the poet. "You son-of-a-bitch. I don't care what you've suffered. This whole problem could have been avoided if you'd not been so spiteful. Bet . . ." He pulled her close to his chest. He could feel her heartbeat, her irregular breathing. Her frailty reminded him of the little cripple he'd carried around in those days on the rancho, except the girl he'd carried too long and so often had been lively, cheerful, and wiggly. "You're not going to die. Nor are you going to spend your life as a cripple."

Zack made a gesture of protest.

Jesse silenced him with a scowl, then turned back to the tiny woman whose pale thin hands were clutching his sleeve. "You can't do either," he said. "Think of Jesse, Jr. He deserves a mother. And he deserves a mother who loves him. I can help you. I know I can. I just have to get you back to the rancho."

"I tried, Jesse." She clung to his jacket, beautifully tailored and of richest black velvet. "I tried. I tried so hard to get out of this bed. But the doctors were finally right. It happened, just like they said."

"What happened?"

"This." She jerked her chin downward, to legs already visibly thinner beneath a thin quilt and the kimono she wore when writing. "I can hardly move them. I've been injured somehow. I can't get out of this bed."

He sat her back gently, lifted the quilt, took her foot in his hand, and kissed it. He thought she shivered, though he couldn't be certain, so he pushed up the night-gown and touched her ankle, the one she used to keep wrapped in ballet slipper ribbons. "Can you feel this?" he asked. She nodded. He raised her gown up to her thighs, ignoring her sound of distress. He stroked her muscles, far more flaccid than they had been in girlhood, except for the days when she'd been a cripple. It was hard to believe this was the same woman who'd insisted on walking over Dead Horse Pass. "What have you been doing since you've come back from the Yukon?"

"Writing." She glanced anxiously at the far corner. "I've been working terribly hard on the novel. It's going quite well, too. We've managed to pay back the library fund, and I've had another offer from Putnam."

Ignoring the musty scent of the paper, he bent down and kissed the inside of her knee. This time she shivered. Of that he felt certain. "Have you been walking?" he asked.

"No, hardly ever," she answered.

"How about riding?" He kept his voice casual, low and unfeeling, but he could sense her immediate reaction. She stiffened and sucked in a breath.

"No." He didn't say more. He could almost hear her thinking, sense her hope flare, subside, and then dwindle. "Oh, Jesse. You don't suppose?"

"Why don't we try it?" he said.

"Do you think Firestriker will still be able to hold me?" she asked.

"Of course," Jesse answered without hesitation. He'd promised Christine to get rid of the mustang, but he'd just have to deal with that problem later. What mattered now was Bet's spirit. Riding Firestriker would help her get better.

"Oh, Jesse, I can't." She sagged back into the flat pillow, her bright-colored ribbons as drooped as a willow in summer. "What would Christine say?"

"Don't worry about her." Bending down, Jesse lifted her out of the bed. The threadbare quilt tangled around her legs. Jesse plucked it off and tossed it away. She felt as light as the child he'd carried so often. The scent of sickness clung to her also, camphor beneath her rose-water. His heart constricted. He stifled an impulse to strangle the poet. Turning, he faced the disheveled writer, fixing him with a look of harsh judgment. He spoke to Bet but glared at the poet. "Christine will be delighted to help once I get you back to the rancho." Jesse lied baldly this time. Christine had reached the end of her patience when she'd entered into the bargain to accept the baby. Her hatred of Firestriker revealed that truth to him, but holding Bet now, clutched tight to his chest, brought back all those old emotions.

He tightened his grip on the frail body. Christine's perspective did not matter at all. He loved Bet Goldman and wanted her back and would do whatever it took to get her. It didn't matter how long the odds, that she'd lied to him about the baby, or even that in some ways she loved this unconventional poet and he, Jesse, tongue-tied provincial, could never compete with that kind of friendship.

What mattered to him was what she was at this moment, a woman with a kind of lunatic courage who'd always be willing to try to be happy, who'd make the best of whatever life gave her, and who enriched herself and all those around her with her grace in the face of life's cruelest moments.

He pushed past the rumpled poet, whose corduroy jacket was incredibly shabby, almost falling off his workingman's frame. "I'm taking her back to my hotel. Then we're going to return to the rancho. You can come with us as long as you're helpful. But whatever your choice, please don't hinder my efforts. I'm completely certain she can get better if you'll just give me a chance."

The poet's eyes widened. He glanced at Bet Goldman.

With his tawny hair and roughened complexion, he seemed right at home in the dingy apartment. To Jesse's chagrin, the poet's poverty simply increased his raffish flair. His face was still boyish and handsome. He carried himself with vigor and passion. Still, Jesse could read fear for Bet in his expression. He also read courage and a sense of compassion.

"Come with us, Zack." Bet held out one hand, pale except where her fingers were ink-stained. "We can keep writing. I know Jesse will let us. But I'd like very much to go back to riding, and maybe, just maybe, he's right about walking."

Zack shoved his hands in his pants pockets, strode to a three-foot stack of papers haphazardly stacked in the kitchen corner. He picked up the first piece and perused it, evidently thinking rather than reading. "This is going to be an odd arrangement. You and I working together. He and Christine engaged to be married. Everyone thinking . . ." He glanced at Jesse, then at the page, and to Jesse's amazement, his weathered cheeks pinkened. "Ah. . . . the poor baby . . ." He crumpled the paper, and it crinkled softly. "What will people say?"

Bet laughed. "What does it matter?" She stretched her hand farther. She already seemed a bit stronger, as if hope itself had strengthened her muscles. "Since when have we cared about those provincials? We'll be like Byron. Like Shelley. Tell stories all evening. And as for the baby . . ." She snuggled her face into Jesse's chest, forehead hot and frail body trembling. "Maybe his life will never be normal, but maybe he could have a mother who loves him."

Jesse sent for a doctor, one of the best in San Francisco, a wealthy man's minion, the kind who made house calls and did not ask questions, no matter how unusual the situation. Bet hated him the first moment she saw him. Neatly tailored, efficient, with a wax-stiffened mustache, he looked like a villain in a cheap melodrama. She wanted to laugh but found she couldn't. Hunkered into the pillows of the gauze-topped four-poster, she felt weepy and crabby, dizzy and fevered. She wanted to strangle him for his manner, wipe the officious frown off his thin face.

She glanced instead at the silent ranchero. "Can Jesse stay with me?"

The doctor tugged on his wax-stiffened mustache. "That's not generally done. Not even with husbands, which I gather this gentleman's not."

"Don't be silly," she said. "I've just borne a child out of wedlock. What do I care for these conventions?"

The doctor coughed, glancing at Jesse, who fixed him with a disdainful stare, princely, exotic, and also quite frightening: "I'm staying." He adjusted the sleeve of his black velvet suit coat. "She's not my wife, but she is quite special. In case you don't know it, this is Bet Goldman, the author."

"I see." The odd-looking physician fished a stethoscope out of his black leather medical bag, then approached Bet with the cold metal contraption. She shivered, but he ignored it. With one last worried glance at the aristocratic ranchero, the physician unbuttoned the back of her new white lawn nightgown. "It's a privilege, Miss Goldman. I've read your horse stories. And, of course"—he stopped halfway down—"there are the poems. . . ."

"They're fiction." Jesse edged toward him, then stopped. He turned abruptly to the towering bay window overlooking the hills of San Francisco. The gauze curtains floated in on the breeze, and he stared intently out at the ocean.

She couldn't see his expression, but she sensed his tension in the line of his back, in his stiff posture. She sighed. How had her life become so peculiar? All she'd wanted was to be normal, to marry Jess and give him a baby, to live on the rancho and write children's horse stories. Now she wasn't even his mistress. Her child might be raised by another woman. She'd rejected three proposals of marriage, and people believed she belonged to Zack English. For all she knew, she might be dying, and it galled her more than all her other troubles that she might be dying more of a cripple than she'd been in the most helpless days of her childhood. "I can't walk anymore," she said to the doctor. "That's my worst problem."

"The least of your problems right at this moment." He flattened the stethoscope to her back.

Bet's heart sped up. He'd warmed the disk with his hand, and it wasn't as cold as she expected. "I don't want to die, but I especially don't want to die this way. As a child they told me I'd always be crippled."

"I can imagine," the doctor said softly.

In spited of her dislike of the metal, she leaned forward to give him better access. "So you do not need to worry. I will not die in this condition. It would be too sad and too ironic if I bore out those doctors' predictions when I've worked so hard to beat them."

"I can see how that would concern you, but let's concentrate on the pneumonia." Pausing, he listened. She tried to imagine what he was hearing, knew she was ill and breathing badly. He removed the disk and felt her spine lightly, outlining the curve with sensitive fingers. "I love your horse stories, you know."

"No. I didn't."

"And also the poems."

In the bay window, Jesse flinched.

Ignoring the movement, the doctor continued. "I've heard quite a bit about your childhood."

"You have?" she asked, surprised. She didn't know anyone knew about her childhood.

"Of course." He moved the stethoscope lower. "It's become something of a legend in medical circles, helped I'm sure by your fame as an author. Your first cure was a miracle really." He bent down and whispered, "Is this the rancher who helped you?"

She nodded, weakened and dizzy from the prolonged

sitting. The ache in her lungs had transformed into nausea.

He closed up her nightgown, then guided her back, as if he had a sense of her limits. "You owe him a debt you can never repay. I don't know how he had that insight, but it was a brilliant, if unconventional, tactic. I don't know if we can repeat it—"

"Why not?" Jesse left the window and strode to the four-poster. He gripped one of its posts with blunt-tipped brown fingers. Bet caught a whiff of his citrusy scent. "We did it once. Why couldn't we do it again?"

The doctor returned the stethoscope to his bag. "For one thing, the first time you helped her, she had youth on her side. For another, childbirth changes the pelvis. She has scoliosis. . . ." He ruffled through the sack, its contents clinking.

"Don't be silly." Jesse's knuckles tightened around the post. He looked as if he wanted to strangle the doctor. "She did it before. She can do it again. I don't care what the odds are. She'll beat them."

"I care," Bet said. She tried to straighten but couldn't. Her back ached. She felt restless. No amount of ribbons or pillows could cheer her. "I want to know if the first time was just an . . . aberration . . . or if you think I can do it a second time."

"A logical question." The doctor removed two dark blue vials from his bag and set them out on a mahogany table next to a brown horsehair sofa. "But one I can't answer. I can tell you the following with some assurance: For you"—he turned back to Bet—"childbirth will always be risky. I don't know what anyone told you . . ." Jesse gripped the poster more tightly. The doctor gave him a nervous glance, but continued. "But you must have guessed . . ."

Bet nodded, fingers playing over the eyelet of the lavender spread.

The doctor opened one of the vials. A stinging scent

reached Bet's nostrils. "You didn't hear this from me, but there are precautions—"

"We used a sheath," Bet put in quickly.

The doctor arched a cynical eyebrow and fished a spoon out of his black leather bag. "There are devices—cervical caps—they work much better to prevent conception and interfere less with your pleasure. They're expensive—"

"Expense is no object."

Bet glanced up, surprised, at the dark ranchero, who was staring at her from beneath lowered lashes.

Ignoring the current flowing between them, the doctor poured a liquid into a teaspoon. "You get them from France, and I suggest you use them. Because, for you, childbirth will always be risky. Even if you haven't damaged your pelvis, you'll always have a high risk of pneumonia. As for the walking, I simply can't say. . . ."

"Not even a little?" Bet asked. Her back hurt. She knew she was feverish. She'd forgotten what an easy breath felt like. "I'm so tired of being a freak of nature. I'd just like my life to be normal."

The physician smoothed the end of his mustache, brought the medicine close, and held the pewter spoon toward her. "You'll never be normal. But you're not a freak, just a variation. Now take this." He held out a spoonful of clear liquid.

Bet opened her mouth and swallowed, metal and medicine stinging her taste buds, the liquid burning as it went down.

She stifled a small sound of distress and concentrated on Jesse. He paced to the brown horsehair sofa and sat down abruptly. He picked up the stones from a game of fan-tan neatly displayed on the mahogany table.

The doctor removed a glass thermometer from his bag. "Do you gamble?" he asked, glancing at Jesse.

"Sort of." Jesse sifted the stones through his fingers. "For pleasure. Rarely for money."

The doctor shook the mercury down, then handed the

slender tube to Bet. "Have you studied statistics?"

"No," Jesse answered.

"You ought to." He lifted Bet's wrist, removed his ornate silver watch from his vest pocket, and counted. She tucked the thermometer under her tongue, feeling the tap of her pulse against his steady fingers. After a minute, he rested her hand back on her stomach, then made a small note on a pad of paper. He frowned, then removed the thermometer. "Numbers are lovely. There are patterns and laws. These are things of great beauty. In our hubris, we think we can beat them. But we never do. That's just an illusion."

"I don't believe it," Jesse said. The stones clicked as they flowed through his fingers.

"You should. It's true." The doctor wrote down another number. He tucked his instruments in his bag. As he did, he watched Bet closely, his expression both impassive and shuttered. "If you like to gamble, then you must have noticed that even in the crookedest places sometimes a player beats very long odds."

Bet nodded, returning his study. He'd treated her kindly, but she was suspicious. He had come to the part she always dreaded. Where the doctor pretended to know what he was doing, then condemned her with gloomy predictions.

He made little notes to himself as he spoke. "That's an illusion, I promise. Study statistics. Whatever the odds are, over time you can't beat them."

Bet gasped.

Jesse dropped the stones on the marble, their clicks like the patter of raindrops.

Bet clutched the lavender bedspread. Pain flared in her back and stabbed her. "Surely there can be exceptions?"

"Exceptions, no. Just variations. That's what creates the illusion." He smiled at Bet, his stiff mustache quirking. He closed his bag with a snap. "In nature, variations are normal."

•   •   •

Jesse came into bed with Bet that evening. He didn't approach her in a sexual way, only took off his jacket and boots, climbed in beside her, wrapped his arms around her waist, and pulled her tightly to his chest.

"I'm taking you home." He propped his leg up, making a kind of railing with that part of his body. "As soon as you get a little bit better."

She snuggled in closely, happy for the comfort, though the heat of his body made her more feverish. "And I'll ride Firestriker?"

He didn't answer, only stroked her hair softly, as much of a reply as she needed.

"Do you think Christine will mind?"

"No."

She knew he was lying, that she'd complicated his engagement again, though she couldn't bring herself to regret it. She regretted, however, giving away Jesse, Jr., and hoped that if she got better, she'd manage a way to get him back or at least make some kind of arrangement to see him, whether she got better or not.

"Do you think I can do it?" she asked.

"Of course." He pulled her in closer, his arms wrapped around her. "It worked before. I see no reason why it won't work again."

"What about the doctor's prediction?"

"Forget the doctor, except for his comment that some variation is normal."

She laughed, twining her fingers in his. "Yes. I suppose so. That's a good observation. I've never thought of myself as normal." She kissed his knuckles, enjoying his presence, the sensation of both strength and comfort. He smelled of citrus, as always, and she reflected she'd go to her grave loving that scent. "Ah, Jesse, I'm sorry. I should have asked for help much sooner. But I always felt I owed you so much. I didn't want to feel I was a burden."

"You could never be a burden, even . . . before. I always adored you, even before you were walking.''

''I never did understand why.''

He shifted slightly, his thigh against hers. ''Because you ignored my shyness completely. During any silence, you simply kept talking. No one had ever acted that way toward me.''

''A silly reason to love a woman.''

''Not if you'd had my childhood.''

''Perhaps.'' She tried to straighten but couldn't. She'd never straighten, but if she could just relearn the walking, she'd never worry about the rest of her limits. ''I suppose I loved you for the same reason. You ignored my defects. That's why''—she pressed her hand to her lower back, which ached more intensely than it had in years, though she accepted Jesse's insight that this might be because she hadn't exercised in so long—''it's hard to disappoint you.''

He smoothed down her hair and snuggled in beside her, evidently intending to spend the night. ''You don't disappoint me, except for your lying.''

''That's a pretty bad habit.''

''I'd say so.'' Fever and fatigue had taken their toll. She leaned into his chest, letting his strong contours ease her burden. A silvery light flickered over the gauzy curtains, reflected from the lamplight below. An image of Firestriker formed in her mind, and a stream, and the willows, and a house of adobe. She sighed. ''But you do know telling stories is how I make my living.''

''But you have to learn to distinguish real life from fiction.''

''Of course.'' She remembered the rhythm of the galloping mustang. She snuggled more tightly into Jesse's taut body.

He stroked her curls lightly. ''Are you listening to me?'' he asked softly, in a husky voice that only just barely penetrated awareness.

She nodded. They were close to the sea. She could

hear the waves' rhythm. Smell the salt air. The mustang was sweating. She tightened her thighs.

Jesse drew her in closer. "We're in San Francisco. You do know that, Bet."

"Oh, sure," she said, but she was lying.

Nineteen

"Christine took the news rather well." Jesse pushed Bet toward the high red barn where he and Bet had spent so much of their childhood.

"I don't believe you." She clutched a handful of quartered apples, evidently nervous at seeing Firestriker for the first time in ages. "I don't believe you for a minute."

Jesse didn't like lying, but had thought it important to keep up Bet's spirits as they started this project. He should have known better, however, than to try to fool such a skilled liar. "All right. She took the news badly, but she has not quite thrown me over."

The large red barn loomed before them, an eastern classic, not Californian, one of his father's few Yankee affectations. Still, Jesse loved it. He'd always loved it—the barn, the corral, the stream and the willows, the faint smell of the ocean, the heat and the sunshine, the green oaks against the golden hillside, and mixed in with these always memories of childhood, the memory of his friendship—no, his love—for Bet Goldman.

"I'm glad she did not throw you over." Bet strained

toward the stables, her posture as anxious as she could manage confined to the rattan wicker wheelchair, the same one she'd used when she was eleven, another reminder, although a sad one, of the magical childhood they'd shared together.

He laughed and kissed the top of her head. "I don't believe you. Not for a minute either."

"Honest." She tried to twist around to see him, but she couldn't quite manage in her seated position.

"No dice," he said, touching her shoulder. "I still don't believe you. You'll have to become a far more skilled liar if you're to convince me you're not jealous."

"Okay. I'm sort of jealous and sort of happy." She gripped the wheelchair arms tightly. The apples jiggled on the fringed white shawl tucked tightly over her lap. "I can't say I'm glad for myself, but I'm happy for you, and perhaps for Jesse, Jr."

"Don't be." He frowned, the wicker chair suddenly heavy. "It's mostly because she still needs money, though she likes Jesse Jr., I'm happy to say."

"Does she?"

Jesse couldn't read the tone of Bet's voice. She'd pulled her hair back and pinned it severely, so he couldn't tell if her ringlets were trembling. Her knuckles whitened on the armrests, however, so he guessed mentioning the baby caused her tension. *Good*, he thought, as he maneuvered the metal wheels through the dry brown grass. *I hope this subject causes her worry.* "Yes. And I must say that surprised me, considering her nature."

"Meaning?"

The shawl covering Bet's legs had slipped. He stopped for a moment to help her adjust it. The San Francisco doctor had cured her pneumonia, but the long convalescence had weakened her further. The kindhearted physician remained doubtful about her chances of walking, though he didn't discourage her riding or trying to push her physical limits once he'd declared her free of pneumonia.

Jesse didn't care, at least not on some levels, but walking had been Bet's lifelong obsession. And, of course, there was the problem of money. She couldn't support the child by herself, unless someone took care of him while she was writing. Though he'd gladly give her the help she needed, he wasn't sure she would accept it. She and Christine were opposites that way. Bet might be a liar, but she remained self-sufficient. In that way, perhaps, she'd never be normal. The poverty of her childhood made her crave independence, especially in financial matters.

He'd tucked the shawl under her legs. She smoothed down the lightly woven material, then gripped the wooden armrests as he returned to the back of the wheelchair. She watched for the horse so intently that he supposed she had forgotten their conversation. She surprised him when she spoke again.

"Why wouldn't she love Jesse, Jr.?" she asked.

He maneuvered the chair onto the trail that led toward the stables. "She's like me that way. She loves horses, but she doesn't especially like people. I expected her to look at a child as a duty, but she's actually trying to mold him."

"Really?" Bet's voice pitched up an octave. "How so?"

He wrestled the metal wheels over a hillock, thankful for the cool weather. He never thought of Bet as a burden, but he understood why she hated the chair. With healthy legs, this trail was so easy. In an invalid's wheelchair, even the littlest variation in surface made forward progression a problem. "She looks at him as a little cipher, one she can mold to her own image."

"I think that's a bit naive."

"I agree."

"Have you discussed this with her?" Bet craned upward, frustrated, then glanced back at the stable. "I've

given you Jesse, Jr., for safekeeping. I'd be . . . upset . . .
if he was damaged.''

"He's my child also.''

"I understand that. But I wasn't thinking. . . .
Jesse . . .'' Again she tried to twist upward, but the curve
of her back, the awkward angle, made that maneuver too
hard to manage. She fiddled with the apple quarters.
"He hasn't whinnied.''

He didn't have to ask who she referred to. It had
ceased to surprise him how the horse waited, even over
an absence of years. Still, he didn't think the absence of
a whinny peculiar until he considered Christine's disposition.

"I'm sure he's there.'' A white lie and harmless, he
rationalized, though he strained for the sounds from the
stables. There was nothing really except the bland hum
of nature, a few metallic sounds in the distance, the rill
of the stream if one paid attention, an occasional stir and
bump from the stable. "He just hasn't heard us.''

"He always hears me by now.'' The tone of her voice
made Jesse uneasy. He wondered. He had written Christine from San Francisco, telling what he planned for Bet
Goldman. Christine had been cold, distant, and angry,
but she'd remained at the rancho supervising the nanny.
He hadn't come out to the stables since they'd been
back. Bet had been sick, and he'd been too worried to
give much thought to his fiancée's feelings. A serious
error, he could see that clearly now.

He pushed the chair quickly, straining also to hear.
He left Bet by the gate when he reached the corral.

"Wait here.'' He entered the stable. A frisson of fear
chilled him. Christine had requested the mustang's destruction, but he hadn't considered that she might destroy him without explicit permission, though the
thought niggled and chilled him more deeply.

"Jesse?'' Bet called out as he stood in the half-darkness, wishing—sheer self-delusion—that the empty stall was an illusion, a trick of eyesight still not adjusted to the dim light. It wasn't.

And he knew what had happened.

He entered the room where Christine was staying, stifling the impulse to hit her. He didn't stop because she was a woman. He would not have observed that particular limit, so angry was he with what she had done, but hitting her wouldn't get Firestriker back. He grabbed her shoulders instead. "What have you done with the mustang?"

She wore her jodhpurs and boots and carried her quirt, and he imagined she was glad of the protection. "I had him put down. I thought we'd discussed it."

"We did discuss it. But I don't believe you. Even you could not be that cruel."

"Why not?" She tried to leave, but he held her. "That horse was ancient, unfit, and not useful."

"Except for teaching Bet Goldman to walk."

He grabbed the lash as she tried to strike him and shoved her against the whitewashed stucco wall. The morning light fell over her face, blond, finely sculptured, and icy.

"I don't believe you," he said, "but this I promise. I'll kill you if you've actually done this. Bet can be cruel, but you've certainly topped her. To condemn a rival to life as a cripple."

"She can learn on any mustang."

There was no fear in Christine's expression. Jesse wasn't sure why. He was lying when he threatened to kill her, but he didn't know if she understood that. His fingers itched to squeeze the truth from her. He tightened his fingers over her shoulders. "She has faith in that particular mustang."

"Yes, well. That's rather foolish." She tried to wriggle out of his grasp. "To put all her eggs in one basket."

He gripped her more tightly, lifting her up by her gray tailored jacket. "What have you done with the mustang?"

"I told you." She arched one finely shaped eyebrow. "I had him put down."

He'd give her this much credit. She was an excellent liar. He hadn't thought she had it in her, but she would have made a good poker player. He pushed her up a little higher. "I know you too well. You don't like people, but you do love horses. You wouldn't have him destroyed, except as an act of compassion."

"You don't think he was old enough for it?"

"Old, yes, but he wasn't feeble. And I'm betting you didn't destroy him."

She fixed him with a gaze of real hatred, and he knew he'd guessed correctly. She could have doomed Bet without conscience, but she couldn't destroy a horse that was useful.

"You really do love her, don't you?" she asked.

He nodded.

"I could have killed him, but that would have been foolish." She touched his hand, tightly gripped over the lapel of her jacket. "When he could be put to a better purpose."

"Such as?"

"I'll give back the horse, but I'm upping the ante."

"That's fair," he said. "If she gets well and accepts my proposal, there'll be even more cash for your rancho."

She lifted the quirt, but not to strike him. She drew it, instead, over his cheekbone. "It's no longer simply a question of money. I have my pride. It's been publicly shattered. And besides"—she touched his lips with the quirt's handle—"I've become quite fond of the baby."

He grasped her hand, gloved in black leather. "But she's his mother."

"She's given him up."

"Only because she's been crippled."

"Why do you bother? She'll never be normal. She's crippled, deceitful. She turned down your proposals. She can't even spread her own legs. I might not be willing, but at least I'm able—"

He slammed her hard against the stucco.

"Why?" she asked without flinching. "Why marry a woman who doesn't suit you?"

He shoved one thigh against hers, felt no reaction, only his hatred. "I haven't a single practical reason. I simply love her. I've always loved her, and in the end that's all that matters."

"Perhaps for you, but not to me. I won't be thrown over for that little cripple. My pride is worth more than you're offering. You've brought this woman into our valley. Taken me into your home to care for her baby. It's not only a matter of a broken engagement. There's the small matter of humiliation."

She smelled expensive. That always amazed him, how she could spend all day with horses and still smell vaguely Parisian. "How much?"

"I told you, it's no longer a matter of money."

"Then what?"

She smiled, cold and triumphant. "The horse for your hand in marriage."

In the end, Jesse agreed to the bargain. He didn't want to, but he didn't see a way around it. If he believed the doctor's prediction, Bet had almost no chance of walking again. He would have married Bet as a cripple, but he couldn't bring himself deep in his heart to condemn her to life in that wheelchair, even at the cost of their marriage.

So Jesse lied. And baldly. The worst lie he'd ever told in his life. He called Bet into the study where they'd played as children and made up the most credible story he could.

"Firestriker's gone to Christine's until the wedding." He looked Bet straight in the eye as he made his pronouncement. "She wanted to fatten him up as a present."

"I see." Bet nudged the wheelchair around the pool table, her head barely clearing its green felt surface. She picked up a piece of chalk and jiggled the small square in her hand. She glanced at Jesse, then out the window. "Will he come back soon?"

"After the wedding. We can move up the date if you want to. You could have him back in less than a month."

She turned pale beneath her new severe hairdo. "I can't ride him before then?"

"No."

She tossed the chalk on the table and rolled to one of the room's deeply recessed windows. Framed by the slanting rays of the sunlight, she stared out at the hillsides. A porcelain clock ticked out the seconds. Jesse waited through many small ticks, as well as the seemingly endless low gong of the imported French timepiece chiming eleven.

Bet spoke as the room fell silent. "You're lying. Tell me what's happened."

He racked up the balls. He didn't know why he felt the need to arrange them. They couldn't play with Bet in the wheelchair, but he needed to put his thoughts in order. "Christine's frightened."

"Of what?"

"Of us, I suppose. She'd rather we did this after the wedding."

"Do you agree?"

"Not exactly." His heartbeat sped up, and his chest tightened. He couldn't believe what he was saying. "Yes. I suppose so. It would be wiser."

Bet made a little sound of distress.

"Bet. We can't go on like this forever. You've turned down three proposals of marriage. We've created a baby together, but I need someone to raise him."

"You don't think I can raise him?"

"Not in that condition." Another lie and even a worse one. She could raise a child without even moving. Look at that damnable street urchin Zack English. She'd raised him up from the gutter and she'd barely known him. He gripped the pool cue and studied the wheelchair, the tiny woman trapped there forever, if he didn't get back the mustang. "If I proposed now, would you accept me?"

He couldn't believe he just said that.

"No."

He didn't believe her answer either. She'd marry him in an instant if he could just get back her mustang. But he couldn't, and that was the problem.

"You couldn't be happy living your life in that wheelchair?" he asked.

She laughed, touching one of the leather volumes on a bookcase that stretched toward the ceiling. "Happy, yes. I'm always happy. That's the greatest gift of a writer. We carry our world around inside us and can never be made truly unhappy. But happy is not the same as normal." She gripped the arm of the wheelchair. "I hate this now more than ever. All I ever wanted was to be normal. Marry you. Give you a baby. But I won't come to you as a burden. Not now. Not ever. That's why I never accepted before. I didn't know if I could have children, and I knew you wanted an heir for this rancho."

"And now?" he asked.

"I want Jesse, Jr., to have a normal childhood."

He wanted to go down on his knees, but he didn't. He finally understood all those rejections. It wasn't a logic he agreed with, but she did have reasons he could respect. "So if I gave you a choice—marry me and spend the life in that wheelchair or give me up to Christine and get Firestriker back—what would your answer be?"

"Is that her condition? If you marry her, she'll give back the mustang?"

He nodded. He hadn't meant to tell her this, but both

Bet and Christine were far better liars than he'd ever be, no matter how hard he practiced.

"What will happen to Firestriker if you don't accept her proposal?"

He didn't answer. He didn't have to. Bet had enough insight into human nature to understand Christine's vengeful disposition.

She rolled herself around the pool table, eyeing the neatly racked balls as she did. "You can't get the horse back some other way?"

"Not without risking his life. Christine is clever enough to keep him well hidden, and her vaqueros are perfectly loyal. Their lives are tied to the fate of her rancho. They'll do what she asks in this matter."

Bet touched the place on her neck where a ringlet should have fallen, as if she missed it without really knowing. "I can't let her kill him." She fiddled with the bare neckline of the brown velvet dress she was wearing. "I love you." She rolled herself back to the window and stared at the hillsides they'd ridden as children. "I'll always love you, and the baby also, but I won't marry you in this condition and I won't let her destroy that mustang." She looked up at him, her clear-browed expression made even more frank by the new upswept hairdo, her green eyes frank and appealing. "Do you understand me?" she asked.

He nodded, although he was lying.

Bet went to her baby that evening. Ignoring the young señorita rocking in the corner, she wheeled her chair next to the crib and touched the sleeping infant through maple spindles.

"I love you," she whispered. "I'll always love you, no matter what happens. You won't remember what I'm saying here, but I've written it down." She took a fat envelope from beneath the shawl covering her legs and held it up for the baby to see. "I don't know if you'll get to read it, but I've tried to explain myself in a story."

Jesse, Jr., snuffled at the sound of her voice, turning his head from one side to another, his silky black hair standing up like antennae. Inside her bosom, her heart constricted. This had been the first of her failures, when her milk hadn't come in because of her illness.

"I don't know if you'll ever read this," she said as she brushed the fuzzy head lightly, "and I don't know if you'll understand it. But this is the best I can do for you now, unless I really accomplish a miracle."

He had this scent. She could smell it, the powdered scent of all pampered infants, but beneath that a musk that marked him only, the scent of her own little baby. "I love your father, and that isn't Zack English. I hope you believe what I'm saying, because you really are the child of my passion. You'll need to ignore what's said by the poet. He's a wonderful boy, but never believe him." She touched tiny fingers through the twisted spindles. "Except, of course, in interior matters."

His hand fisted gently, as if in protest. From the corner, the young nanny watched but didn't comment on Bet's presence.

She stroked Jesse, Jr.'s, soft skin. "I wanted to give you a normal childhood. I still don't know if I can do it, but I promise you, Jesse, on the grave of my father, I'll try my damnedest to give you a mother and to give you a mother who loves you."

Bet went to Zack English for help. She wanted Jesse back. She wanted Jesse, Jr. Perhaps she wouldn't ever be normal, but she wanted her baby and to marry his father, so she was going to take a very long gamble.

She met Zack out by the stables, the high red barn filled with half a dozen highly bred horses, but not her beloved brown mustang. "How much do you know about horseback riding?" she asked.

"Very little." He eyed the pale cow pony with an Arabian face circling the dusty corral. "I'm a city boy mostly. A skilled oyster pirate but a terrible rider. I can count on one hand the times I've been on horseback.''

She pushed the shawl off her legs, cringing at the sight of their thinness, obvious beneath a calf-length skirt she'd hauled back from the Yukon. ''We're going to ignore that limitation. I need you to help me, at least a little. If you get me on him, I'll do the rest.''

He frowned, touching the wicker, his gaze skittering off legs that were spindly and useless. ''Isn't this where Jesse is supposed to help you?''

''In theory, yes, but he'll be busy.'' She pushed herself upward, ignoring the sharp stab of pain in her back. ''They've moved up the date of the wedding.''

Jesse didn't see Bet the day of the wedding. He stood at the front of the small chapel, dressed in his finest black velvet jacket. He ignored the brown-robed Franciscan before him and waited for Christine to enter in triumph. He hadn't seen her wedding dress yet, but he knew she would shine in traditional white, an emerald glinting on a long slender finger. He would have liked to see Bet one last time, but she'd disappeared, as she'd done often in the past few weeks, ignoring both Christine and the baby, to spend most of her time with Zack English.

Jesse tugged on the sleeves of his velvet suit coat. The organist started into a song, the kind of low background music intended to soothe as the audience waited. Jesse shut out the sound, as well as the spectators, the handful of ranchers from around the valley, a few of his father's vaqueros, and Zack English, tattered as always. Once more, Jesse adjusted his sleeve. He thought Bet's attention to the poet peculiar, but she had always been odd and never more so than in the long days before the wedding. She studiously avoided his gaze, pushing herself around in the wheelchair and steadfastly refusing all offers of help. Her behavior hurt him, and yet it didn't. She wanted to do right by her baby. He wasn't sure he agreed with her decision, but he understood better now that they'd talked. He could see quite clearly her heart was breaking, but she was determined not to burden him or the baby with the limits caused by not walking.

The low music continued, a change of song, but still not the triumphant oration announcing the bride. Jesse shifted slightly and glanced at his mother. Time hadn't diminished her unhappy beauty. She stared at the front of the chapel, her dark eyes hidden beneath a black lace mantilla. He avoided the gaze of Don Wheeler and glanced instead out the mullioned window at those golden hills he'd known since childhood, the hills his father had once sold his soul for, the hills he'd pass on to Jesse, Jr.

Jesse sucked in his stomach and turned back to the altar, his gaze averted from that of the priest. He wished Christine had allowed the child to grace the wedding. He'd asked her, but she'd refused bluntly. In her view, this was her moment. No squalling infant was going to mar it.

The organ burst into a high crescendo. All eyes turned toward the back of the chapel. A small figure appeared, tiny, almost childlike, seated in a wheelchair, her embroidered dress topped by a lace collar, her hair done up in bright-colored ribbons, a cluster of ringlets flowing over her shoulder.

Jesse swallowed.

Christine appeared behind the wheelchair-bound figure, her white satin dress rustling softly. Like a low wave on a glass ocean, a murmur traveled over the crowd.

"Move out of the way." Christine's voice didn't carry, but Jesse could tell what she was saying. She grabbed the wheelchair handles and twisted. A collective gasp burst from the churchgoers.

Bet stood. Christine stepped back, evidently astonished, then raised her hand as if to hit her.

Jesse launched off the dais. He strode down the aisle,

reached the two women, and grabbed Christine by the wrist.

"What are you doing?" He turned to Bet. "Sit down. She's going to hurt you." He tried to push Christine away from the wheelchair, but she resisted, surprisingly strong. He wrenched her back firmly and flung her away.

"Jesse." Bet stepped into the aisle, speaking so softly only he could hear her. "We have to talk."

"Here?" he asked. "In front of these people?"

Before she could answer, Christine grabbed the wheelchair and shoved. The handles cracked against Bet's steel-ribbed corset. She gave a quick cry of pain and slumped forward. Jesse caught her, stopping the wheelchair with his free hand, giving Christine a look so vicious, the horsewoman stepped back a few steps.

"Are you all right?" He lifted Bet by her elbows.

She struggled to straighten, but he could see she was hurting. He was vaguely aware of movement behind him, his mother, Don Wheeler, even the poet. The latter two reached Christine and restrained her. Bet steadied herself with her hand on Jesse and glanced at her rescuers in real gratitude.

"Walk with me, Jesse." One hand on her back, the other tucked in his elbow, she took a swinging step foreword, her old gait exactly. He walked down the aisle beside her, amazed by her progress. She walked almost as well as before the baby.

"Where did you learn this?" he asked.

"Zack."

Jesse scowled. When they reached the foot of the altar, she turned and put both hands in his. "Ask me again, Jesse."

He glanced at the crowd, his old shyness rising. He ignored the visible stir and muttering, the astonished look on the faces of the ranchers. She couldn't possibly reject him in front of these people. Or could she?

"Would you accept?" he asked softly.

"If you would have me."

He took a step back, creating a gap between them, so he could no longer feel the heat between them, no longer hear the creak of her steel-ribbed corset. "Can I ask why you'll finally have me?"

"I'm walking," she said, as if that were an answer.

He looked out at the crowd, consumed by his shyness, but his questions burned more deeply in him. "You were walking the first two times I asked you."

"True," she said as she glanced at the poet, who was still restraining the furious horsewoman, "but this time I learned by myself."

"You had help from the poet."

"Only a little. I taught myself really."

"Why does that matter?" He touched one finger lightly. "I always thought that's why you loved me—because I taught you to walk."

"To ride." She lifted her chin, trying to straighten. She'd never achieve a true normal posture, but for the first time in her life perhaps that did not matter. "You did, but that was the problem exactly."

He sighed. "Why do you always talk in such riddles?"

She smiled and swatted his arm, then turned him to face the brown-robed Franciscan. "It's just a metaphor, silly, but I'm too fine an artist to ignore its truth."

Jesse frowned, fishing a small gold band out of his pocket. He placed his free hand on the small of her back, where he could feel the steel-ribbed corset, the spine she could never quite straighten.

"It isn't just that I want to be normal," she said. "I thought that was my problem, but I can see now it wasn't." She clasped his fingers and squeezed them tightly. "Maybe I am just a variation. I can accept the truth of that statement." She slotted herself beneath his arm, fitting so neatly he'd have thought someone had built her for that spot exactly. "But I needed to learn to walk on my own, because it didn't matter how much I loved you . . .'' She leaned into his side. He could feel her heart beating, but she wasn't trembling. ''I'd never make a suitable wife until I had proved to myself that I could stand on my own without you.''

Epilogue

Firestriker died of old age, but not before young Jesse rode him. Hank, Hal, and Handsome made the moment immortal with their moving pictures. Bet remembered the day as she stared into the darkness, sitting on an overstuffed parlor divan, its nubby texture pricking her skin through the thin material of her silk blouse. Firestriker's image flickered on the flat wall before her. Ten year-old Jesse, Jr., slept beside her, his dark curls nestled in his father's lap. Jesse, Sr., was playing the Jew's harp, a seafaring ditty, one she remembered from the days at Lake Tagish. The tune and the pictures combined to create a subtle magic. Layer upon layer of interior voices mixed with memories and complex emotions . . .

"They're going back to the Yukon," Zack had announced. He was standing beneath the spreading banyan whose deep green leaves sheltered the front porch of the rancho. Sunlight dappled his hair, tawny as always. Bet noticed the fray of his corduroy coat and the smiles of the brothers arrayed behind him, still sporting those memorable black-and-white houndstooth trousers.

"Are you crazy?" She tightened her grip on the boy in her arms. Terror and pity swept through her, but also nostalgia. She'd come to think of that trek as golden. In spite of her trials, perhaps *because* of her trials, she somehow remembered only the beauty, the soaring adventure and deep satisfaction of having tested herself on every level. She shivered, staring at Hank, Hal, and Handsome. In spite of the haunting pull of the memory, she had no desire to repeat the experience. "Don't you know it will kill you? And why would you go there? The boom is over. You won't find any gold there."

"Ah, but they will." Zack pulled his hands out of his coat pockets. "I already have. My poems are selling like crazy. And I see you have also." He chucked her chin. His gaze wandered to Jesse, who had appeared in the doorway. "I see you've included the setting in your latest novel."

"So write from memory if you have to." She moved from the porch into the sunlight, still chilled by the memory of those icy passes. She put down Jesse, Jr. Zack ruffled his hair. The toddler ignored the raffish poet, as well the trio of dandified gamblers. He climbed into the roots of the banyan, crouched into its gnarled embrace, formed his fingers into a gun, and squinted up at its branches. "You don't have to revisit such a harsh place."

"I'm not." Zack leaned against one of the porch posts. "But I'd like to help them." He glanced shyly at the youngest brother, and Bet knew suddenly what he was up to.

Jesse drifted out of the doorway. He was dressed like a rancher, in faded blue jeans and a well-worn white cotton shirt. Bet liked him best when he dressed that way, devoid of the trappings he affected with strangers. "That doesn't seem very helpful," he said, "sending them back to the Klondike. I don't think it's become kinder to gamblers."

"We've given up gambling." Handsome stepped forward, his mustache quirking. He held a highly polished wood box, whose varnished surface gave no clue to its contents. "Mr. English has staked us for another purpose. Do you know what this is?" He lifted the shiny box higher.

Bet and Jesse shook their heads in concert. All three brothers stepped forward in one jerky motion.

Handsome spoke for the others. "It's called a Kinetoscope."

"I've been reading about that." Jesse moved in closer, a glint of interest in his dark eyes. "Have you purchased one of Edison's patents?"

The three gamblers looked down at their shoes.

Undaunted, Jesse took the box from the youngest brother, casting Zack an appreciative glance. "You smuggle this in from France?"

Zack nodded. "They're going to capture the Klondike in pictures." He gestured at the waiting brothers. "They're going to film the scenes in my poems. Make a little visual story. We think it will be very successful." He took Jesse by the elbow. "And we also thought a shrewd man like you, one with an eye to the future"— he shrugged toward Jesse, Jr., then smiled at Bet— "might take a risk on a long-term investment with potentially limitless profits."

To Bet's surprise, Jesse had invested. He'd never found copper as a result of the voyage, so he'd staked the three brothers in a movie business, which turned out to be a wise decision. Their movie company turned out steady profits, as steady as Don Wheeler's salt mine, even more profitable than investments in copper.

But the real treasure flickered before them. They'd recorded Jesse, Jr., learning to ride on an ancient mustang with a star on his forehead.

"Can you believe they could do this?" she asked Jesse softly.

He paused in the song he was playing, stroking her

arm. A familiar magic tingled through her. "It's a miracle really." He turned sideways gently without interrupting the sleeping boy. "If the house burned down tomorrow, I'd rescue you and the baby, then this would come next."

She nodded down at her son. "What about him?"

"He'd rescue himself."

"True. Too true."

She watched the child in the flickering image. He rode as if life had no limits, having no idea of how she treasured the mustang, of how much she'd miss him when he died the next winter. He did relish, however, the animal's power. She smiled as she watched her son grin in triumph, much the same thrill she remembered from riding.

She watched Firestriker longer, however. Not because she loved him better. Only Christine had that particular limit. But the horse had died, and this moving picture was the only way to experience the mustang, unless, of course, she reread her stories. She enjoyed them both, but especially the pictures, simpler, more vivid, than her portrait in words. Because there was her horse, captured for always, in light and shadows, with the star on his forehead and three-year-old Jesse riding him gaily while his father loped along beside him, the way he'd done with her in her childhood.

"Do you ever regret that we didn't have more?" she asked as she snuggled more deeply into his shoulder.

He didn't answer. He didn't have to. He didn't seem to regret a bit of their marriage. She'd used the French cap always and always, which still hadn't prevented a second baby. But this time Jesse had gotten her doctors, good ones, the best in California. And this time she had been smarter. She'd kept up her riding and hadn't done badly, though after Jenny, Bet had not wanted another. And so far she hadn't had one.

Jesse had never said a word on that subject. He'd hired a nanny, worked on the rancho, and kept silent while she'd written her novels, enjoying both her fame and her money, though never as much as he enjoyed the children. He'd bought up every red volume of poems he could. Zack had never published another, sobered by his regard for Jesse, Jr. The few volumes that had escaped Jesse's grasp and were now in the hands of private collectors were each worth thousands of dollars.

"Do you ever regret you married a writer?" she asked.

"Never." Jesse smiled, stroking her gently. "No, that's not true. Maybe not never. I do have one complaint on that subject."

"You do?"

He nodded gravely, regarding her from beneath those eyelashes that scarcely softened his distant expression. "You know when you're asked who inspired the hero?"

She nodded. She got asked that question quite frequently, at least when they traveled to San Francisco, though here at the rancho they seldom saw strangers.

"Why don't you tell them it's me?" he asked.

"I'm trying to protect you."

"I always think you should be truthful."

"You do?"

"Yes."

"I'll do as you ask." She touched his thigh, wondering how they'd act on his burgeoning interest without waking Jesse, Jr., from his sleeping position. "But don't you think it's a little deceitful? After all, the novels are fiction. You only inspire them. You're not really the hero."

"True. But I would think it a pleasant illusion, believing a man like the hero existed. And besides"—a glint appeared in his eyes—"there isn't anyone else who inspires them, is there?"

"Of course not." She kissed him because she was lying. And badly. For years she believed that Jesse was the hero, but the longer she wrote, the more she realized she had that in common with Zack English, the poet.

Just as he was the virgin in his erotic sonnets, *she* was the hero of her adventures, and also the heroine, of course, and the villain, and each smaller person, and sometimes even the trees and the horses. No matter that the novels were fiction, the emotions expressed by those stories were as real as the pictures that flickered before her, capturing her soul by some mysterious process that had explanation, but didn't.

"Look how well he rides him," she said.

"He's a marvelous rider. Almost as wonderful as his mother."

"He had a good teacher."

"And a good horse."

"I miss him." Tears welled up. A stray droplet splashed on her hand. "I'll miss him always."

"Be happy, Bet." Jesse wiped her cheek with his thumb. "You don't need to miss him. You've made him immortal."

She smiled, glancing again at the flickering picture. "Perhaps not immortal, but awfully famous. But I'm glad we have memories to pass down to our children."

"Memories and the rancho," Jesse murmured, nuzzling her earlobe.

"Memories and the rancho." She didn't say more, though she could have, but Jesse understood the implicit finish. She snuggled instead into his shoulder, savoring the sharp scent of citrus.

He stroked their son's black curls in silence, his gaze fixed on the flickering pictures. Slowly he slipped from beneath the boy.

He turned her toward him, stroking her back. "Memories, the rancho, and a mother who loves them," he whispered, then kissed her.

Author's Note

Horseback therapy is a known treatment for improving coordination, muscle tone, and self-esteem in the disabled. Regaining the ability to walk through such therapy is rare, though not unknown. There are many local programs in the United States that offer such therapy, and persons interested in the programs should contact their physicians.

Special thanks to Dr. Jeanette Donley for helping me with the medical details of Bet's condition. If I got them wrong, it's not her fault.